Legends:
The Den Anthology 2017

A Collection of
Winning Entires and
Honorable Mentions from
Grey Wolfe Publishing's
Writing Contests 2015-2016

Edited by
Robert McCrandall

Grey Wolfe Publishing, LLC
145 East Fourteen Mile Road
Clawson, Michigan 48017
www.GreyWolfePublishing.com

© 2017 Grey Wolfe Publishing, LLC
Published by Grey Wolfe Publishing, LLC
www.GreyWolfePublishing.com
All Rights Reserved

Print edition ISBN: 978-1628281903
E-Book edition ISBN: 978-1628281910
Library of Congress Control Number: 2017963724

Legends:
The Den Anthology

Edited by
Robert McCrandall

About This Book

This is a culmination of the Monthly Writing Contests that Grey Wolfe Publishing has offered since 2015. Each month, we challenge writers to create short stories that follow a prompt. The requirements are loose, with the only real expectation being that each story is 2,000 words or fewer, and follow the prompt as closely as possible.

Our calls for submissions were met with a wonderful collection of short stories from writers from all over the world, of every age and stage of their writing careers. Our goal in offering these contests each month is to assist writers in developing publishing credits to add to their writer's platform. Also, we understand that creating a regular writing practice can be challenging. We also know that the more frequently we write, the better we get at our craft. And we know that bribery works! We're happy to help in any way we can — and if that means a little bribery in the form of a prize to get you to write more often — then so be it. ☺

We have included the winners and honorable mentions of each Monthly Writing Contest in this collection. The stories are arranged alphabetically by title; and of course, because we received multiple submissions each month, you will notice a similarity between the stories.

We hope that readers enjoy this collection and perhaps discover a new author – Google their names, many have written novels, short story collections, poetry, and other works both in print an on the Internet.

We also hope that this book spurs you to engage your imagination and write for one of our upcoming Monthly Writing Contests. You can view the full list of prompts for 2017 and 2018 on our website. Enter as early as you like and as frequently as you like. There is no entry fee to write for any of our contests.

Enjoy!

Keep Reading, Keep Writing!

 Grey Wolfe Publishing's
2017 Monthly Writing Contests
Free To Enter
Enter Early, Enter Often
Max Word Count: 2,000
Monthly Prize: A $25 Visa Gift Card

www.GreyWolfePublishing.com

⮌Howl With The Pack

⮌Writing Contests

Contents

A Day in The Life Of A Favor-Saver
Matt McGee

Kevin had agreed to give McCoy a ride to the airport. They'd known each other almost eight years, and Kevin was McCoy's go-to guy. But it was a little more than that.

Kevin had done everything a man could do behind the wheel of a vehicle, from delivering pizzas to driving lab samples to piloting a taxi. And in his years of driving, Kevin had found there are two types spending money.

There are Tippers. If their ride home is nine dollars, they'll hand over twelve and say 'have a good night, man! Thanks!'

Then, there are the Favor Savers. For them, every dollar spent equals ten dollars' worth of goodwill down the road. The Favor Saver uses a service once, pays full price, then expects a lifetime of Groupon. If the recipient refuses or doesn't answer their phone, the Favor Saver moans something to anyone listening: "yeah man, that guy is just all about the money."

McCoy had paid full price for a taxi ride three years earlier, and by Kevin's count, he was now on his sixth or seventh favor. So when his phone rang, and McCoy's number appeared, Kevin groaned, paused, then picked up. His head was a hurricane of excuses.

"Bro!"

Bad start, Kevin thought.

"How's it going, McCoy?"

"I'm screwed."

Here it comes.

"Yeah bro, but, how are you?"

The old soft soap, Kevin knew. "I'm good."

"Cool. Bro, look. I'm in a jam. I gotta get to the airport in the morning. Can you hook a brother up?"

Gotta be something in it for me, Kevin thought. He was surprised by just how much there was.

****

Being a bit of a night owl, getting at McCoy at four o'clock in the morning didn't much inconvenience Kevin. He stuck an arm out his car window to type in the gate code McCoy had texted. A light rain had begun. Kevin pulled the retired cop car he'd picked up at auction into McCoy's driveway like he lived there. Then sprinted thru the rain to the front door.

McCoy was single. He also wasn't prone to original thought. So, while Kevin waited at the door, he wasn't surprised to see McCoy's fake-rock hide-a-key squatting in the dirt for any gardener to find.

Thunder sounded, then the sky opened up. As overdue California rain cascaded off the roof, Kevin tucked himself under the eaves. He knocked again. A full three minutes passed before McCoy answered.

McCoy slid a wheelie-style airport bag onto the porch. "Here you go, bro." He went back inside. Kevin left the bag and walked inside. The ceilings in the McCoy mansion invited echoes.

Kevin looked up.

"So, why didn't you get a shuttle?"

"Those jokers want twenty-four-hours' notice. Some of us don't roll like that, bro. Dude, when did it start raining?"

"Just now."

McCoy was a big guy, the pride of a local gym his uncle owned. The uncle, Kevin knew, also owned the house.

When McCoy tried to slip by, he merely turned his shoulders another angle. "Bro, is my bag out there?"

Kevin shrugged. "It's weatherproof. And no, it's under the eave."

"You don't think we should put it in the car?"

Kevin looked up and around. "This place is monstrous."

"Bro. Speak English."

"Your house is really big."

"Four thousand square feet. Pool table in the den. Total chick magnet."

"You live here alone?"

"My uncle stops in once in a while."

"How often is a while?"

"I don't know. Couple times a year. Not likely to happen soon, he was just here a couple weeks ago."

McCoy opened an entryway closet; he passed up the raincoat, parka, leather jacket, and pulled out a flat-billed baseball cap. He twisted it at a hip-hop angle then flexed his shoulders.

"Ready bro."

****

It rained steadily as they started down Decker Canyon Road, away from McCoy's hilltop neighborhood. The car felt good, handling the way civilians only pay top dollar for. Craggy rock outcroppings flashed by through the downpour.

"This canyon is pretty hairy, huh?" McCoy observed.

"Good thing I've been driving it twenty-five years."

Another half mile of windy canyon weaved by before a well-paved boulevard took over and, soon, Kevin swung onto the Ventura Freeway. He gave the Impala some juice and joined the flow of traffic.

Gonna be a sedate ride, he was thinking.

"So. Do the cops give you a lot of breaks?"

Kevin shook his gaze from the road. "Huh? Give who a lot of breaks?"

McCoy waved his hand around the car. "You guys that speed around in these old cop cars."

Kevin looked at the speedometer. "Not much of anyone bothers me when I'm only doing sixty-two on the freeway."

The roads were slick and, typical to LA, drivers fell into two categories. There were the Same-as-Evers, those who maintain that 80mph is a God given right. Then there are the Shirley Slow-

Downies. Inspired by panicky news reporters, they proceed at 20mph under the speed limit *because you can never be too safe.*

Kevin had hoped the ride would lend a little bonding time. Seeing his friend's eyes soaking in the LED of his iPhone, Kevin figured conversation was going to be his duty.

"If you could wake up as a different person tomorrow," Kevin said, "who would it be?"

McCoy's fingers moved slowly around the text box. He was trying to tell someone something, using as few letters as possible.

"Bro. What?"

Kevin held the wheel against hydroplaning. "If you could wake up as a different person tomorrow who would it be?"

McCoy kept texting. "Nicki Minaj. And when I woke up I'd feel myself up."

Kevin nodded.

McCoy kept texting. He never responded or asked, 'and who would you be, bro?' It didn't matter. Kevin knew who he wanted to be when he woke up tomorrow.

****

Kevin only needed the front door key. McCoy hadn't set an alarm code because there was no keypad. When he turned the key in the deadbolt and entered, Kevin looked around for any sign of a security system. Apparently, neither McCoy nor his uncle cared enough to pay for one. But, just to be sure, Kevin left his car on the street a few houses away and made sure he wasn't being watched.

McCoy kept the fridge completely stocked. The cable was premium, and the pool and hot tub were well-maintained. The pool table was mostly unused.

The smallest upstairs bedroom was twice the size of Kevin's master bedroom at home, and the master was bigger than his whole condo. Kevin wasn't greedy; he settled into one of the smaller rooms.

Then he changed his mind.

Kevin stripped off all his clothes, found a robe fit for a Hilton, then walked downstairs to the laundry room. He threw all his clothes in the washing machine with a little detergent. A few quick cycles later he threw them in the dryer, went back upstairs, and crawled into bed with a remote control.

He could stay up all night watching premium movies or any show on cable. He had only begun to scroll through the channel guide when, through the sound of the TV and the falling rain, he heard a noise downstairs.

He muted the TV. The doorbell rang again. Then it rang again, and again, four times quickly.

Kevin leapt out of bed. He threw on the robe, sprinted out of the bedroom and down the stairs. He grabbed a graphite driver from a golf bag McCoy likely never used; he hid out of sight from the front doorway window and peeked around the corner. The doorbell rang again. Then a fist pounded.

"Dammit!" a female voice said. "OPEN THE DOOR! IT'S RAINING OUT HERE!"

Kevin swung into sight and pulled the door open. He held the knob in one hand, the driver in the other. The woman crossed her arms over her chest and stepped quickly in.

"Oh my GOD it's literally pouring outside. What took you so long?"

Kevin didn't answer. He couldn't take his eyes off what she'd decided not to wear that night. Behind her, an Uber drove quietly away.

The woman looked right at him. "Wait. Who are you?"

Kevin held up the club. "Tiger Woods," he said, "are you my three o'clock appointment?"

"Huh?"

Kevin lowered the club. "I'm... housesitting. Sorry, I thought the doorbell was from the TV."

"I love TV. What were you watching."

"Porn."

"I love porn." The woman smiled mischievously. "I'm Nicki." She looked Kevin up and down. "Tiger, huh?"

"It's a family name."

"Really. What else did your family endow you with?"

Kevin stepped back and let Nicki into the house, though judging by the way she went straight toward the liquor cabinet, she'd been there before.

In the morning, after Nicki had redressed and called herself a ride, Kevin's cell went off. He looked at the alarm clock; 10:26am. He grabbed the cell. The screen displayed a familiar number. He picked up.

"McCoy."

"Bro! I'm getting in this afternoon at four-ten. Need you there, bro."

Kevin noticed McCoy wasn't even trying to call himself a shuttle. He also noticed he was still naked and the bed smelled of damp bodies.

"Yeah. Which airline."

"Southwest. You got it?"

Kevin started getting out of bed. "Yeah."

"Okay, see you then, bro."

Kevin said a sleepy 'yeah.' McCoy had already hung up. Kevin set the cell down and plopped back on the mattress. He got out of bed a half hour later, had a shower, then stripped all the bed sheets and walked them down to the washing machine. He set the water temperature on HOT and dropped in some detergent. With the machine in motion, he opened the dryer. His clean clothes felt like a gift.

Kevin made himself some coffee, toast and three eggs. The dryer buzzed. He retrieved the sheets, remade the bed, did the dishes, then made sure he had all his belongings and walked down to his car.

McCoy's plane was on time. The cab drivers in line tried to stare Kevin down, likely because of the Chevy's familiar body style. McCoy threw his own bag into the waiting open trunk then dropped in the car. He slammed the door behind himself and started texting again, slowly.

"Bro."

"Hey."

Kevin started to navigate the airport roundabout. Signs for Century Boulevard appeared, followed by a freeway on-ramp. Soon they were up to speed with the rest of LA.

The Grey Wolfe Den Anthology

"So. Have a good time while I was gone?"

"Yeah. You know. Work. Shit like that."

"Uh-huh."

McCoy kept tapping at his phone.

"Well, I appreciate you at least washing the sheets," he said. "Least you coulda' done."

Kevin decided to play confused.

"I don't."

McCoy smiled a huge grin. He held up his phone. "Bro. ADT has a remote alarm system. No more code box."

Kevin still didn't answer.

"You wanna see the video footage?"

Kevin shook his head. "No."

"Gotta hand it to you bro. I don't know who that chick was, but you nailed her pretty good. You're okay."

"Thanks."

"Who was she?"

"Don't know. She came to the door and asked for you."

"You're kidding!" Then McCoy snickered thru closed teeth, the way he'd heard hip-hop stars do it. "Oh *snap*! You tapped one of *mine*, bro?"

Kevin shrugged. "Hey, no homo bro, but good work."

"Thanks."

"Good endurance," McCoy added.

"Um."

"She's really one of mine?"

"I guess."

"Damn. Looks like you were taking care of all *kindsa* business while I was gone."

"What can I say, except..."

"Say it..."

"Thanks for the loan."

"You're welcome. Glad someone was having fun. But seriously, bro. It took everything I had not to call and say *get outta my house*."

"Well, yeah. But thanks for the mini-vacay," Kevin decided to say.

"Bro...?"

"I know," Kevin said.

"Yeah. You *effing owe me*, bro."

Kevin knew. The price of getting caught was that he was now committed to this Favor-Saver for life. He guided the car along the freeway, resigned to the slow pace of the Car Pool lane.

"Okay," Kevin nodded. "Deal."

A Dream Amusement Park
Sue Ann Whitston

"Hurry up, Karen! You should see this!"

"I'm coming, Beth. You know I watch my footing since tripping on that root last year. Spraining my ankle was no fun for me."

"I know. But you won't believe this."

"Believe what—" Karen began ducking under a tree branch and stopped. "An amusement park? Here? I don't believe it."

"How come we didn't see this before?" Beth queried. "Our families have camped in the park for at least ten years. We've hiked around every year. I can understand why we might have missed last year after your injury, but not in previous years."

"I was wondering the same thing," Karen answered. "Now, *what* do you see? I see a Ferris wheel and a roller coaster."

"Do you see the helicopter and flume rides, too? And I see one with little cars on a track weaving around buildings."

"I'm seeing the same rides. There's the merry-go-round with *horses*."

"Your favorite. Especially if there are horses."

"Yeah. But it-it's spooky. How would anyone know our favorite rides?"

"But, shall we explore?" Beth asked. "I'm willing."

"Let's!" Karen answered.

The girls moved towards the entrance to the deserted and dilapidated amusement park. As they neared the archway, the midway lights illuminated. Calliope music played from the merry-go-round.

The girls stopped and looked at each other.

"This is spooky," Karen stated. "Did we venture into *The Twilight Zone*?"

"I don't think so," Beth added.

The girls studied the rides before Karen said, "Shall we continue? This could be a trap."

"Maybe. But we could have fun."

"We could," Karen conceded. "Where do we start? I haven't been on a helicopter ride in ages. Could we do that first?"

"Let's!"

The girls rushed through the entrance to the helicopter ride and mounted the two wooden steps to the octagonal boardwalk. They chose individual cars. Karen crawled into an ultramarine blue copter while Beth settled into an orange one. They buckled the belts and practiced moving the bar which controlled the copter's flight movements as a shadow at the control station pressed the starter and the copter lifted. Karen pushed and pulled the handle fore and aft, moving the copter in a zigzag motion.

"Whoopee!" Karen chirped until the motor stopped and she felt the gentle bump against the boardwalk. "Now it's your turn, Beth."

"The roller coaster," Beth replied.

The girls raced to the roller coaster and crawled into one of the yellow cars under the awning. A shadow appeared at the control panel, and the four attached cars crawled along the steel track to the first incline. At the top, the cars turned right and sped downward in four arcs with centripetal force. A hundred-foot flat space – relief to the girls – led to another incline and four more downturns before returning to the awning and stopped.

They paused to catch their breath. Karen sighed, "That was fun."

"If you don't mind feeling like a ham sandwich," Beth answered.

"But that is part of the fun for riding a roller coaster."

They turned and walked to the Ferris wheel. A shadow started the motor after locking the girls in the car. The car moved up and stopped at the top. They looked over the trees.

"This is strange. We should be able to see the campsite," Beth remarked.

"You are right. We did not walk that far. The campsite is in a clearing," Karen said. "We seem to be alone. There are no other people here."

The Ferris wheel moved again, stopped at the pedestal and the girls unhooked the bar and walked away.

Undaunted by mysterious circumstances, the girls raced for the flume ride. The plastic log bobbed in the blue trough as Karen and Beth settled on the gray upholstered seat cushions and grabbed the aluminum rails inside the log.

Karen, being lighter than Beth, sat in the front and asked, "Ready?"

"I am," Beth stated. "Did you remember to turn your watch around? They won't get wet when we splash."

"I did," Karen said. "Hopefully, we won't get too wet."

Swoosh, and the log swerved into a channel, floating to the inclined rubber conveyor belt. The log thundered and plopped into an overhead channel. Water lapped over the log's side. A bird chirped. An owl hooted from a tree. Sunshine sparkled on the water. Silence. They heard the rushing water plunging ahead. Their log flew down an incline and into the lake.

"Did you get wet?" Beth asked when she stood on the boardwalk.

"Not much," Karen answered. "The weight distribution worked."

Now they found the car ride and chose separate vehicles. Karen climbed into a white convertible while Beth clanged the bell on a fire engine after a shadow pressed the power button. The girls steered the vehicles around the buildings on the steel track.

"That was easier than steering my car through heavy traffic. I didn't have to brake for traffic lights, either. No worries about someone hitting you from behind," Karen said.

Beth chuckled, "Ah, our carefree youth."

They saved the merry-go-round until last. Karen used the stirrups to climb on the white horse in the middle. Beth found a dog nearby. The calliope music started, and the animals moved on the pulleys.

As the ride ended, Beth looked at her watch. "Time to head back."

"Yeah," Karen agreed. "But it was a fun afternoon."

"How do we explain what we did?"

"Ah, that might be difficult. Our parents won't believe us."

"We could walk back with them."

"And do it again?"

"Why not? Feel like a kid a third time."

The girls turned and walked across the clearing to the path which brought them from the campground. They stopped under the tree and looked back at the amusement park.

The lights were extinguished and the amusement park dilapidated. Rust and peeling paint covered the steel and wooden surfaces on the helicopter ride, roller coaster, Ferris wheel, flume ride, car ride, and the merry-go-round.

Puzzled, they looked at each other.

"What happened?" Beth asked.

"I don't know," Karen answered. "We were riding minutes ago on the merry-go-round. What do we tell our folks we've doing for two hours?"

"I have no clue," Beth replied.

Karen shook her head as they started on the trail when they heard a voice shriek, "Oh, my! It's an amusement park!"

The girls stopped, looking across the clearing as four people emerged from the other side of the woods as a second voice screeched, "Ooh! There's a roller coaster, and a Ferris wheel, and a tilt-a-wheel, and bumper cars!"

Now, this was another mystery.

A Glorious Thing
Linda Tyler

From the prow of his pirate ship as it sailed across the sparkling blue Mediterranean, Marcos spied the white sails of another ship gleaming on the horizon.

Catriona saw the shimmering sea, felt the warm breeze on her face, tasted the salt on her lips, softening her at last.

Silhouetted against the sky, he lifted his spyglass and brought the enemy into focus. Marcos's black curls were wet with spray, and he laughed as he shook off the droplets.

The sun blazed, the sea was a dazzling blue, as the ship beat its way through the glittering waves.

Catriona stirred in her sleep. "I'm yours," she murmured to Marcos, her blue silk shift fluttering in the sea breeze. She raised eager lips.

The rocking motion of the ship increased, the swell of the waves grew louder. She opened her eyes.

She was standing in a ship's cabin. Catriona looked down and saw she was wearing a loose white shirt and baggy black trousers. She gazed around the room and drank in the panelled walls, the oil lamp hanging from the ceiling, sunlight streaming through the porthole as dust motes danced in the air. *Oh, bliss!* She was a character in a thrilling novel! A short, stocky man lounged in the open doorway.

The words slipped out of her mouth. "Well, Mr. Morgan?"

"Ship on the horizon, Cap'n."

"Whose colours?"

Her First Mate shook his head. "None flying."

"Best to prepare the men."

She sprang to the ladder, Mr. Morgan following at her booted heels.

As he reached the main deck, he shouted, "Clear the decks for action! Gunners in position!"

The crew ran to their posts, their oaths mixing with the crash of the waves against the hull. Catriona climbed to the poop deck, pulled a spyglass from her trouser pocket and raised it. The other ship was under full sail on the horizon. As she tried to make out its origin, it slowly changed course.

It was coming towards them.

"Raise the colours!" She would show them she meant business.

Their opponent was gaining speed.

"To starboard, making for us!" cried the lookout.

Catriona kept her eyes focused on their manoeuvres. She could see the gleaming round muzzles of cannons through the portholes in their hull. As Mr. Morgan joined her, she snapped, "Who is this insolent captain?"

"No idea, ma'am."

She lowered the glass. "He's too far off to sink us, but we will soon have him in range."

Catriona slipped the eyeglass back into her pocket and took the megaphone from Mr. Morgan. Raising it, she shouted the orders to her men. "Come about to face the enemy! Starboard guns in position. Fire the cannons when I give the order."

She waited, holding her breath until the right moment. "Fire!"

Each of the three big starboard cannons on the *Celtic Dragon* recoiled on their tracks from the shock of discharging its load. Their boom echoed across the sea. Catriona felt the familiar temporary deafening and the smell of powder tickling her nostrils. When the smoke cleared, she could see the other ship had not been hit.

Mr. Morgan swore. "Now we have to be careful. He knows it takes time for us to reload."

She watched as the enemy changed course again, making an arc to avoid her cannons. It moved with swiftness, its sails set. "He's going to double back and try to sink us."

She raised the megaphone again to the crew. "Get ready to face him."

Catriona and the First Mate waited as the *Celtic Dragon* began to swing round. "If we can take this position, he'll have to sail against the wind to get at our side," she said.

The other ship seemed to be adjusting to their new manoeuvre and for several moments there was a heavy silence on both ships. Then, in the distance, Catriona saw the enemy returning towards them as she had predicted. It flew over the water, then suddenly stopped and turned into the wind.

"Clever!" Catriona laughed. "Pity he's our foe."

She turned to Mr. Morgan. "Have the cannoneers reloaded?"

"Aye, ma'am."

"Then fire at once when I give the order."

But the cannons on the enemy ship fired. Debris soared into the air around them and a deafening explosion echoed from side to side. Catriona struggled to recover her breath and an enormous wave crashed down, nearly knocking her off her feet. Soaked to the skin, she clung to the deck rail as the *Celtic Dragon* slowly righted herself.

"I'll check the damage," said Mr. Morgan. He jumped down to the main deck.

The white sails of the enemy flapped in the wind, almost on top of Catriona. The smoke from the firing hid part of it from view, but she could see the varnished wood of its hull glisten in the sinking sunlight and the figures of musket-armed men standing in the gunwale.

In the prow, silhouetted against the sky, stood a tall, slim man watching her through his telescope. His black curls were wet with spray, and he laughed as he shook off the droplets.

From the other ship, long boats were being launched, their oarsmen rowing through the smoke lingering from the cannon fire. The long boats bumped against the side of the *Celtic Dragon;* men jumped from them onto the ship's ladder and mounted the rungs.

On deck, the fighting was hand-to-hand. Knives flashed in the last rays of the sun and bloodied men on both sides fought on or lay groaning or silent where they fell. Catriona was in the middle of the fighting, but exhaustion was taking over. Her knife still shone in the air, but her movements were slower. Above the turmoil, she heard a voice behind her and turned, gripping her knife. The tall, dark-haired man she had seen in the prow.

"Everything okay?"

Catriona looked up from filleting the fish. Her husband was home from work.

A Memorable Shopping Trip
Kimberly A. Wisener

I was rummaging through the attic and found something that made memories flood back. I was going into fourth grade and was school shopping with my mom and older brother. We lived in a small town, so shopping involved a thirty-minute drive to a nearby larger town and was a big deal.

We went into a shop in downtown Denison, Texas, that probably was a more expensive place than where we normally would have shopped. We were K-Mart shoppers, or mom made our clothes. I saw the most beautiful brown velvet jumper with a matching bright-colored flowered top. I fell in love. It was so soft. It was belted with a gold buckle. I actually tried it on and it was a perfect fit, but the price was more than my mom could afford. The staff at the shop were also not terribly friendly, so we left.

I can remember being so sad about it and probably a little pouty. My older brother, for some reason, who could not have possibly been having a good time, told my mom we should get the dress. He was my hero pretty much all of the time as he still lived at home and was not too embarrassed to be around his little sisters, although I do remember having to hide in the floor board of his car if he saw his friends.

He went to bat for me over the jumper. I don't know why or how she was able to pay for it, but we did go back and get it. I can remember feeling so happy and just knew that my school year would be the very best when I wore that outfit. I still have my class picture wearing the outfit, sitting in the front row.

My mom is gone now but was always willing to make sacrifices for her five children. I was the next to the youngest, and she had me when she was thirty-eight. She was older than most of my friends' moms but was always the first one willing to ride the roller coaster with the kids. She was a person that could make everyone feel special. This was a day she made perfect, and I have no idea how she was able to do it!

A Mysterious Call
Lisa Ginsburg

The harsh ring of my landline pushes me out of the dark abyss of a dreamless slumber and into the cold reality of three o'clock in the morning. I don't know why Max, starting to stir beside me, insisted on keeping this land line active. After all, we had embraced the world of smartphones a long time ago. In fact, the only person who ever dialed this antiquated line, my mother-in-law, passed away over a year ago. Perhaps Max is keeping this line more out of sentimentality more than anything else. I do not know why I am even bothering to pick this up. In fact, this is the first time in fourteen months that this phone has rung at all. Even the spam advertisers and political campaigns have long since found our smartphones.

"Hello!"

I say this in an irritated tone, fully expecting to slam the phone down, roll over, and go back to sleep. A voice that sounds familiar but I cannot place says cryptically, "There is a car waiting for you outside your house. Get inside. You don't want to ignore this."

Max, mumbles, his eyes are in a squint, and he is not fully awake, "Everything okay?"

I glance at him not wanting to wake him up for something that is most likely a wrong number. *What could either of us have done to have received this type of call?* We are just insignificant middle-class people who will be sending our daughter off to college this fall. In fact, a few hours ago we hosted Kate's graduation party. Max has already fallen back into his alcohol-induced sleep. My head is pounding a little bit, reacting to the glasses of wine I indulged in while talking to my best friend, Bree.

I further ponder, *it could be some of Kate's friends, trying to prank us after a long night of partying.* I sigh, stretch my muscles, and get out of bed reluctantly. *It wouldn't hurt to check things out, even if it were one of Kate's friends, they would have texted her, rather than using this number but better to be safe.*

I walk down the stairs and Lilly, my sixteen-year-old basset hound, follows. She has lost all concept of time, and I know now that if I don't let her out, there will be an accident. I throw on a robe, grab the leash from the end table and make my way outside.

As I open the door, I am nearly blinded by the glare of headlights. I stumble in shock as the horn blares. Not really thinking, I wander over to the car and admonish, "Shhh! You'll wake the neighbors."

The window opens, and I belatedly remember about my safety. I start to back up and then an unmistakably familiar voice half-whispers, "Joanie, you are as beautiful as I remembered."

I look into those unforgettable blue-green eyes and gasp. It's him, Trevor Patterson, the one who broke my heart. He joined the Army shortly after our passionate fling the summer after my senior year of high school, right before I started college. A lifetime ago, I was the same age my daughter is now.

I close my eyes and the smell of rose petals, mixed in with Trevor's spicy cologne and his cigarette smoke, comes wafting back into my nostrils. I remember the way my body tingled with anticipation as he kissed me, deeply and plundering. It was the first time where a man's kisses left me wanting more but at seventeen, not quite eighteen, despite my desire, I always stopped him.

He seemed sophisticated and worldly as an older man of twenty-five, and my parents, sensing my passion, wholeheartedly disapproved of the idea of us. It did not stop me, however, as I frequently argued, "I am an adult now, a high school graduate. I can do what I want." Looking back, I can see how naïve I was, and I pity that girl. In fact, I had a drunken conversation about this a few hours ago with Bree. Bree's son, Steven, and Kate were falling in love.

We looked at the two of them holding hands. Bree gave a long, drawn out, breathy sigh.

"Ahhh! Young love. Have you ever felt that if you couldn't have somebody that you would just die?"

I looked over at Max, holding a beer and barbecuing hot dogs and hamburgers for our guests. Sweet, solid, reliable Max. He sees me looking at him, gives me a brief smile, and waves, I half-heartedly wave back and take a long sip of my wine.

Bree looks at me and then at my husband of almost twenty years and nods. "The two of you always seemed to be the perfect couple of the neighborhood. If things develop between our children beyond puppy love, I know that Kate has come from good people." I nod, willing myself to stay in the present and not letting my mind wander to what might have been. I have the ideal husband, the type that dreams are made of. Max is nice looking with sandy blond hair and kind gray eyes. He is calm and steady, with none of the wild nature and sense of adventure that eventually tore me and Trevor apart.

Maybe fueled by the alcohol, I look at Bree and confide, "Maybe Max isn't the love of my life."

She raises her eyebrows and lets me continue.

"The summer after I graduated from high school I fell hard and fast."

My confession brings me back to the grocery store where I had a job as a cashier for the summer to earn money for books. The manager walks me over to a man with dark, almost black hair which provides a nice contrast to those hypnotic eyes, the color of the sea. "Joanie," he introduces, "this is Trevor, our head cashier. He will be training you."

He smiles at me, and there is an energy pulsing through my body that I cannot give a name to. My heart is racing, and I feel tongue-tied. I nod as he gives me basic instructions on working the register, dealing with customers, etc.

After our shift is done, he wipes his hands on his jeans, looks at me, and says in that husky voice, "How about we go get some dinner?" I nod and say quietly, "I biked here and need to take it home first."

He lights up a cigarette, takes a long drag, sighs, and replies, "No worries. I have a bike rack, we can strap it on the back of my car."

From that moment on, we were inseparable, and I knew his kisses drove me wild in the way no other boys that I went out with in the past had. I realized that compared to those previous, insignificant dates, Trevor was not a boy but a man. I wanted him in a way I never had anyone ever before, and pushed things to the limits. But maybe it was my upbringing, both moral and religious, we always stopped before I lost my virginity. I remember several nights, in the back of Trevor's car or in the room in the house he was renting for the summer, where he would reach for the button on my pants, I'd say something like "I think we should stop now." He never argued with me, only sighed deeply, and went outside to smoke.

Then one night it was different. It was the week before I left for college. As usual, after our shift, we left the store together, with the plan of us going out. He looks me up and down, "Let me take you out someplace nice tonight. I'll drive you home to get dressed up." He pulls up to our house and slows down as he reaches the driveway. My parents are waiting for me, and I call, "Trevor is talking me out to dinner tonight. Don't wait up." In fact, I had decided on my own that tonight would be the night and even went to the doctor earlier this week for protection. My mom looked at the window at Trevor sitting in his old beater. My dad says, "Invite the man inside, it's about time we had a talk."

With both of my parents watching, I walk out to him and say, "Why don't you come inside and wait for me there?" Without saying a word, he nods and follows me inside. As I am walking upstairs to my bedroom, I hear my dad inviting him to sit on the couch. Given his tone, I decide it would be best to change as quickly as possible.

I walk into the room finding all three sitting there with a silent tension between them.

Trevor gives me a tight grin and says, "What do you say we get out of here?" Dinner seems to have an awkwardness to it that I cannot describe. He orders a beer and sips it wordlessly. He pays the bill, and we walk out to the car in silence.

I break the heavy, strange silence and say, "I'm ready. Let's go back to your place, and I promise I won't stop you this time." I reach up to kiss him, but he pulls away roughly. I stumble backwards, almost falling.

He says gruffly, "This isn't going to work. I can't be with a child like you anymore. I am leaving town, and I don't want to see you again."

I argue, "Trevor, I think I lo—" He doesn't let me finish, "I don't need to hear this, I'm taking you home. It's over and don't try to find me. I'm joining the Army and don't want to be tied down."

He pulls in my driveway and watches me walk away from him as I'm crying hysterically. He doesn't even say goodbye.

That was the last I had seen of Trevor until tonight, and despite twenty-five years and a marriage later, my heart still races. I raise my eyebrows.

He explains, "I never wanted to say goodbye. I loved you, too. But your parents made me see that I wasn't good enough for you and the best thing I could do was walk away until I was. I've been through four tours, fought the demons of PTSD and addiction that goes along with it, cleaned myself up, went to school, got a degree and a career with a future. I am finally ready to say that I might possibly be good enough to be someone you deserve. Come away with me right now and let's find out."

For a moment, I look into those eyes that remind me of stormy seas and am tempted. I can get the excitement I had craved when I was with him that never did get fulfilled. Then Lilly whines, tugging me towards the house, bringing me back to reality.

I look at the house where Max is sleeping peacefully with Kate in the next room. Max, who two years after wallowing around wearing my heartbreak on my sleeve, made me want to move on. He was the one who stuck around for the tough times in life, cheering my every triumph and commiserating every setback. *How could I do this to him?*

I glance at Trevor one last time, aging has only made him more attractive, but a feeling of regret washes through me. We might have been incredible together, but I can never find out. I look at him one last time, drinking him in. He looks back at me with regret knowing my answer. I shake my head, tug on Lilly's leash, walk back to the house, not daring to look back.

I wipe away a stray tear as I hear the car pull away. I stand in the kitchen for a moment, stroking Lilly's fur. Finally, I go back upstairs and climb in bed next to my husband.

Alaska (Or Bust)
Sue Ann Whitston

Sheila Neilson stared at the final transcript in her hand, pausing at the front door.

She thought, *Dad, can't refuse to take me to Alaska now.*

She was certain the subterfuge would not be detected by her father. This *must* work since he promised to take her to Alaska if she passed English. She had made a copy of the transcript, cut an 'A' from a previous semester, and with rubber cement, positioned the letter over the 'C' listed for the current English grade. She rubbed away any excess cement with the pickup. She repeated the process for the final grade point average.

This was too easy.

Now, she took a deep breath and exhaled as she opened the door. "Dad!" she screeched. "I've got my final grade report!"

She waved the transcript in front of her father.

"And what did you get in English?" Mr. Neilson queried, his voice lower than normal as he reached for the transcript.

"I got an 'A'!" Sheila replied, giving him the paper. "Now, you've got to keep your promise to take me to Alaska."

"Oh, right," he answered.

"What's wrong, Dad?"

"Nothing to concern you. But, may I see your final essay?"

"Later. I'm so happy to be going to Alaska with you at the

end of this month!" Sheila paused, twirled on the blue-gray carpet which made her full skirt billow. Then she continued, "I can't wait to get to Juneau and see Mendenhall Glacier. I want to see the sheep through the high-powered binoculars, clinging to the mountain which you can't see with a naked eye. I want to experience the breathless view of Mendenhall Glacier through the sanctuary window at Auke Lake Church. Oh! Taste the salmon grilled over Alderwood and roast marshmallows on the fire pit."

"Ah, before you continue, may I see the final essay?"

Sheila ignored the request as she expounded on their adventures in Skagway. "I would like to hear my steps on the old boardwalks, ride the train into the Yukon Territory to where the Gold Rush began. Maybe lick an ice cream cone before we sailed to Glacier Bay National Park. What an adventure for viewing Humpback Whales as they breach, Sea Lions reposing on icebergs, Orcas pacing the ship, and the Captain pulling the whistle to make the ice tumble from the glacier as they 'berth'."

"The essay, please."

Now, Sheila expounded on the Russian Icons in St. Michael's Cathedral in Sitka after they rode the tender from the ship docked in the bay. She hoped there would be numerous Bald Eagles and Grizzlies on the Wildlife Cruise near Sitka.

"And what about the pre-cruise tour in Vancouver?" She wanted to see the Gas Clock in Gastown, Chinatown, the Vancouver Aquarium, the infamous Totem Poles constructed by the First Nations, and Victoria before they boarded the ship.

Sheila paused.

"Stop, young lady!" Mr. Neilson commanded.

Sheila gulped. "Yes, Dad?"

"Show me the final essay, the one which gave you the 'A' in English."

"Er, the teacher kept it."

"She did? Why?"

"She keeps all of the 'A' essays."

"She does? She returned your brother's 'A' essay two years ago."

"She did?" Sheila replied. "Oh! Now, I remember. She said she changed the policy after someone last year used their sister's essay."

"Oh? That is not what she told me during the parent-teacher conference."

Sheila stammered, "Um, I lost it."

"Really? You lost the fabulous 'A' essay so you wouldn't have to show me."

Sheila looked down before she turned to her backpack. She sighed, opened the flap, and rummaged for the English folder. She mumbled, "I have to confess. I really did not get an A in English. I did try! Honestly! I did so want to go to Alaska!"

"I'm afraid we can't. I lost the money at the track."

"What?!" Sheila screeched. "You promised to stop betting on the horses!"

"Well, someone told me this horse was a sure winner."

"And the horse came in last?"

"No. The horse came in fourth, out of the money for place."

"Then, you've lied."

"As did you, Sheila." Mr. Neilson was rubbing his thumb over the transcript. "You did a fair bit of cheating yourself to cover up the real grade in English and your final grade point average to prove yourself worthy of a trip to Alaska."

"You're right, Dad."

"Then, I'd say we are both guilty of a crime," he concluded.

An Ominous Call
Lisa Scuderi-Burkimsher

Restless from the heat and broken air conditioner, I twisted and turned in bed. My husband, Mark, grumbled and rolled over.

"Well, if we had gotten central air like I wanted, we both would get some sleep," I said as I turned on my side. Mark ignored my comment.

Mark had been an alcoholic for seven months after losing his managing job due to budget cuts. My family was well-off financially, not to mention I had a great job, but I stayed in the marriage for our six-year-old son Charlie's sake.

I finally got comfortable, and the damn phone rang.

"It's midnight, who could be calling at this hour?" I mumbled to myself. "Hello."

"There is a car waiting for you outside your house. Get inside. You don't want to ignore this." The scratchy voice had been disguised cacophonously with a voice box.

"Who's that, Alyssa? Everything okay?" Mark asked annoyed rolling over and squinting his eyes.

"It's my boss, Sue. There's an emergency down at the office," I lied.

"Damn, that place! Can't she get someone else to take care of it?"

"No, she's counting on me. I'm her right hand on this month's issue. If you had a job, you'd understand." Before he could

---

answer, I tossed my pillow at him and left the room.

I threw on some clothes without showering, sprayed lavender perfume on my neck and arms, put my hair in a bun, and headed out the door to the waiting car.

I stood motionless, afraid to enter the black sedan that was parked with the back door already open. *Who could it be,* I wondered? My stomach churned, my legs shook, and my body trembled. I must've spaced out because the next thing I knew; I was sitting in the car. I took a deep breath and exhaled. I smelled cologne, a familiar scent. I checked my surroundings. I sat on grey leather seats with a cup holder in the center, coffee smoldering in a styrofoam cup. I wouldn't dare drink it. Stupidly, I tried to open my window, but it had been locked. A black screen blocked me from seeing who the driver could be and my nerves got the best of me. Suddenly I had the urge to urinate.

"I've been waiting for you. What took you so long?" the ominous voice asked.

I ignored the question but asked where he/she was taking me.

"You'll just have to wait, Alyssa."

"How do you know me?" I asked clearing my throat and twitching in my seat.

"No more questions!" The voice was blunt.

I closed my eyes, leaned back and prayed to the good Lord to help me.

"Okay, we're here."

My body still trembling, I nearly fell getting out of the car onto the sidewalk. I steadied myself and looked around.

"Oh my God," I said, when I saw the building.

"So, are you ready, Alyssa?" the man asked walking towards me with that recognizable voice.

"You're an idiot, Jack! What were you thinking scaring the crap out of me? All you had to do was call me on my cell phone, and I would've met you." I yelled so loudly; that one of the neighbors opened their window and told me to shut the hell up.

"We've been seeing each other secretly for six months, and I wanted to do something exciting. Just meeting at Zen's Garden for Chinese food and then going upstairs to my apartment is getting old. Wasn't this exciting, wondering what would happen once you got out of the car? Now I'm all revved up, and we can get it on." He kissed my neck, and my body shuddered.

"You're romantic. Get it on. Nice way to get a girl in the mood. If you weren't so damn hot, I'd punch you in the stomach for this stunt. But I'd rather head upstairs. Let's go, sexy."

I didn't want to admit it, but after the shock had worn off, I wanted to do him right then and there on the sidewalk.

Baby Blue Garment
Nick Johnson

The buzzing electrical motors and simultaneous hammering of a hundred sewing needles made a hectic but numbing atmosphere. Even in such crowded conditions, the workers were careful never to let their weary eyes meet those of the people around them, especially the overseers that stalked the roads looking to make a brutal example of his absolute authority. The heavy air hung stagnant with sweat and fear.

Their worn-out bodies were vulnerable to the infectious diseases that ran rampant through the workforce. Piali had worked at the factory for nearly four months. She hadn't seen the sun once in that time. She was part of her machine; she had to feed in the fabric and press the peddle with her foot. She performed the repetitive task with mechanical precision. One error in the stitching, a single inconsistency in the hem and she would be discarded.

The operators of the machines were far more easily replaced than the machines themselves. It was part of Piali's job to make sure it always ran, to assure that motor was always humming. Their blood was what fueled the comfortable illusion of childhood for those who were insulated from the suffering that was the foundation of modern life.

When they hugged their dolls, they would never think of the children whose pain created the merchandise that symbolized their parent's love.

She kept her head low and her eyes down at her hands to avoid the piercing gaze of the overseers. Piali was pregnant, and she feared somehow, he would know. Pregnancy would render her useless to him, and she would be condemned to starve among the hordes of emaciated and destitute bodies haunting the areas around the factory. Their decaying bodies putrefied in the streets. They were refuse, just meals for stray dogs and insects.

Piali finished the stitching on yet another baby blue pajamas designed for a plastic infant. She had stitched together thousands of these garments; she wondered how many prosthetic children could have been manufactured.

She clutched the soft cloth article in her hand. She remembered the child her sister had. She was born small enough for the dolls clothes to fit her. Her life had been brief, though. She lived long enough to feel the torments of starvation, crying futility for a mother whose body was being ravaged by infection. It was a brief and brutal existence, and she knew she couldn't expect anything much different.

A sharp pain tore through her. She cringed and clenched her torso. She felt warm blood streaming on her thigh. Her baby was gone. She crossed her legs and hoped no one would notice the growing stain. She threw the garment she had just sewn into the waiting plastic bin and began to stitch together a new one, a new outfit for a synthetic child who would be afforded far much more in its imaginary life than her real child could ever have.

Being A Goddess
Izabela Jeremus

My eyes are closed, my body relaxed to the point that I can barely feel it. I am floating inside myself, weightless. As my breathing slows, I feel myself lifting out of my physical prison and floating up, up above myself. As my spirit drifts, I turn around and see my corporeal body lying on my queen bed, nestled among the rose comforter. My blonde hair is fanned over the fluffy pillows, framing my pale face, dark lashes resting peacefully on my cheeks. My heart shaped lips are parted slightly. The rest of me is beneath the blanket.

I turn away from myself and drift higher, through the ceiling, toward the pregnant moon and brilliant stars. The farther I go, the faster I travel. Tree tops soar by me in flashes of dark green and black-brown. There is a rushing in my head, like wind in a tunnel, as I move past the tops, higher still. I float through the troposphere, stratosphere, mesosphere, thermosphere, then out through the exosphere. A look back shows me the shining blue marble that is the Earth, quickly retreating from me.

Shooting across the Milky Way, I barely see the streaks of lights that comprise the planets and stars. They're just a jumble. The blur eventually subsides and before me lies a blinding star, brighter than the Earth's sun. Orbiting around it is a planet much like the Earth with brilliant sapphire water and emerald patches of land. As I head toward it, it becomes bigger, at least three times the size of Earth. It has three moons, all different sizes.

Gently, I'm planted on a patch of kitten-down grass.

"This is yours now," booms a voice from the sky. "Craft it well."

Sitting down, I run a hand over the rich soil, concentrating. Where my hand has touched, flowers pop up, fully grown. They are a cross between roses and lilies, the petals winding in like roses, but large like lilies. I color them in with every shade of the rainbow. Pointing to a spot several feet away from my new flowers, a tree springs forth. Its trunk is comprised of three smaller trunks winding together to make a larger one. I make it shine like white marble. The leaves sparkle as brilliantly as black diamonds. Next to it, I create an identical one, but invert the colors.

With my eyes closed, I envision an entire forest of these trees, spanning miles of this land. Before me, I imagine a crystal lake, the water so clean, you can see straight to the bottom. The surrounding land fills up with the rose-lilies. When I peek, my visions have come true.

Moving toward the lake, I dip my hand into the cool water. A silver Koi fish with four legs tucked beneath it appears and begins swimming happily. Leaving my hand in the water, a gold one follows. A silver one after that, then another gold one, until the lake is filled with them.

Turning away from the water, I establish a ring of giant mushrooms near one of the trees. Within it, I plant little faeries to be guardians of the element of earth. They're no bigger than my thumb and come in all sorts of colors, their delicate wings fluttering with their specific shade. Each one lands on a mushroom and gets to work carving out a little home.

My forest finished, I imagine myself on the beach until I am there. The water that is already rolling in Is the color of a blue jay's wings. I fill the ocean with my own creations: fish with wings, dolphins with legs, sharks with arms. I paint them all in colorful hues, so the water is filled with rainbows. I make crustaceans with precious gems for shells. Deep on the ocean floor, plant life of every color and shape springs up. As protectors of the water, I choose mermaids and mermen, their fins and hair as vibrant and different as the fish. Each one stops to wave at me before disappearing into the waves.

After the ocean, I travel to the equator of the planet and build the tropics. Palm trees that look like rubies and coconuts without the tough outer layers begin to fill the land. Flowers that are bigger than the average human head surround them. Sweet fruit and berries in all colors grow on bushes and trees, all of them mixing together to form a harmonious painting. Long rivers cut through the rain forests on their way back to the ocean. I fill these with more merpeople and fish.

Here I choose to place the fire elementals, the phoenixes. Their beautiful fire bodies roar from my fingers and lift to the skies with ear-splitting shrieks. I litter the ground with their prey - guinea pig creatures with gazelle legs, mini elephants, buffalo-sized antelope, and other manner of spliced animals. The only other predators I set down are the wolves, just a little smaller than lions. I then copy all of the animals I have created, adjust them to fit other parts of the world, and set them down world-wide.

Satisfied with my tropics, my last stop is the northern-most part of the world. Here, I crack the earth open so I can mold mountains. The highest peaks disappear into the clouds. Topping the giants are piles of aquamarine snow. To protect the air, I craft dragons. Each magnificent creature has different color scales. Their children will be a mix of both parents. For instance, if a red dragon and a blue dragon procreate, their child will be green. Their thick skin keeps them warm on the mountains, while their fire breath melts the snow into their lairs. A wave of my hand turns the animals here white for better camouflage.

While I'm contemplating whether or not I'm finished, the biggest dragon of them all sets himself down in front of me. He is a mountain of an animal, as big as two elephants, and blacker than the night. His eyes twinkle like two stars in the sky. He pulls out one of his smaller scales, like a seashell, and puts it down in front of me—an offering. Smiling, I accept and pick it up. He then takes to the skies, searching for his new mate.

The dragon has clearly shown me that this world is done. Clutching the gift he has bestowed upon me, I plop down and close my eyes. Picturing the Earth, I ascend from the ground of this planet and begin the journey back. This time is much quicker than the first; I only see flashes of radiance as I travel back to my home planet. The sound is more like a shrieking jet now, only getting louder the closer I get to Earth. Instead of slowing down, the closer I get, the faster I go.

I slam unceremoniously into my body. Gasping, I shoot up in bed. Paralyzed at first, it takes me a few minutes to realize that I'm holding something. I turn on the lamp next to my bed to examine it. It's a smooth, gleaming, black scale - the one the dragon had given me. With a smile on my face, I lie back down and silently thank the Universe for having given me the opportunity to create something wonderful.

Brain Child
Arthur M. Doweyko

"You called *me,* Doc. So, what's going on?" I looked up at the camera and threw it a grin. When Riddles opened the fire door, my jaw dropped. His head was wrapped in aluminum foil. But that wasn't the worst of it. I pinched my nose. "You look like... crap, and you smell like—"

"I know, I know. Get in here. Put this on."

He handed me a silvery foil hat. The hollow look of his eyes and the dark stubble kept me from hurling more insults.

"What's this?"

Riddles leaned out as if making sure there was no one else outside. Entering through the loading dock of the BioGentics Research building gave me a bad feeling.

"Keep your voice down, Jimmy, and put the hat on."

"Doc, you are beginning to scare me." I put the hat on.

He eased the fire door shut and grabbed my sleeve. "This way—hurry."

We jogged the length of a hallway lit up by a blue-white emergency light at the far end.

"No power?"

Riddles steered me up the stairs. Four floors later, my chest pounded. "Hold on, I need to catch my breath."

"We're here."

I staggered into an office that looked like a doctor's waiting room and plopped into the closest chair. "What gives?"

He swung the door shut. A red ceiling light flashed over his head, giving me the willies. "It's out of control."

"You're not making any sense. What's out of control?"

He pressed an ear to the door. "I don't know how much time we have, so I'm going to make it short. Someone has to know." He sucked in a long breath. "Jimmy, you know what we do here?"

Princeton's BioGentics was famous. "Yeah, you grow organs—for transplants—right?"

"And we've been very successful." His gaze wandered to the door.

"Go on." I noticed that the wall clock wasn't running. No lights on the phone console, either.

"You heard about our tissue work—in vitro generation of livers and kidneys. We use stem cells, so that—"

I waved him off and nodded. "Doc, I get it. What do you want with me? I'm just a high school chemistry teacher."

"Last year, management thought we should take on something more challenging."

The floor shook for a second, sending Riddles back to the door. He turned the deadbolt.

"What was that?" I asked.

"So we started with mice, Jimmy. Just to see if the fundamentals would apply."

I couldn't help but raise my voice. "Get to the point."

"Then rats, of course." Riddles adjusted his hat. "It's getting hard to think."

Maybe it was contagious. I was getting a headache. "What the hell did you do with mice and rats, Doc?" I felt another tremor.

The man slid down to the floor with his back against the door. "We tried it with human brain tissue."

"What the hell for?"

"The idea was to grow specific sections of the brain—you know—to replace damaged or missing tissue. Human stem cells— we transformed them into brain cells. And it worked."

"You already said that. And?"

"We didn't expect them to grow into a whole brain."

I pictured an isolated brain floating in some kind of soup with bubbles and wires.

Riddles gasped. "Do you see the problem, Jimmy? Do you see it?" His eyes fluttered for a moment. I thought he was out, but a twitch later, he was back. "The problem—"

"I'm sorry, Doc. I don't get it."

"Senses, Jimmy. It had no sensory input."

That got me to pause—a brain grown from scratch, not connected to anything. No input. I got a really bad feeling.

"It kept growing—like it was searching for some physical way to connect with the outside world. Jimmy, you can't imagine."

Sparks began flying off his little foil helmet. I threw mine off, maybe a little too late. I smelled burned hair.

Riddles tore at the foil. His mouth opened into a silent scream like in Munch's painting. That's when the door got all wavy-like. The next thing I knew, he was stretched out on the floor. My head felt like it was going to explode. All I could think of was getting away. Something was coming.

The pain was so bad that I forgot about Riddles and fumbled with the deadbolt. The door opened, and I fell on my face. Crackling and popping sounds echoed up the stairwell. The concrete cracked, walls were crumbling into sand.

I heard a voice—maybe it was more like a feeling than a voice. This was a cold, lonely, and very upset feeling.

I took the steps two and three at a time—fifth floor, sixth, seventh—through the last fire door and onto the flat asphalt roof. I ran to a parapet looking for a fire escape. The building lurched, almost sending me over.

I thought about a giant brain that had grown without any restrictions, without senses. No duties set by language or custom. The damn thing had no limits—it was just pure thought—maybe struggling to discover its purpose.

The streetlights went out. The rumbling in the building stopped. The stars jiggled for a second. Then they all disappeared. I floated in pitch black, surrounded by complete silence. Then that lonely feeling came back, and I heard a voice like a bell got rung in some humongous church.

Time to start over.

****

"Please turn on the lights, Jimmy."

I waited a moment longer for effect, and then flicked the switch. "Let there be light."

The laughter from the class filled me with joy, as did seeing the children's wide eyes, their grinning faces. Miss Molly, our teacher, sat back down at her desk and thought about what she was going to prepare for dinner tonight.

Even with the fluorescents, the classroom felt a bit confining. A few windows would fix that. Of course, that meant bringing up a sky with a sun and a whole bunch of other stuff.

Carlos/Carlita
Janet Garber

Carlos discovered a tiny sweater in a box in the back of his grandmother's closet. He was looking around for her stash of coins—she kept changing the hiding place. He needed to find it fast—the latest Superman comic had just hit the stands! He had bragged to the kids at school that he had already read it. He'd really just seen the cover and made up the rest. He had to get his hands on it to find out how the real story ended. Darn Grandma, always keeping him begging!

What was this stupid thing anyway? He picked it up from the floor. It was nothing she would have worn: a watery pink color with a white ribbon at the back. He threw it down on her bed in disgust.

Jumping down to the floor, he looked under the bed but found nothing but fuzzy slippers and one long black sock. "I gotta think," he mumbled to himself, getting up and sitting on the edge of the bed. It was getting late. The store was ten minutes away and usually closed at five o'clock. The clock on the night table read 4:20.

Grandma stood in the doorway. "Carlos, what are you doing here?!" she asked as he jumped off the bed.

She had her hands on her hips. Bad sign.

He fished around in his mind for an excuse. He had... nothing. She knew he knew that her room was off limits.

He decided charm was called for. "Abuelita, how nice you look," he said, all sugary. He noticed her shiny white hair, what was left of it, was newly crimped and curled.

She took the bait. "Oh, Yesenia in 1-A set it for me. Nice, yes?"

"Very nice."

She walked in to get a look in her bedside mirror and spotted the reflection of the tiny garment on her bed.

"Look what I found," he said hurriedly, holding it up by one corner. "What is it, Abuelita?"

She stepped forward, reaching out a trembling hand. "Where did you find that? Give it here."

Handing the garment over, Carlos glanced at her watch. "Grandma, do you think I could have a dime?"

She did not seem to hear him. She seemed lost in her thoughts, kneading the dress between her bony fingers, holding it up to her face to sniff. "I meant to get rid of this a long time ago."

She sat on the bed. "Carlos, sit down next to me. I have something to tell you."

****

Abuelita was really losing her mind, Carlos concluded as he ran the short blocks to the comic book store. Maybe she was tilting that Mescal bottle, the one with the green worm inside after he went to sleep at night? Blecch, he could just see the caption above his head. And the sweat pouring off his face as he spied on her guzzling the stuff—in the comic book of his life!

Where did she come up with such a story? Of course, she was his grandma! She had always been his grandma. His mother? He was too little to remember; that's why he couldn't remember her face or really anything about her. That was her picture on Abuelita's nightstand, wasn't it? Wasn't that proof?

It was 4:50, and he was running now. One more block. His heart was dancing around in his chest, so he stopped. He leaned with both hands against the window of the Five and Ten and looked at his reflection. He was on the small side, true, and his muscles so far had failed to materialize. The other second grade boys were taller; some were tougher, meaner. So what!

At 4:55, he got to Archie's Comic Stop. It was closed! What the heck? He wiped the sweat off his brow with his cap. Unbelievable! The new Superman issue was still in the window.

He glanced around – the street was empty. He picked up a brick.

****

"Abuelita, I don't want to hear this. Really. You're confusing me and, you know, I'm getting sick to my stomach every time I think about what you're saying."

"It's my fault, Carlos. I'm so sorry." She dabbed at her eyes with an old embroidered hanky from the old country. "But... the police are coming, my boy. Do what I told you!"

"Why are they coming? I left the quarter on the ledge."

"No, my boy. That's not enough. Now, hurry and do what I said."

He went into his room and put on the shorts and pink top and sneakers she had bought for him. His hair was already on the longish side, so it wasn't a problem.

The police were coming any minute. She looked him over. "Basta."

"My daughter, Carlita, is very shy. I am very strict with her. You see, I had her very late in life..."

"Okay, tell me again."

"The sweater, Carlos, was yours. When you were little…"

"A little boy…"

"No, Carlito, listen. I was alone. And I didn't know what you were!" His grandmother paused to blow her nose. "I went to the priest, and he said you were a little girl."

"Why couldn't you tell? I had a pipi like a boy… didn't I? Don't I?" Carlos shivered and looked wildly around the small apartment for a way out. Then he looked back at his grandmother. He went over to her sitting in the kitchen chair and put his hands on her shoulders and shook her. "Tell me, tell me!"

"Stop, hijo. You're hurting me. Listen: when you were very little, I dressed you like a girl and called you Carlita."

"NO! NO! NO!"

Grandma nodded her head sadly.

"You still call me that sometimes for a joke."

"Yes, but not a joke. Then one day I had to leave you with a neighbor. For a week. When I returned, she said to me that you were a boy. She was so sure. I looked at you. She had dressed you in boys' clothes. I saw a boy too. So from that day, you have been Carlos and not Carlita."

"Grandma, are you making this up? WHAT AM I?" Carlos ran screaming from the room.

"What do you feel you are, Carlos?" Grandma yelled after him. "The doctor said you could choose when you were older.

Maybe you're old enough?"

****

"Abuelita, are you home?"

"I'm here."

"Sit down."

"Okay. Do you have a story to tell me?"

"I want to show you my new comic book. I made it myself. About Juan and Juanita."

"Yes, I want to see it. Hmm. Interesting. Oh, this is naughty! Why is his friend Pepe pulling his pants down and he's watching? I can't look at this!"

"No, see, Grandma," Carlos said, pulling her hands away from her eyes, "Juan wants to see what a boy's pipi looks like. Look!"

Grandma looked at him. "And that's not what you look like?"

Carlos shook his head, and a little sob escaped him.

"So you believe me now?"

"Why, Abuelita, why am I like this?"

Grandma gave him a big hug. "You know I love you any way you are. And if you like, the doctor said he can make you look more like your friend. When you are older."

Carlos brightened up. "What? How old?"

"You want to do that? Maybe five more years. Maybe sooner."

"Sooner sooner sooner!" Carlos was jumping up and down now, clapping his hands, grinning.

"I want you to be sure. When you're a bit older. You're sure you don't ever want to be a girl?"

"Ugh. I hate girls! No way!" Carlos paused. "What does the doctor do to me?"

Grandma thought how to explain. "You know when you are drawing your comics? Sometimes you make a mistake, and you erase it and draw it again?"

Carlos nodded.

"And if you are playing with clay, you break a piece off and shape it, and then press it back on? So that's what the doctor will do."

"Will it hurt?"

"Does it hurt to look different from your friend?" Seeing him nod, Grandma continued, "We will think about it and decide in a few years, okay? Meanwhile, Pepe called you. He wants you to meet him in the schoolyard to play some stickball. I said you could go as long as you're home for supper."

"Thank you, Ab... Mama." Carlos grabbed his bat and ran out, slamming the door.

Then he ran back. "I took a dime from under your bed. HaHa!"

"What a bad boy!"

He kissed her on both cheeks. And then he was gone.

"Gracias a Dios."

Chetric The Grand

Jean Davis

Lightning flashed outside the basement window. Chet Wykowski gripped his controller, praying to the game gods that the power wouldn't go out while he was in the middle of the quest he'd been working on for the past two hours. Rain beat against the house and thunder rumbled, but the TV and game console stayed on. He relaxed into the couch, reaching out blindly for the bag of nacho chips that had been his sole source of sustenance since downloading Wizards and Warriors six hours ago. His fingers met with nothing but greasy crumbs. Wiping his hand on his pants, he reached for the can of lukewarm soda beside him and settled back into the game.

As he took yet another beating from the heavily armored Orc Lord, and applied his last healing potion, he began to consider that he might need to waste more time on side quests to level up his character before trying for the Orc again. A level five wizard just wasn't cutting it. But he was sick of delivering items from one town to another or providing safe passage for hapless travelers in exchange for a rusty knife or a threadbare rug posing as a magic carpet.

The Orc battle promised enough experience to gain him several levels and enough gold to purchase the rune-covered cloak and spell book he'd seen in the last shop.

The Orc swung his tree-trunk size spiked club at Chetric the Grand again, knocking the wizard into the wooden wall of a livery across the town square. The stupid chickens that seemed to be milling around in every town scene scattered with crazed squawking. The wood shattered with a crack that came through the sound system so loud that he thought his eardrums burst. The room around him flashed white. Chetric's body slid down the wall and landed on the ground with a pathetic grunt and a puff of dirt. Everything went black.

Chet opened his eyes, blinking away the fog of heavy sleep. He didn't remember falling asleep. Or shutting down the game. His heart raced as he fumbled around, searching for the controller to verify that he'd hit save before nodding off.

The damned controller was nowhere to be found. And no matter how much he blinked, he couldn't quite clear his aching head. In fact, his entire body ached, even worse than his doomed two-week stint on the wrestling team in high school. He hadn't liked all the aches then, and now, three years after graduating, he didn't like them even more. Grimacing, he worked his way into a sitting position.

He tried to find the can of cola to wash away the grit he discovered on his teeth, but that was gone too. The sun beat down on him, making him sweat. Why was there a sun in the basement? And what the hell was this long-sleeved tunic he was wearing instead of the t-shirt and shorts he'd fallen asleep in?

Chet's eyes and mind suddenly clicked into working order.

A worn backpack lay by his side. He reached in, pulling out three turnips, a leg of mutton, and a three-page book. His eyes bulged as he read. It was the beginner spell for shooting balls of energy that worked for hobs but not much else. On the last page was a weak healing spell. Both useless.

Chickens clucked nearby. A woman in a peasant dress wandered over to him.

"Do you have a ring for me?"

"No. Go away."

"Very well. Find me later. I'll be at the Inn."

The only thing keeping Chet from losing it entirely was the fact that the Orc wasn't in the square with him. All that remained of their battle was a broken wagon and two broken boards on the side of the building where he'd been landed after being smacked with the giant club. No wonder he ached all over.

But that meant he was in the game. Like *in* it. Chet leaned against the livery, hunched over with his hands on his knees, hyperventilating.

The sun was arcing downward before he'd gotten himself under control. If he'd somehow gotten into the game, there had to be a way out. He spotted a rusty sword in the dirt near where his backpack had been. Upon picking it up, he realized it fit in the scabbard that hung from the thick leather belt around his waist. With his backpack slung over one shoulder and the sword at his side, he ventured out into the street.

A large, grime-covered man wearing a leather apron and reeking of smoke and hot metal, took a lumbering swing at his head.

Chet dodged out of the way. "What the hell was that for?"

The big man scowled. "You're the wizard, right? You can send me home."

Revealing that his powers were not quite up to that task as of yet didn't seem wise. "I am a wizard, yes. Where is your home?"

"The north coast."

Chet did his best to recall the map in the lower corner of the screen that had slowly revealed itself during his travels. "Right. If you take this road to the left, you'll come to the port and from there you can take a ship. That's the fastest way."

"Can't you magic me there? I don't have gold for a ship."

"Sorry, no."

The blacksmith snorted. "Some wizard you are." He stormed back to his forge on the other side of the street.

Not even ten steps later, someone hit him in the back of the head with something hard. Chet put his arms up, trying to defend himself, and spun around to face his attacker.

"Send me home," cried a young boy with a long stick in his hands.

"What is it with you people?" Chet finally got out of range enough to muster his energy ball spell and send the kid flying backward.

"My uncle stole me away. He sold me." The boy got up from the dirt, tears flowing down his face. "Please, sir, you can help me?"

"Sorry, I can't." Chet hurried down the street, trying his best to avoid everyone. Sore and hungry, he sought out the inn the woman had mentioned. The more he walked around town, the more he remembered about where he'd been and where things were. Once he got his bearings, he made his way to the inn.

As he walked, more footsteps followed him. He turned around to see two men, one with a large fish, the other with a game board under his arm, and a woman with a rolling pin following close behind. All three of them stopped when he caught sight of them, smiling nervously but all with the same determined gleam in their eyes. He started walking faster, the muscles in his neck and shoulders tensing further and further.

Finally, he could take it no longer. He turned around again to find a well-dressed man with a deck of cards had joined the other three stalkers. "What the are you people doing?"

The four of them looked from one to the other, shifting their feet in the dirt and pursing their lips.

The woman spoke up, "Your sign, we just want to go home."

"What sign?"

"The challenge pinned to the back of your shirt," said the man with the fish. "Beat me, and I'll send you home."

Chet tried to twist his head around to find the note. He contorted his arms to try and grab it, but his muscles were too tight. "Where?"

The man with the deck of cards approached slowly and after a tug, handed Chet a hand-written note and a pin.

"I did *not* put that there. I'm not sending any of you home, or anywhere else. Now, leave me alone!" He crunched the note in his hand. That's what he got for blacking out in the middle of town. Some stupid kid had probably thought he was being funny.

Chet stormed off to the inn. No one else accosted him along the way.

On the boardwalk outside the inn, sat a row of beggars. One of which was the urchin he'd sold the threadbare rug to before he'd gone off to battle the Orc. The kid looked happy to have a rug to sit on, though the rug looked even worse for wear, covered in mud and food crumbs.

"Looks like you're not starving then," he said to the urchin.

"No, sir. Are enjoying the stone?"

Chet had to trace back his transactions. He'd received the rug as payment for returning a doll to a girl, but then had accidentally started a riot and killed two men with his sword when his performance skill was too low, and instead of the simple trick he'd meant to do to win the favor of the miller's daughter who had promised to teach him another spell, had set the town's wooden granary on fire. To gain back some of his good karma, he'd traded the urchin the rug for the boy's favorite stone. The stone fit in a hole in an old woman's wall, sealing her home against the wind and earning him three turnips. He still had no idea what he was supposed to do with those.

He nodded to the urchin.

Dust puffed from beneath the boy, making the beggar next to him cough. The boy pressed his hands firmly on the front corners of the rug, but the back corners continued to flap. Chet swore he heard a muffled voice, but the boy nor the man next to him said anything.

"Who is that?" He peered around.

The boy's eyes grew wide and he rocked back and forth until he was violently pitched forward, rolling head-first out into the street.

The rug rose up, standing end to end, as if it had legs. It walked forward on two corners, slapping Chet in the cheek with the third.

"You idiot," said a feminine voice. "I could have brought you anywhere you wanted to go, but you traded me for a stone? You took one look at me and thought I was worthless, didn't you?" The corner drew back as if it were going to slap him again.

Chet stepped back. "Uh, sorry?"

The rug pointed to the wad of paper in his hand. "I see you found my note."

"Yours?"

"Look at me. I mean, look at this mess!" The rug twisted side to side. "That kid hasn't had a bath in, well, ever and his feet are covered in mud. I'm filthy."

"So..." Chet bit his lip, not sure whether to run screaming or laugh. "You want me to... beat you?"

"I thought the note was quite clear. You clean me up, trade the kid something else for me, and I'll send you home."

He removed his three turnips and set them on the boardwalk. "Those are for you, kid."

Chet motioned the rug over to a grassy lot with two chickens scratching about. "Go stand over there."

The rug floated over the street and stood in the lot. Chet summoned three energy balls one after another, hitting the rug and knocking the mud and dirt away. On a whim, he threw a health spell its way too.

Color ran over the rug, bursting into intricate patterns. Long golden tassels dripped from its corners. The rug leaped into the air, laughing, rolling in tight spirals.

"You can call me Nora. Promise you won't trade me again?" it purred his ear, rubbing up against him and running a silken tassel against his cheek.

"Wouldn't dream of it, Nora."

"Then hop on, it's time for you to go home."

Daisy for One Day
Mark Hudson

I walked home discouraged. I was so depressed! I was an artist and a writer, and people just didn't understand! I was on the proverbial pity pot in this gloom and doom town. And everybody around me was so depressed. My forty-sixth birthday was coming up, and what did that mean? Cake and ice cream? Choo-choo trains? I was growing old, and I was bald as an eagle, but without the dignity, nor the cult status. I couldn't fly like an eagle when I was crawling like an inchworm.

As I entered the elevator, I saw my neighbor, the attorney, who had his dog Daisy. That dog was spoiled by his owner and everybody in the building. Why, the people in the building loved that dog more than me! If I only I could be a dog!

I got home and still felt sad! Should I end it all? I took my bottle of Fred Flintstone chewable vitamins and downed the bottle. I prayed I wouldn't wake up, or at least if I did, I'd wake up in a better place.

When I woke up, I was Daisy the Dog! I had somehow been magically transported into my neighbor's apartment, and I was his dog! I was lying on a beanbag, sweating under a heavy air conditioner! My master was feeding me tons of pizza. I needed to go number two. But I didn't know how to tell this to my master. I was new at this dog thing.

He must've read me like a book. "Oh, you want to go poo-poo, don't you Daisy?" I guess I must've nodded my head, wagged my tail in agreement. Could it be more obvious?

So, my master put a leash on me and put me in the elevator. In the elevator, there was a gorgeous woman in the elevator! She said, "Oh, your dog is so cute!" and pet me on the head, and massaged my ears! Why couldn't that ever happen to me when I was human? All I could do is drool like a fool, and stick my tongue out, panting! It's what I secretly wished to do as a human being, but I couldn't do, my parents taught me manners!

My master brought me out to the front lawn, and I let out a fresh poop to decorate the grass. Suddenly, I didn't feel so cute. A bunch of grade-school kids were laughing, and I felt self-conscious! They better be grateful they're not a dog! Their parents better monitor how many Fred Flintstone vitamins they take, or they might be the next one to be a dog!

Then, my master took me inside, and put me in a cage and said, "Good night."

Good night? It was dark and uncomfortable! Ouch! What was this? Oh, if only I could only be a human again, I'll never complain again! I begin to think like Dorothy from 'The Wizard of Oz" There's no place like home...

Then a weird thing happened. I found myself in my own bed, in my own apartment and Daisy was at my side, licking my face.

"Yuck!" I said.

Then, Daisy disappeared. Everything was back to normal. What happened?

I checked my wastebasket, and there were no bottles of vitamins that I took. Then I found it. A can of bad tomatoes must've given me the bad hallucinations, and guess what had also been mixed into it: dog food! I smelled a lawsuit on my hands!

So I consulted the very same neighbor, the attorney, and he helped me sue Happy Foods where I got the tomatoes. Needless to say, they were not too happy. I won the case, I had a million dollars, and I bought a mansion in Lake Forest, and I became like Howard Hughes and bought an anorexic poodle that refused to eat.

Then he peed on my thousand-dollar rug which was the last straw. I threw him out on the street, and then ten minutes later I cried, and packed all my belongings in a bag and a stick, and took off to find my dog looking like Charlie Chaplin, or a tramp, or something.

We got to about Rogers Park with all the bull dogs and killer canines, and we got scared, and we both ran back home, where we eat tons of pizza, and my philosophy is,

"Don't read newspapers, it's too depressing. Put them on your rug so your dog can pee on it."

I may be nothing but a "hound dog", but at least I wasn't Elvis Presley. Every dog has his day.

Fame Can Be Lame
Mark Hudson

I had been invited by Grey Wolfe Publishing to appear at one of their summer festivals. Being from Chicago, and being rather bad at directions, and furthermore, by not being a driver, I had taken a train to Michigan and gotten close to Detroit. But when I got off, I realized, "Wow, I'm here in Michigan, and I am lost."

I called Diana and she came and picked me up. I was to spend a weekend promoting my latest book of short stories to the Michigan crowd.

I arrived for the weekend, and I was staying in a comfy lodge in town. The book-signing event was to go on all weekend, and I was thrilled. I'd been working on a book of short stories, and with the help of the editors at Grey Wolfe Publishing, I had produced my masterpiece.

The first day was a thrill. I met local Michigan residents, all lovely people. They were so kind and encouraging that I knew the trip was worthwhile.

Then up walked a slender blonde, a country girl with that look of innocence, yet definitely not naivety. She approached my table and said, "Are you Mark Hudson? I'm your greatest fan!"

I was flabbergasted. My face turned beet red. My pride and ego soared like an eagle, while my insecurity bubbled at the surface.

"Really?" I stammered.

Later that night, Grey Wolfe had a campfire in the woods. The blonde and I shared marshmallows over a campfire.

"You didn't mean what you said, that you are my number one fan, did you?" I asked.

"Yes, I did. And I want to show you my dedication to your craft. Follow me into the woods," she flirted.

With adolescent enthusiasm, I followed her into the woods. We kissed under the moonlight. Then, came the kicker.

"Oh, Mark Hudson, will you join me in the circle?"

And with that, she shape-shifted into a wolf! She chased me till the break of dawn, but I got away.

I told Diana about the experience in the morning, and how traumatized I was.

Diana looked me dead in the eye and said, "Well, why do you think we call it Grey Wolfe Publishing?"

Fanfare
Sujoy Bhattacherjee

Sujan Kumar is a pop singer of immense popularity all over Asia. He has been gifted with a melodiously robust voice. He has been trained by his godfather, Afjal Ali Khan, a great classical maestro. Sujan Kumar has numberless fans all over the continent. He has many crazed fans. Among them, Sunita is the craziest one. If anybody says anything against Sujan, she becomes lunatically irate. She comes to a fray with him and ultimately ends up in shedding tears of mental agony.

Sunita is a student of engineering at a college of good repute. She is a bright and promising student, but her craziness for the pop star often puts her in awkward situations. She embarrasses herself and makes others embarrassed, too. She keeps all information about her adorable singer — what he likes to eat, what colors he likes, what he dislikes and where he goes walking, his favorite car; his all oddities and specifics are known to her. She writes letters to him regularly. In the beginning, her letters were given careful reply. But gradually, the content of her letters took the form of a love letter. Sujan Kumar smelt a danger and stopped replying to her letters. She still goes on writing letters to Sujan Kumar, making amorous soliloquy and sending them to her dear singer. She has not been receiving any return letters from Sujan for a long time. She is so badly obsessed with her hero that she does not mind not getting any reply. She talks to him over the telephone, though Sujan has changed his phone number. But she dials the old, obsolete number and talks for hours as if she is a mad woman. Yes! She has turned mad for Sujan. She tells false stories to her friends that she is going to marry Sujan Kumar soon. Her friends mock her ruthlessly, but she never takes it to heart.

One day, the National Herald published the news that Sujan Kumar was going out for a world tour. Sunita read the news and reacted lunatically. She packed her luggage as if she was also going with Sujan. She contacted a travel agent and confirmed her tickets with a Visa and other relevant things needed for a world tour. She spread the news to her friends that she was going on the world tour with Sujan and, as evidence, produced her airline tickets and other ancillary papers. Some of her friends accepted that what she used to say regarding her relationship with Sujan was true. She boastfully danced in joy.

Sunita accepted Sujan as her favorite idol, and a morbid possessiveness forced her to take him as her lover. She never met him personally, but her one-sided love made her psychology disturbed. She was not only a diehard fan of Sujan Kumar, but her strange obsession made her a crazy person. She set out for a world tour to chase her hero.

She was fortunate to confront Sujan in Egypt. Both of them met each other in a park for the first time. It was a most coveted moment for Sunita, but to Sujan Kumar, it was a problem. He wanted to get rid of the unwanted hazard at any cost. He said to Sunita, "I am going to marry my girlfriend within a couple of months. I can't marry you. You are my fan. I also adore you, and I can give you anything you want except love. Please understand." Sunita listened to what Sujan told her with heedful attention. She wore a queerly calm and quiet air on her face and hurriedly galloped to her hotel. In a perturbed mood, she committed suicide by hanging from the ceiling fan after making a noose from her saree. She could not even write a suicide note before killing herself. Thus, abnormal craziness nipped a promising blossom in the bud.

There is no harm to be a fan, worshipping idols, but when the craziness of the fans reaches an alarming height, we should consult a psychotherapist. Otherwise, any fatal mishaps might destroy our lives.

Sujan Kumar is not to blame for the baleful fate of Sunita. Numberless fans sent him marriage proposals. He received many letters written with the blood of his crazed fans. They also threatened to kill themselves if he did not agree to marry them. Fans are next to God to all celebrities. They adore their fans as living deity. They do not look upon their fans as common beings. So, fans should treat their idols not as a personal, but public property.

Hunting Golden Carrots
Izabela Jeremus

"Girl, I say, girl, what are you doing there?" are the words that wake me up.

I open my ten-pound eyelids to a strange sight. Before me stands a giant rooster, all white, with a red head and tail feathers. His large yellow beak is only outdone by his gigantic feet. He peers at me with tiny, squinting eyes.

"Who *are* you?" I ask, attempting to stand up.

My knees give out, but before I can fall, the rooster catches me.

"Foghorn J. Leghorn at your service," he responds, stabilizing me.

"Thanks," I reply, looking around. "I'm Linda."

The field around me seems to be colored in with pencil, perfect greens for the trees and grass, but the details are scarce. The trees rise in solid brown, no variation to the color. Behind me is a small white house, red roofed, with a white picket fence. A hound-like dog sleeps in a kennel. His long brown ears twitch every now and then; his white body rises up and down rhythmically.

Another dog marches around the yard. He's a grey bulldog, wearing a black collar with silver studs. A scowl paints his face.

"Do you live here?" I ask Foghorn.

Foghorn laughs. "No, I say, no. This is Granny's house."

Just as Foghorn says this, a little elderly lady in a white shirt, blue skirt, with glasses and grey hair comes running out. Granny seems to be in a panic as she approaches the bulldog.

"Hector!" she cries out. "Sylvester is at it again. Tweety is gone. Please find him!"

Hector, the bulldog, nods and takes off. Granny returns to the house.

"Well, I say, well, here's my chance with Barnyard Dawg!" Foghorn exclaims.

Foghorn grabs a two-by-four from a pile near the fence and sneaks up to Barnyard Dawg. He smacks the hound dog with the two-by-four, laughing maniacally.

Barnyard Dawg yelps and jumps up growling. Seeing Foghorn, he takes off after him, barking up a storm. Barnyard Dawg pulls harder and harder, until his lead snaps. At this point, Foghorn takes off in the direction of the woods, Barnyard Dawg on his heels.

I stare after them for a moment. Now that the chaos has settled down, I realize that I have an inexplicable desire to go hunting. Rabbit hunting. I go and knock on Granny's door, hoping for some answers.

Granny answers on the third knock and smiles at me.

"Um, hi, Granny," I say, uneasily. "My name is Linda and I'm a little lost."

Granny throws open the door. "Oh, you poor soul! Come in for some tea and cookies!"

I walk into a tiny kitchen. A large golden cage, fit for ten parakeets, sits in the corner. Staring at the open cage door, I miss the man sitting at the table until he bounds up and shakes my hand enthusiastically. He's just a huge nose with a pudgy little body. Dressed in what seems to be a hunting outfit, brown and red, he's full of energy.

"Elmuw Fudd, hewe, young lady," he introduces himself.

Gingerly, I pull my hand away. "Hello, Elmur, I'm Linda."

Granny brings me a cup of tea and bids me to sit down.

"Elmur here is a dear friend," Granny explains.

"I'm just westin' before I go back out," Elmur states.

I take a sip of tea and am surprised to find that it's delicious, sweet with honey and a little tart with lemon. "Back out to do what?" I ask curiously.

Elmur pulls a double barrel shotgun from under the table and strokes it lovingly. "Wabbit huntin'."

My eyes widen despite myself. "Rabbit hunting?"

"Yes, ma'am."

My mouth says the words without my permission, "I know this is going to sound strange, but can I go rabbit hunting with you?"

"Suwe, Winda! The mowe the mewwiew!"

After some of Granny's sugar cookies, Elmur and I set out. He leads the way through the field, the grass getting longer.

Out of nowhere, my ankle falls into a hole and, yelping, I tumble face first to the ground.

"Caweful! That's a wabbit hole."

Elmur helps me up and continues creeping forward. I hang back a little, making sure I don't step in any more holes. Suddenly, I feel a tap on my shoulder.

"Ehh, what's up, Doc?"

Spinning around, I see him. His long ears make him a foot taller than me. A blue-grey coat covers every inch of his body, except his fuzzy white belly. Nibbling a carrot, his huge buck teeth are set in a grin.

"Elmur! It's the wabb- I mean rabbit!" I call.

Grabbing a nearby rock the size of my fist, I advance on him. He backs up, still grinning that maddening grin.

"Ehh, not smart, Linda," he says, dancing around me.

I pause. "How do you know my name?"

He stops and considers me seriously for a moment. "Bugs Bunny knows everything."

"Do you know how to get me out of here?"

The grin of the insane returns. "Maybe, maybe not, Doc."

Jumping on him without warning, I strike with the rock. Moving like lightening, the attack only gets his shoulder, but he seems as perplexed as I am that I got him at all.

Advancing on him, I wave the rock like the desperate woman I am. "Can you get me out of here?"

Bugs throws his carrot at me and says, "Get me the golden carrot and we'll talk."

With that, he turns and bounds away on all fours before disappearing into a hole.

A shutgun blast to my right catches my attention. I run in its direction to discover Elmur firing at a black duck. He has a little white stripe across his neck, like a priest's collar, and a large yellow beak with webbed feet.

"Elmur, what are you doing?" I exclaim.

"I'm wabbit huntin'."

I push his gun down just before he fires again. "That's not a rabbit; that's a duck."

Elmur puts down his gun. "A duck?"

The duck slinks over and gasps, "Thank you! Bugths told him I was a rabbit! Ithn't that dethpicable?"

I wipe his spit off of my face. "That's not very nice."

"No thir, it'th not," he says. "And I thought Bugths was a friend!"

"You're friends with Bugs Bunny?" I ask, hope blossoming in my chest.

"I thought tho."

"Do you know anything about a golden carrot?"

"Is he thtill looking for that? I have a lead, but I don't think he detherves it."

"He may not, but I just saved your life."

The duck hesitates, then sighs deeply. "I thuppose tho. Daffy's the name. Let'th go!"

I leave Elmur still rabbit hunting and follow Daffy. He leads me to three small cottages. One is made of straw, one of wood, and one of brick. Daffy heads to the brick house and knocks loudly.

"G-g-g-go a-a-a-away!" comes a voice from the inside. "I'm n-n-n-not l-l-l-letting y-y-y-you in, w-w-w-w-olf!"

"It'th Daffy," the duck shouts, "not the wolf! Open up, Porky!"

A piece of wood slides to reveal a huge, scared eye. Then the sound of multiple locks being slid open fills the air. A round, pink pig in a blue jacket and hat with a red bow tie opens the door and beckons us to come in quickly. Once we're piled into the micro kitchen, Porky hurriedly rebolts all six locks.

"W-w-w-w-w... How are you, D-d-d-d-affy?" Porky asks.

"Fine, thankth," Daffy replies. "Thith here ith..."

"Linda," I fill in.

"She's looking for the golden carrot," Daffy continues. "I believe you thtill have it?"

"Shh!" Porky ducks, as if there is a sniper outside, rifle raised to take him out.

Daffy goes to the window. "There'th no one out there, Porky. The golden carrot. Do. You. Have. It?"

"I'll g-g-g-g-g-g- let you have it. For a p-p-p-p-p-rice."

"What is it?" I ask.

Porky turns his beady little eyes to me. "G-g-g-g- take care of the wolf for the village."

"Stay here, you two," I tell them and let myself out.

I run back the way we had come and look around frantically.

"Elmur!" I call.

He comes to me, pulling me to the ground, a finger to his lips. "Shh, be vewy, vewy quiet."

"Yes, I know, you're hunting rabbits," I finish for him. "I know where there's going to be a huge rabbit soon."

Elmur's eyes widen. "Where?!"

"Come with me!"

Elmur follows me back to Porky's village. I explain to him on the way that the rabbit is going to be dressed as a wolf to disguise himself.

"Twicky!"

"That's right, Elmur, he's trying to trick you. But you won't let him, will you?"

"No!"

I knock on Porky's door, and after reassuring him that neither one of us is the wolf, he lets us in.

"This is Elmur," I explain. "He's going to take care of your wolf problem."

"H-h-h-h-ow?"

"I'm goin' to hunt him, of couwse!" Elmur replies.

Just as we finish laying down the plan for the hunt, we hear squealing from outside. Porky opens his door just in time for two other pigs to come running in, panting.

"He's here!" they shout in tandem.

Then, from the other side of the door, a gruff voice says, "Little pig, little pig, let me in!"

"Not by the hair of our chinny chin chin!" replies one of them.

"Then I'll huff," he replies, "and I'll puff and I'll blow your house in!"

I nod at Elmur. He gets in front of the door, with Daffy and I on the sides. Daffy undoes the latches and I throw the door open. The wolf has only enough time to look startled before Elmur discharges his rifle in his face.

The pigs surround Elmur, profusely thanking him for being their rescuer.

"Glad to be of sewvice!" says Elmur, proudly throwing his bounty over his shoulder, before leaving.

I turn to Porky. "Now, about that carrot..."

Golden carrot in hand, I find my way back to rabbit hole where I last saw Bugs. I stand above it, feeling silly for a minute, before crouching down and calling, "Bugs?"

"Eh, what's up, Doc?" comes a voice from behind me.

"*Must* you do that?" I complain.

Bugs just grins and nibbles his half-eaten carrot.

Repressing the urge to slug him, I hold up the golden carrot.

"Great!" Bugs exclaims. "Let's go then!"

"Go where?"

Bugs points down the rabbit hole.

"I am *not*..."

I don't get to finish my sentence as Bugs jumps down into the hole. Seeing nothing else to be done, I gingerly crawl in behind him.

Much to my amazement, I end up in a large room lit by several electric lamps. Bugs is standing in front of a black cauldron, the fire already going beneath it. He's throwing things I don't recognize - and don't want to look too closely at - into it.

Finally, he holds up his hand for the golden carrot. He gives me his half-eaten one. "Hold that for me, Doc."

I shove it in my back pocket as I watch him shave a few peels of the golden one into his bubbling pot. He goes over to a shelf filled with all sorts of mysterious things and produces a piece of chalk with which he draws a door on the side of the wall.

"As promised, a door home," he says, then throws the entire concoction onto the door drawing. It begins to glow with a heavenly blue light.

"Go fast," he says, "it won't stay open for long."

He doesn't have to tell me twice; I run through it.

I wake up on my bed, with my back sore. Looney Tunes is playing on late night TV. Chuckling to myself, I roll over to pull out whatever it is that's hurting my back.

To my astonishment, it's an oversized, half-eaten carrot.

If You Have a Rotary Phone
Reynold Junker

I couldn't help staring at her. I knew there was nothing unusual about my wife standing at a kitchen counter, chopping fresh vegetables into a salad. I'd seen her doing it countless times in our kitchen in California. It's just that this had been my mother's kitchen, and my boyhood Brooklyn memory of my mother's kitchen and her cooking was of one endless string of pasta — not a vegetable in sight. There'd been tomatoes, of course, peeled, crushed, pureed and pasted beyond recognition. But those tomatoes had been peeled, crushed, pureed, pasted and canned by some invisible hand - not my mother's.

Chop. Chop. Chop.

Now my mother was gone. She'd passed away quietly, cursing under her breath in Italian at the rest home attendants tending to her passing.

"I haven't seen one of these things in ages," I said now toying with the heavy old black Bakelite rotary dial phone. It hefted like something that the police might find chained to the ankles of a body submerged in Sheepshead Bay—someone else who might well have also passed cursing under his breath in Italian.

"My mother used to keep a lock on this phone," I said. "That old lock is probably still hidden in a drawer around here somewhere."

Chop. Chop. Chop. A tomato. A fresh tomato. No invisible hands here.

My mother had kept a lock on the phone to keep my brother and me from using it without her permission. In those days, you were charged for telephone use by the call, ten cents per local call. We lived on a very limited budget based on a small allowance provided us by the uncle in whose house we lived. Every penny counted, every dime, certainly.

Chop. Chop. Chop.

"A rotary phone," I said. "Honest to God. You know how these new voice mail systems run you through a menu of choices before ending with 'If you have a rotary phone, please stay on the line...'?"

"I hadn't really thought much about it."

Chop. Chop. Chop.

"Have you ever wondered what would happen if you had a rotary phone and stayed on the line?"

"I hadn't really given that much thought either."

Slice. Slice. Slice. A cucumber.

"I think I'll try it."

"Try what?"

"Try to call somebody. I think I'll try to call John Doyle!"

This time she stopped chopping, slicing and scraping and turned to look directly at me. "Joe, it's been years since you lived in this neighborhood. You were a child. How could you possibly think that John Doyle could still be living around here?" My wife couldn't understand many of the things that I'd told her about growing up in Brooklyn. She was from New Mexico - the land of the jalapeno pepper.

Chop. A tiny jalapeno pepper secreted from some remote farm village in New Mexico made even tinier by my wife in my mother's kitchen. *Chop.*

"That's something that I could never explain," I said, explaining. "John Doyle didn't just live in this neighborhood. For us as kids, John Doyle was this neighborhood. He was its driving force. Everything that we did as kids, we did with or because of John Doyle."

It was true. John Doyle had been our fearless leader. He'd also been our court jester and master prankster. Our parents did not appreciate John Doyle. John Doyle was one of the reasons that my mother kept a lock on our phone.

One of the games that John Doyle had invented for our after-school entertainment had been a telephone game. You had to think of a name that had seven letters that could be dialed on a phone. Stanley was, for example, a name with seven letters that could be dialed S-T-A-N-L-E-Y on the phone. You dialed S-T-A-N-L-E-Y and...

"Is Stan there?"

"There isn't any Stan here."

"Are you sure he's not there. This is his number."

"Listen, kid, I told you, there isn't any Stan here."

"But I dialed S-T-A-N-L-E-Y. That's his number."

"Listen, kid..."

"Ask him to call me when he gets in."

"Listen, kid. God damn it..."

M-I-C-H-A-E-L

"Is Mikey there?"...

"Anyway, I'm going to give it a shot. I'm going to try to find John Doyle. What's the number for Information?"

"411," she answered.

Chop. Chop. A mushroom loses its head. *Chop.*

"That's another thing."

"What's another thing?" she asked without turning.

"We used to dial 'O' for the Operator when we wanted Information. Who decided on 411? Who decided that we had to go metric to make telephone calls? We used to have exchanges that meant something. Some had romantic or exotic sounding names. I remember that when I was a boy, ours was ESplanade 5."

"ESplanade. That sounds just like Brooklyn. You can't go anywhere in Brooklyn without running into an esplanade."

"No. Really. There was a MUrray Hill. There was a BUtterfield. They made a great movie with Elizabeth Taylor called 'BUtterfield 8'. Can you imagine Elizabeth Taylor starring in a movie called '288'? Or how about the old Glenn Miller tune, 'PEnnsylvania 6-5000'? Can't you just hear Frank Sinatra crooning '736-5000'?"

I dialed 411 feeling the toneless uniform analog clicks march individually and smartly back into my fingertips from the old black phone.

"Information. This is Harold. What city please?" my mother's telephone asked.

"Brooklyn, please."

"Yes."

"John Doyle, please."

"Thank you."

A humanoid metallic voice clicked at me. "The number is 687-8000."

"That's kind of funny," I said.

"What's kind of funny?" both my wife and the phone's metallic voice asked simultaneously.

"That number," I said into the mouthpiece.

"What's so funny about it? The 687 part or the 8000 part?" the voice from the phone asked.

"The 8000 part. I always figured that only large businesses and organizations had numbers like 8000 and 1234 and number combinations like that. Make them easy to remember. You know. Like the old Glenn Miller tune, 'PEnnsylvania 6-5000'."

"You mean the old Glenn Miller tune 736-5000, don't you?"

I started to explain. "But. No. No. Never mind. It would take too long to explain."

"Anyway - the number is 687-8000. Thank you for using A, T, and T." I'd half expected to hear him say "Thank you for using 1, 8 and 8." I guess it's different when you're in control. When you're in control, you get to make the rules.

"Thank you."

"Did you find him?"

"I've got a number," I responded. I dialed MUrray Hill

7-8000.

"You have reached Murray Hill Consolidated, Manchester."
The voice was clearly properly clipped English in accent. "Please
listen carefully before choosing from the following menu options.
They have been changed within the past fortnight. If you know the
four-digit extension of your party, you can enter it at any time. To
order..."

"I don't believe it."

"What's wrong?" my wife asked.

"I got a voice mail. It sounds like it's someplace in England.
My mother never had long distance service. I can't imagine my
mother calling anyone outside of Brooklyn, much less England."

"...If you have a rotary phone, please stay on the line, and
one of our agents will be with you momentarily. Your call may be
monitored or recorded to ensure..."

Then, from the phone, not metallic—"Of course it's England.
It's Manchester, and this particular Manchester is in England. There
may be other Manchesters in the world, but this one is in England."

I could hear another voice from the phone in the
background asking "What's wrong? Didn't you tell him that his call
might be monitored? Is this one we should be recording?"

The phone voice again, this time to the voice in the
background—"Some bloody fool doesn't believe he's reached
England."

In the background—"Maybe he doesn't believe you're really
a licensed monitor."

"What else would I be? That's what I'm doing. Isn't it? I
mean I am monitoring. If he keeps on like this, I may have to report

him. That would look nice on his permanent record. Serve him right, cheeky American bugger."

"I'm going to record this one. Can you get him to hold on for a bit longer?"

From the phone again—"Look. Let's try this one more time, shall we? '...If you have a rotary phone, please remain on the line, and one of our agents will be with you momentarily.'"

I replaced the headset in the cradle as the tone whined into my ear.

"Now that's really strange. I can't believe that."

"John Doyle?"

Mush. Mush. Mush. California avocado. Another alien intruder in my mother's kitchen.

"No. I actually got a voice mail someplace in England."

I dialed 411 again.

"Information. This is Harold. What city please."

"Brooklyn, please. John Doyle."

"Didn't we just do this?"

"We tried, but I got a wrong number. I got someplace in England."

"Must have been monitored. Did you get the monitor's badge number?"

"No. I didn't get the monitor's badge number. I wasn't even aware that monitors had badge numbers."

"It really would have made all of this much simpler. I may have trouble getting you credit for your wrong number. What number did you dial? Is it at all possible that you failed to keep all of the numbers that you dialed in the approved range between 0 and 9?"

"I dialed 687-8000," I lied.

"Are you sure? Are you sure that you didn't just maybe dial Murray Hill 7-8000?"

"How would you know?"

"We have our methods. This is the twenty-first century you know. I have the monitor's flash report right here. You were calling from a rotary phone, and you didn't remain on the line as instructed."

"Will this go on my permanent record?" I asked.

"That's not my decision. This is, I assume, your first offense of this kind. My guess is that you will be let off with a warning. We will have to run a background check, however."

I waited.

"Now, is that 'B' as in Boyle or 'D' as in Doyle?" he continued.

"That's 'D' as in - I don't know as in A, B, C, D. A, B, C, D," I tried.

"One moment please."

After a minute of silence, he was back on the line.

"I have that information for you, now. Very sad about John Doyle. He was around for a while mooching drinks and doing all sorts of odd jobs."

"What happened? Where is he now?"

"He died about a year ago. Very sad. All of his troubles started a while ago, actually, during his childhood. Something about a bit of mischief with the telephone company, a violation of the A, T, and T nuisance rules."

"Thank you," I said, shaken.

"No, thank you. Thank you for calling A, T, and T. And in the future, please be more careful."

"I will. I promise." I replaced the headset in the cradle one last time.

"Well, did you get him?" my wife asked turning to face me. "You look like you've seen a ghost."

"John Doyle's dead. He died about a year ago."

"How did you find that out? Did you get his family?"

"No, I just called Information. I mean I called 411." You can't be too careful.

"How in the world did they know?"

"That's why they call it 411, I guess."

"You're the computer whiz," she said. "Let me ask you a question that has puzzled me."

"Yes?" I expected her question to have something to do with vegetables. It didn't.

"Why do they call it voice mail anyway. It isn't really mail at all."

"It must be an A, T, and T rule like 'Don't ask. Don't tell'," I answered.

"I didn't know that 'Don't ask. Don't tell,' was an A,T, and T rule," she said.

"A, T, and T has a lot of rules that you don't know about," I answered. "Now where did my mother hide that lock?"

Chop.

In the Halls of Knossos
Irish Goat

I opened my eyes to a labyrinth. Upon its ivy face hung a brass marker that read "You Have One Hour. Do Not Touch the Walls." A small narrow path led forward, then branched at right angles. To my right were acres of flora continuing in an endless maze, to my left, an impressive and foreboding structure.

The edifice was marble, with iambic columns supporting a richly sculpted portico. Fluted pilasters framed the doorway. It had two solid, oaken doors, with heavy hinges to support their weight. They were gothic, with a parabolic top. To get there I had to enter an iron gate and walk a winding path. It was well-designed, but a bit unkempt. The hedges and ornamentals still held their basic shapes, but it had been a while since they had been pruned and trimmed by human hands. The rocks were un-raked and leaf-strewn.

The white facade was obscured. Only the path could be seen clearly. Periodically, stone benches appeared in seemingly random areas along the route. The wood-line was thick and intertwined; there was no opening within its tangled barricade. As I approached the manor, the shadows condensed into a woven fabric of shadows. The trees were an interwoven network of oaken boughs, with minute patches of sunlight visible through holes and natural irregularities.

I approached quietly, cautiously. I did not know how I came to be here. I paused a moment and stared at the powerful facade of this grand structure. It had the masculine attributes of several styles —all reflecting wealth and power. I heard the hinges before I saw the door opening. A tall, extremely thin servant pushed it wide. He was clad in a hooded, woolen robe, with nothing but pale talon-hands protruding from umber sleeves. Behind him was a darkened hall. Nothing else could be seen. I thought, for a moment, I smelled lamp oil and paraffin. It was a faint, but tangibly viscous scent —old, stale air. I began to back away.

My retreating steps somehow left me leaning against the broad double doors, but from inside the house. My withdrawal failed, and now I stood within the mysterious sanctum, in that broad and wooden hall. It, too, bore the plaque "You Have One Hour. Do Not Touch the Walls." I wondered if my elapsed time walking the grounds counted against me. I hoped it did not.

Everything was constructed of similar, interlocking, mahogany panels. There were beaded ceiling boards carved from the same material, and a wooden parquet floor that displayed a rhythmically repeated pattern of geometric shapes. Every few feet, an oil lamp hung from chain tethers.

My heart raced, as panic seized me. I could hear each breath and rhythmic beat. I wheeled around to the doors to escape, but no handles remained. The gothic outline, hinges, and seams were now a continuous sheet of wood. My only exit had vanished. There were only walls, the endless surfaces I could not touch. All avenues leading ahead were identical. Forward was my only option.

I forced a fragile calmness; controlled my breathing and fervent mind. I began walking slowly, looking for identifiable differences along my route. Finding none, I devised a method of marking my progress. As I passed each alcove or turn, I pronated my shoe heel to scrape a polish scuff against the parquet slats. It was faint, but discernible. If need be, I could retrace my steps.

The air was thick, almost tactile, and was laced with the heavy scents of oiled wood. A pungent, musky odor would waft periodically, but was not consistent. I listened intently for any noise, but could only hear the clacking of my own heels as I walked. At each opportunity, I made a right turn. That seemed a logical way to traverse the entire labyrinth without getting lost. But after the fifth right turn, I realized that logic had no weight here. My straight paths were not changing, and I continued to make right turns. Yet I had not returned to an area that bore my scuff marks. Mathematically, I either was traveling in a perfect, repeated square, or should witness longer or shorter legs as I meandered in a cubist's spiral. After several minutes, I stopped and closed my eyes to think.

I reopened them after my brief period of meditative reflection, and found myself standing before a door. It was closed, but not seated. There was a minute crack through with I could see a faint light. I nudged it open, slowly; the soft creaking seemed exaggeratedly piercing in the complete silence of the hall. Once inside, I faced a life-sized mirror. It was old, with flaking silver nitrate under clouded glass. It was free standing, with a heavy metallic base and gilded frame. I took a single step towards my distorted image, and I dropped through the floor.

I awoke unscathed, aside from a sore ankle. Dust stuck to my right side, where I lay in a mix of pale grit and sand. I could see the trap hole above me. It was beyond reach. There were no doors here, no windows or breaks. Stranger still, there were no corners. The room was oval —a seamless interlocking pattern of grayish stones. In the center of this ovoid cell was a mirror identical to the one above; but in this reflection, my image was reversed.

I lifted my right hand and observed how my mirrored-self did the same. Not the same, in the sense of a true reflection. This 'identical image' literally raised his right hand —on the reflected, opposite side. His right. I stared, trying to comprehend. He stared back with similar perplexity, then smiled at me without my initiation.

"Before you speak," my image began, "Know that I am you. The forgotten you. The 'you' you have lost being... well, the 'you' of now."

I gaped at him.

"I can see that this is going to take some time," my reflection continued, "and you have precious little to spare. I'd like to move this along if that's quite all right with you..."

"So... what do I need to do?" I asked.

"Remember me," he said. "Remember 'you.' Piece together those shattered shards of self that you lost in life's trials. Reopen those wounds that scarred your perceptions, suppressed your ambitions. Find yourself. Recapture the passion and zeal of who you were. It is the only way to rekindle who you are."

"But how?" I asked.

"You have to reunite with me. Until our reflections truly mesh into a perfect Janus, you'll be stuck here. You have no time to waste. You need to hurry."

I delved into those forgotten haunts; those inner cells I had mortared into my mental wall. I sat down, and relived those moments that had made me jaded —the hatred, judgement, envy. Those lost opportunities I let slip in times of discord: her death, his betrayal, their abandonment. The losses. The failures. The closures.

I forced myself to accept responsibility and blame for my chosen paths. It was inadequate reactions to these trials that ruined me. The triggers were irrelevant. I felt the memories wash over my mind, as I saw my doppelgänger blur into our shared image. As the final pieces slid into place, we rejoined. The wall opened behind me, and I exited into the heart of the maze.

I was within in the ivy walls I saw earlier. The space was open, and I was alone in a courtyard with a tiled mosaic floor. The image was familiar, but too large in scope for me to realize exactly what its image revealed. Ornamental shrubs formed a low barricade around a fountain that seemed the heart of this labyrinth. I could not find an opening through this hedge. I pressed my hand against the leaves, to find razed thorns beneath its silky plumage. I began bleeding. As I wrapped my palm with my shirt-tail, I remembered the warning on the plaque.

There seemed no way to push through, even though I could easily see beyond this lush, razored barricade. I stood and pondered over options. The fountain's soothing melody lulled me into a relaxed state, as its water cascaded over ceramic tiles. I found myself unexpectedly tired. I continued to listen to the water's dance, and without realizing the extent of my exhausted state, collapsed like melting wax. A deep sleep overcame me.

I awoke within the circular hedge. My doppelgänger sat beside me, in a very relaxed pose. He smiled and told me that I succeeded in navigating the labyrinth. I was confused, disoriented, and I asked what this journey had been.

"It will be revealed," was his reply.

He took my hand and walked me into the fountain's brisk waters and held my nose. Then he leaned me back into their soothing embrace as a baptism of rebirth. I awoke on a sterile bed, in a sterile room of sterile tope. A nurse hastened over and checked my vitals. I observed my bandaged body and felt the immediate pangs of broken bones, a sore ankle, and my lacerated hand.

"What happened?" I asked.

"You were brought in last night after an attack," she explained. "The police report stated that a child witnessed the assault and called 911."

I began to remember. The depression. My pain. Her death. I had succumbed to the grief of losing her, and drank myself into a stupor. During the binge, I collapsed in an alley and had been mugged, beaten, and left for dead. Even in this state of semi-consciousness, I had welcomed the thought of death's release.

Apparently, I was received by the hospital in a coma. The labyrinth was my mind's adaptation to these events in my life. My subconscious was making sense of my path, my role, my reasons to live. The maze was quite simply a construct of self; a rebuilding of who I had once been.

My double was the better 'me'.

The nurse watched me in reflection. After a minute, she asked me how I felt.

I could feel none of the self-loathing, fatalism, I had endured for years. I smiled a bit, as I considered my response to her... and answered.

"I feel good, ma'am," I allowed a heart-felt smile to burgeon. "...I really do feel quite well."

Inside the Game
Daniel Por

"Yeah, mom, I'll be sure to lock the door!" I called after my departing mother.

"Remember, no going anywhere, sweetie. The money is on the table, yeah?" she called out.

I gave a grunt of noise. I was itching to try out the new game my friend had lent me: *Wizards and Warriors*. My fingers drummed on the sofa armrest, trying to smile convincingly to my mother. She gave a last wave and then she drove off.

Immediately, I sprang to my feet and dug out the game cartridge from my bag. Eagerly, I slotted it into my console. *BEGIN*, the screen read.

The world of the Wizards and the Warriors have been torn apart by the evil sorcerer Allerask. He has sown hatred among the two races, and they are heading towards WAR! Choose your side in this epic adventure now...

I clicked the button that said 'Wizards'. Then, I started gaming my life out, determined to maximise the time that I had while my mother was away. I was plunged into the incredibly detailed world of the Wizards and the Warriors, battling the ugly and grotesque armies of the Warriors using my Gauntlet of Power and my trusty Staff and the army that I had at my disposal.

I furiously mashed my controller's buttons, racking up combo after combo and crushing the enemies that stood in my way. Occasionally, I encountered Allerask's evil forces, only to be destroyed because I hadn't paid enough money to unlock the really powerful characters.

Then, I reached my first boss battle against the warlord Ehernar. I furiously tried my best attacks, but I was losing health quickly. Then, thunder struck. I paused the game, and I looked outside. I had seen something outside there.

A shape had moved, just outside my window. Rain poured down. A bolt of lightning struck something far away in the distance. My heart was pounding. I looked outside again. Another bolt of lightning lit up the night, and then I saw a human head, clearly defined. I backed away.

I heard something. Thunder sounded directly over my house. Then I saw something pass through the window, and lightning struck the house. I blacked out.

****

Something crowed above me. A bird flew over me. It blurred, and then it came into focus again.

There was a thing that was pressing into my back. I reached for it and pulled out a metal sword. I hadn't seen it before. A bag lay next to me. There was a note on my shirt. I reached for it and pulled it off.

Beat me, and I'll send you home.

I had no idea who had sent it. Inside the bag, there was only food and water.

I struggled up and put the bag on, but not before pulling something out and chewing on it. It tasted horrible. I was in some kind of forest. Trees surrounded me. I was dizzy.

I headed towards a random tree, and on it, I saw, a message carved into a tree: *Head west and you shall find help.*

Having no other idea of where to go, I looked up at the sun. It was setting. I decided to take the advice seriously. Walking forward as fast as I could go, I stumbled forward through the undergrowth.

I felt dazed, almost as if I couldn't feel anything. Something had removed everything inside of me. I didn't care about anything. It was as if I had lost something.

I just kept going west. I hacked through the shrubbery when I couldn't get through it. Soon enough, I got scratches on my arms and legs. I just kept going. Something seemed to be pushing me forward, prodding me in the small of my back whenever I felt tired.

When the sun set, I found myself in front of a village. It felt old and dated, a ghost town. It was clear no one had set foot in here for years. I entered it.

There was only a small, tinny noise coming from one of the houses. I unsheathed the sword and went in cautiously. Something jumped out at me. I killed it. It was a rat of some kind. I stepped over it and continued.

Someone sat there, watching an old TV screen. He turned once he heard me come in. "Well, well, well, look what the devil dragged in." He wore an eyepatch over his head and a shawl covered the rest of his face. He had a black cloak on.

He told me to sit down. "We didn't know when and where you would arrive, so we carved messages all over the forest." I was confused.

"Who are you?"

"Don't act stupid." He continued on before I could say a word. "Allerask's forces are getting closer. We've lost a huge number of Wizards. Even the Warriors are feeling the loss."

"I'm sorry, what?"

"We need you now. You are the only one who can rally our forces against Allerask. You see, he's marshalled his forces here —" he pointed to a point on the map he had spread out in front of him. It showed a giant mountain and on top of it was written: *Allerask's Fortress*.

"I really don't get you." I was bewildered. *Who was this man, and what did he want with me? What about Allerask? He was just someone in a game, wasn't he?*

"Good God, man, don't tell me that you don't know about the war between Allerask and the Wizards and the Warriors?" The man then launched into an incredibly long description of what had happened in the war so far. The only thing I could think of: *I'm in the game?* Slowly, slowly, it sunk in. I was in the game.

I finally understood the note. Allerask had pulled me into the game and challenged me to defeat him. I stood up. This was not a game. This was life and death. The man cleared his throat. "You, sir, are the One Who Stands. There was a prophecy made about you. You are the only one who holds the key to defeating Allerask and ending his oppressive reign over our people now."

"I don't know anything." The words just fell out of my mouth. I really did not.

The man sighed. "The prophecy told of you not knowing things, but I didn't know that you wouldn't know so many things."

He got up and shook my hand. "I'm Jake, by the way. Nice to meet you."

He took me outside, and then we took a horse and rode on. Jake had an amazing sense of direction. I fell asleep on his back. In the middle of the night, we arrived at the main headquarters of the Wizards and the Warriors. He introduced me to everyone. I forgot all their names.

In the morning, he trained me, teaching me sword-fighting skills, defence, keeping up my fitness, making me do exercises, over and over again. I felt stronger. In two weeks' time, he told me, Allerask would be able to collect all the Crystals he needed from the Mine. Then, he would forge a new weapon that could be used to destroy everything and everyone and would allow him to remake the world as he saw fit. Jake said that we needed to attack him when he was at his most vulnerable, when all the Crystals had been input into the Machine. Then, he would have no Crystals left, and we could attack.

It all seemed so arbitrary. This-this-this-that, this-this-this-that. I hated all of it. But what could I do? No matter how much I tried to do my own thing, something always restricted me. It was as if something was controlling me with strings and I was the puppet, dancing for people's amusement.

The day we attacked, Jake put me at the front of the army. Races of all kinds, Wizards, Warriors, Elves, Dwarves, and even some weird octopus-cat-hybrid thing gathered in their armour in front of me. Jake gave a speech. I murmured a few words. We saddled up.

I tried not doing anything. My body still moved of its own accord. I had no freedom. I *was* being controlled by something. I didn't know what.

Together, we charged. Riding towards the mountain, I realised that there was nothing glorious about war. There was nothing fun or exciting or anything that had been depicted in the movies. It was only me riding on a horse.

Soon enough, Allerask began attacking. His archers only attacked the people whom I didn't care about. They avoided Jake on purpose.

I got to the top of the mountain, and my body started to attack Allerask. Even though I knew that attacking his left flank would be easier and would lead to me being able to kill him more easily, something kept making me attack his right flank. My head and my left arm were vulnerable. And even though Allerask repeatedly thrust his sword into my heart, I was able to get back up and continue being the puppet that I was.

"Enjoying yourself?" His ugly face breathed into mine. It smelled of disgusting things. It *was* disgusting. Then, he suddenly went into an elaborate ritual, making weird hand signs and chanting. I couldn't do anything. He blasted me with his staff and then monkeyed over to his Machine.

I felt no pain. I just kept lurching on, controlled by whatever was controlling me. "YOU'LL NEVER ESCAPE MY CLUTCHES! YOU ARE TRAPPED HERE BY YOUR OWN DEVICES!" he screamed.

Something clicked inside of my head, and I had my first independent thought since I had arrived here. That word 'device'...

It sparked something inside. An image, of a console. Of a TV screen. Of a game...

A game!

That was it! I was in the game! I wasn't playing myself! I was merely the puppet of whoever was playing. I had no freedom because I was the character!

And then it all made sense to me. Why I couldn't make moves on my own, why I had to randomly speak sentences that I would never say, why I couldn't do anything when he was dancing around. It was all because I was in the game! I was only the character.

And, by the look on Allerask's face, he knew that I knew. "No! You can't know! You're playing the game! You can control yourself!" he desperately tried to convince me.

I knew what I had to do. "I can beat you. Because I am a person, and you are merely a character. I'm being controlled as a character in the game. And I know it." My eyes gleamed, and the last thing I saw was Allerask screaming, "NOOOOOOOOOOOOO!" before I closed my eyes and felt my body ascend towards somewhere.

****

I started.

I was back on my couch, the game paused, still at the first boss battle.

I had realised that all I had to do to beat Allerask was to recognise that I was a character the game, being controlled by some person. His power only held over me when I submitted to the lie that I was actually in the game and could do what I wanted. Once I recognised that I had a life outside of the character in the game, I could escape.

As the saying goes, what is known cannot be un-known.

It was morning. Sunlight streamed in through the window. Then I realised someone was standing over me. He looked vaguely familiar. He looked... like a woman.

I shook my head, and then I saw my mother standing over me. "What is this?" she demanded furiously. She pointed at the screen.

My eyes widened. I looked at her, and then at the screen with Ehernar still snarling at me.

"Oh no," I murmured. As the saying doesn't go, all's not well that ends well.

Jack's Crazed Fan
Lisa Scuderi-Burkimsher

I'm sitting at the kitchen table, sipping hot coffee, and chomping on toast, while reading the top news story. I nearly choke, and spit out my toast. A fan of my novels, had been arrested at a local bookstore for stealing all of my books. The man, his name is Hank Thomas, according to the paper, is quoted as saying: "I just want to be their best friend!"

I can hardly breathe, my heart pounds heavily, and I feel faint. My body trembles, and thoughts of this man freak me out; I curse out loud. I count to ten, and take deep breaths. Slowly I stand, and make my way into the living room. I sit on the couch, close my eyes to relax my body, until the phone startles me, and I jump.

"Hell, I have to calm down. This is ridiculous. The man's in jail," I say and pick up the receiver.

"Hey, Jack, I just read the newspaper," Charlie says abruptly. "As your agent, I'm advising you to take a vacation until the dust settles."

"I'm so nervous because of this, I don't know what to do. I'm having a panic attack over here." I feel my body tremble again, and hold onto the end table for support.

"I'm coming over."

"No, I'll be fine. I just need to process this. I don't need you coming over here, and babying me."

"Fine, but do what I said, and take a vacation," Charlie says, and then hangs up, the dial tone buzzing in my ear.

I take two tranquillizers, and finally calm down. *It's just a lunatic fan. He's not going to get to me. Even if he gets released on bail, he doesn't know my address or phone number. I'm not listed, and I always wear sunglasses, rain or shine, to hide my face. No one recognizes me.*

I lay down on the couch, close my eyes, and drift off to sleep. I awake the next morning. The tranquillizers really did a number on me, but I needed that. I put a pot of coffee on, and check the front porch for the newspaper. I couldn't believe my eyes. The headline now read that the crazy fan of my books hanged himself in his jail cell because he couldn't live without knowing me. I should've felt sympathy. Instead, I was relieved. This time, I call Charlie.

"Charlie, did you see the newspaper heading today?"

"I was just going to call you. No need for that vacation now," Charlie says reassured.

"Listen, I need to get myself together, and get out of this house today. Meet me at Spruce's Diner, twelve o'clock, for lunch. We'll talk about my next novel."

"Sure thing, I'll see you then."

Sipping my coffee, I wonder what kind of life this man had that he fixated on me. Then I clear my mind of him, shower, dress, and get ready to meet Charlie to discuss my next bestseller.

Jet Glass Buttons on A Crimson-Red Dress
Karen Sallee

The musty smelling cardboard box contained three old baseball T-shirts, five yellowed love letters Dad penned to Mom years ago, a piggy bank, a plastic coffee cup and more old pictures than I could count.

I pulled a framed 5x7 black-and-white photograph from the box, blew off the dust and placed it on my desk. It is displayed in a simple gold tone frame with imitation mother-of-pearl inlay. The frame is old, older than the little girl looking out from behind the glass, who flashes a big smile with a bright sparkle in her eyes. She sits up straight and proud.

Me. Age seven. Fifty-six years ago.

I was a stocky child with crooked buckteeth and straight, wispy brown hair. I didn't think I was much to look at. People often commented on my eyes, "Such pretty, big brown eyes. And those lashes." But as far as I could tell, my eyes were my only redeeming feature.

I was sandwiched in the middle of two sisters, always comparing myself to them—the older being long-legged and tall with a mass of golden, wavy hair; the baby a blond-haired, blue-eyed bit of adorableness.

I felt out of place, brown eyes and lush lashes no match for my sisters' prettiness. I was the shy, ugly duckling.

In the photo, my stick-straight hair was fashioned in my least favorite style. Puffs of curls adorned the top of my high forehead. Princess Leia-like puffs covered my ears, drooping unevenly on each side. This was Mom's go-to hairdo for me.

I remember feeling pretty as I was photographed, despite my teeth and hair. When I look at the faded black-and-white photo, I see the reason for my rare bloom of confidence.

My mom was a wonderful seamstress, who sewed the majority of our clothes when we were young. Her black Singer sewing machine with its gold leaf lettering hummed from the corner of my parents' small bedroom.

Their tiny closet was used as a fitting room where unsewn garments, pinned to tissue paper patterns, were slipped gently over our heads, pins sticking us, Mom's warning, "be still, don't wiggle," mumbled from her pin-filled lips.

The rustle of the fragile tissue was magical. Mom created soft, gauzy Easter dresses trimmed in fine lace, embellished with tiny, pastel-colored silk flowers. We wore delicate dotted Swiss over stiff petticoats and scratchy wool jumpers over simple blouses. Mom sewed matching baby-doll pajamas for each of us. Our summer shorts sets were cool and breezy; winter flannel gowns kept us toasty on cold nights. Every August, Mom fashioned sturdy cotton dresses for the upcoming school year.

In our mid-century household, a growing family meant the milkman's paycheck Dad brought home each week was stretched thin. Sewing was Mom's way of contributing. More than just a way to manage the family budget, though, sewing was her creative outlet. Each new article of clothing was fresh and new and stylish. She might have used a stock Simplicity pattern, but the extra touches were all her own. No one could match Mom's smocking or ruching. Her detailed handwork set her apart.

Mom's attention to detail resulted in wonderful and serviceable clothes. But of all the pretty clothes she sewed, she never created a more loved dress than the one she crafted for me to begin second grade.

The dress was a deep crimson-red, dotted with small white flowers outlined in black. The poofy short sleeves were just right— not too tight, allowing free movement, but not so loose they got in the way of play. Mom attached a two-inch sash that could be tied in front or back—the front if my small hands were tying the bow; the back if Mom helped.

Black ricrac zigzagged around the sleeves and neck. The bold trim perfectly framed the deep red fabric from the neck to the knee-length hem.

Polished jet glass buttons were the finishing touch that secured the dress all the way down the front. The buttons were like jewels—shiny, glitzy and expensive-looking. I wore them like a society-maven wore her diamonds. They were my Bling before there was Bling.

Red. Black. Shiny glass buttons—a more gorgeous dress there never was.

The red was a perfect complement to my brown eyes and hair. My olive skin glowed against the warm color. I felt like a beautiful Mexican senorita, exotic and bold.

I felt pretty for the first time in my life.

I began second grade with a new attitude. I wore my dress with pride as I headed to school that day. I walked taller, laughed more, and raised my hand often.

My usual shyness receded when I donned my red dress. I felt like a mild-mannered reporter emerging from a telephone booth in blue tights and red cape. I was strong, self-assured, powerful. I could do anything.

The feeling of confidence that first day of school carried over to the next day. I rushed through my morning routine—breakfast, face washing, teeth and hair brushing—then went to the closet and carefully removed my red dress from the wire hanger.

The soft fabric was slightly less pressed and starched from the monkey bars and swings of the previous day's play, but its beauty remained. I pulled on my dress of armor, brushing the glossy buttons with affection, and tied the sash. I was transformed once again, my inhibitions vanquished.

By the third day, Mom gave me a look that said, "Really? Again today?" My confidence answered back. I wore my dress. I felt pretty. I was mighty.

My dress was gone the fourth day. Mom picked out a suitable replacement—a green dress with blue flowers—cute, but a poor substitute. I was crestfallen. My red dress wasn't dirty. It wasn't wrinkled. "Why can't I wear my red dress?" I wanted to know. Frustration and tears threatened my self-assurance.

Mom explained I just couldn't wear the same dress over and over and over again. It needed washing, starching, ironing. It needed to be saved for something special.

The next weekend, Mom styled my hair in puffballs, dressed me in my much-loved dress and sat me down in front of a photographer, my confidence restored.

Fifty-six years later, black-and-white memories morph to living color and place my favorite dress front-and-center each day. A perfect smile, shining eyes, and a reminder of the jet glass buttons on a crimson-red dress worn by the mighty middle sister who could.

Licking Lizards in
The Gizzard Desert
Shawn McDaniel

Skiddles slings the bus, halting himself and Mars seven-full.

"Fork-tine, funky friend?" Mars glows.

"Buttress that button, Mars Magenta, there's a stamen straight tomorrow." Skiddles hops down to survey the ground. Sure enough, a fatty stamen sits sprung not a slurp ahead, spewing saliva like a Savanna sunset.

"Looks like a lotus doodle - what to do?"

Spunky succulents wave along the shoulders. "Wasn't us, honest, we've been sucking little since the last thumb."

"Newton's anus, I know!" Skiddles skulls.

Mars twitter pates around the stamen, semen splashing his cudgels, which begin to sizzle, causing poor Mars to start back, losing a long stream of alligators, "Look at my cudgels! They'll never be the same now."

Suddenly, the stamen deflates like a clown, spits out one final globe, and sulks back into the skanky ground, leaving behind a white smarmy puddle.

"Get over it mouse, back on the bus!" Mars dives headlong through the window as Skiddles bounds back into the driver seat and guns it gung-ho. Shadowbox wretches, lurches, lumps forward through the stamen's liquid, sparring the succulents with a wave of sticky white stuff. They pump their spiky fists in a *how rude* kind of way, but the two are long gone.

The countryside extends to an endless horizon in all directions. The Gizzard Desert is something of a wasteland, pocked with tiny oasis portals. Mars navigates...

"Louse! Are we on track?"

"Don't fuss, Skid, we'll make it. You didn't do what they say anyways, right?"

"What have I told you about lousy questions, of course I'm innocent."

Mars takes up the manuscript in question: *The Proverbial Pride of Lions,* by Skiddles Brown; a pseudo-fable spiced with a plethora of feline puns, fun enough for a comic... "You ever consider standup, heck, Broadway, this stuff is gold!"

"I am a writer, not a performer," Skiddles drives with his knees while polishing a gleaming .45 caliber handcannon. He takes aim out the window and sends a slug into a turtle-crossing sign, blowing a hole the size of the ozone in its center. "WHHOOOOOEEEEEIIIIIII! See that shot?!"

Mars pulls his fists from his ear holes, "What'd you say?"

Skiddles exorcists his neck backward with a glare to scare a gorgon, just in time to see Mars' eyes grow to the size of grapefruits and his hand shoot up with an extended index. Skiddles whips back to the front as the bus comes upon a giant spinning turtle shell. With the flick of the wrist he whirls the wheel, sending Shadowbox into a spiral barrel roll.

When they finally come to a sliding halt, the bus is on its head, whining shamefully. Mars's eyes are still money melons, and his calico cowlicks stand straight to the floor-once-ceiling. Skiddles is sprawled about the cabin. He slimes out the space where the window once lived and kisses the hot sandstone. "Thanks for the cushy landing, love." His companion is frozen in time. "Well come on, we have to give that rock a piece of our minds." The turtle shell is still spinning as if the bus had never come.

"Hey you, spinning top, what's your deal? Doesn't anybody know this road is for drivin'!"

A head pops out, a very round, featureless face, smooth as a piece of bubblegum. Then slits form, eyelids part and three, dopey cornea'd balls find a very disgruntled Skiddles rolling up his sleeves. The smooth turtle face opens his beak, and with deliberation in every single syllable, responds:

Whhhhhhheeeeeeeeeeeennnnnnnnnnnnnnnnniiiiiiiiiiiiiiiiiiiiiiiiiii iwwwwwwwwwwwwwwwaaaaaaaaaaaassssssssssssssaaaaaaaaaaaaaaatt ttttttttttttttttttttaaaaaaaaaaaaaaaaaaaaaddddddddddddddddpppppp pppppppppoooooooooooooooooooolllllllllllllllllllllllllttttttttttttttttttthhhhh hhhhhhhhhhhhhhiiiiiiiiiiiiiiiiiiiiiiiissssssssssssssssssssssrrrrrrrrrrrrrrrrrrrrrr ooooooooooooooooooaaaaaaaaaaaaaaaaaaaaddddddddddddddddddd dddwwwwwwwwwwwwwwwaaaaaaaaaaaaaaaassssssssssssssssssssaa aaaaaaaaaaaaaaaaaaaaffffffffffffffffffffffffffffiiiiiiiiiiiiiiiiiiiiiieeeeeeeeeeee eeeeellllllllllllllllllllllddddddddddddddddddddddooooooooooooooooooo ffffffffffffffffffffffffffffddddddddddddddddddddddaaaaaaaaaaaaaaaaaaaa ffffffffffffffffffffooooooooooooooooooooodddddddddddddddddddddd dddiiiiiiiiiiiiiiiiiiiiiiiiilllllllllllllllllllllllllllllllllllllllllllllllllllllllllllllllllllllllllllllllllssss ssssssssssssssssssssssss

 "Wowwo you need a linguist slow poke, or some sort of fingerless signal, but because of you, our ride is trashed, and I ought to show you some respect!"

The turtle's head retreats as Skiddles performs a people's elbow on the solid shell with a thunderous crrrrACK!... his arm hangs noodle limp.

"Skid!" Mars sobs from the upsidedown Shadowbox as Skiddles executes a fury of kicks.

"What now? I'm in the middle of something here. Bring your cudgels and give 'ol Skid a hand, won't ya Mars bars?" But Mars just keeps crying. With an indolent sigh, Skiddles ceases his senseless kicking and the shell continues his defiant spinning. He returns to the overturned ride. "Out you go," he whips his weeping friend back into the world. "What's gotten into you huh?"

"You know I abhor violence. Why must you... *sniff... hick....* why must you ..." a bubble spews from Mars's wide nostrils and he gave up entirely.

"I'm sorry, sweetheart, but that turtle-dum deserves some schooling."

"Besides, we're gonna be late." Mars unravels the map, "Look, see, there's a portal right over there."

"Fine, here, hitch a ride. Let's get rollin' piggy," Skiddles loads Mars on his back, and they hike for a few miles off-road, passing succulents.

"Howdy-ho!"

"Who-doggy!"

And Lizard Logs,

"Ssssalutations"

"Salad"

Mars loved when Skiddles held him so, their scaly faces rubbing together on the rugged terrain, Skiddles rougher than six o'clock on a Saturday. From this vantage, his long face looks like a topographical map. Underneath the cloud cover of long, green-blonde sideburns reaching nearly to his chin, Mars could make out a Great Divide of blemishes and soars, more canyons than the Rockies, more craters than the Moon, and the hair in his ear-holes like gnome forests. The stubby Mars could hardly contain himself. Skiddles felt something moist entering his most sacred hearing space - "Release thine mouth member from betwixt mine beeswax scoundrel!" and Mars retracted his red slithering organ.

The Oasis came into sight, sticking out of the barren landscape like a swollen jungle-thumb hitchhiker. "Now that's the girdle of a diamond," Skiddles awes. Mars' jaw drops down to his waist. It was the greenest piece of fresh air and wily tentacle life the pair had ever seen, jutting from the cracked badlands. Green and amethyst foliage, geysers spewing turquoise, spiders big as semi-trucks spinning crystalline webs, elephantsauries, walnutmaples... as if everything in the universe had come to this one spot to have a wild, spontaneous orgy. Plants devour other plants at one end, only to have them shoot off at another, vines with twenty thousand fingers, webs wrapped around a square mile, and everyone lounging as if in hammockland.

"Alright enough gawking. We're on a tight schedule Marmalade. Where's the worm hole?"

Mars opens the map, lifts it to his nose, pauses, turns it left ninety degrees, right a hundred eighty degrees, flips it over...

"Neverhead! I'll ask one of the barbarians," Skiddles raises his hands to his eyes, cupping them like a brontosaurusstronomer. This is what he saw:

Giraffedactyls with oversized, star shaped, sun shades; a Skeleton cowboy stroking a stogie, twirling his six shooter bananas, sitting at the bar in a Hawaiian shirt; Camel campers unloading the luggage from their humps; wanderers; vagabonds; vagrants; vandals; Sandshifters cloaked toe to head, a slit for their eyes; palmspruces playing poker; countless, shapeless, winged things in the leaves; long tailed children swinging on the grapevines; herds of striped unicycles, their long nosed seats lifting to the air, then down to the water for a sip; and so on, and so on.

"This is ridiculous, I don't want to be associated with a single one of these loose cannon whackos, let alone have a word or two-"

"Typical Skid, refusing to ask for directions. Why you don't just consort the bones? I'll never know, I'll never mow your mindlawn. Let's just go home! I'm starting to shake and itch, and I swear that tail with a tan just licked her lips at me"

"It's a circus, I say. Ought to waste the lot with my—what tail?"

Several hairs stand ten-hut on the back of Skiddles neck as a breath of hot, sticky, urine-soaked air washes over him. A low purring grows into a growl from the thick canopy above. Skiddles and Mars slowly arch their necks to the heavens to see a pair of fiercely glowing eyes and a light shower of saliva. Like lightning she pounces upon the thin Skiddles and envelopes him in one swift gulp.

Mars gapes in disbelief, his knees made of jellyfish. A slender lioness stands before him, daintily patting her jowls with an embroidered handkerchief, monogrammed in gold stitching: F.L.

"Oh, don't give me those eyes little one, I wouldn't dream of devouring you, not on a full stomach, I have a strict calorie diet going on, in fact-" the feline reveals a slim black device hidden in her fur, jots in a few notes with her claws, then returns it to a hidden tuft.

Mars is at a loss. His good friend's ingestion was just too much to process right now. He smokes a long camel-humped cigarette.

"Terrible habit," the she-lion scolds the quivering Mars. "Wrinkles your skin, fouls your breath, rots your teeth, shallows your lungs, not to mention all the tumors and cancers encouraged by the tar and carcinogens—" she shakes her head.

Mars just keeps puffing until he's smoking nothing but filter, then the tips of his fingers. Finally, he tosses what's left, stamps it, then, standing as tall as ever, with the courage of a nicotine buzz, puffs up his chest and begins to berate the lioness, "You vile femme fatale Homunculus! How could you eat my beloved Skiddles! He was a good soul, a true friend, a stalwart companion, a wiz with a pen, a golden canary whistling in the deepest mine! Sure he could be crude and arrogant, and his temper flared hotter than solar winds, and his face more pocked than a herpes ridden chicken, and he often farted on children and robbed, cheated, and, stole from everyone he ever met—"

A muffled sound emerges from the bowels of the beastly she-lion, who was quite overtaken by Mars sudden outburst. The muffling went something like this: ("shmm mmm you mmff ffmmph") in a familiar voice.

"Skiddo!" Mars bubbles over joy.

The lioness rolls her night vision, "Now I hear you two are—"

("don't worry its—")

"looking for a—"

("quite cozy in her—")

"portal—"

("like a womb—")

Mars scratches his head, unsure of who was speaking. Both voices sail out of the large jaws at once. She, a little perturbed, thumps her stomach a few times to silence the talkative Skiddles.

"There, now, as I was soy saucing, I'll take you there. Why, the portal is closer than you think my edible little dumpling."

Mars can't help but notice the sheer beauty of the smooth legged lioness and he swoons slightly. All he can manage is "What's your name?"

"Fauna—"

("Quit consorting with—")

"Fauna Love—"

("the carnivore and hop-to!—")

"You can call me Fawn," her cat eyes envelope Mars; curvy green slits like knives one begs to be impaled by.

He shakes himself aware, "We have to hurry. We're already late."

Inspecting her claws with blah-blasé, she sighs a tidal wave, "As I said, the portal is only moments away," Fauna Love opens her vast jaws and ushers Mars into the chasm with a long mother tongue

    all

      the

        way

          down...

Lovers in Time
Izabela Jeremus

"Babygirl, you have to look at this!" My best friend comes running in and shoves the morning paper under my nose.

I take it from him and have to read the article twice before it sinks in.

"So this George McIntyr stole nothing but my books from the bookstore?" I ask, making sure I read it correctly.

Lucas Robertson nods. "Isn't that great?"

"I wouldn't call it 'great,' exactly," I reply.

"Look here," he says, taking the paper from me, "'All I want is to be her best friend,' said Mr. McIntyr when asked why he stole only Ms. Annabelle Saphronite's books.'"

I laugh, giving Lucas a hug. "My best friend, huh? Well, I hate to break it to him, but that role is already filled."

Lucas chuckles. "He *must* be your biggest fan to rob a store and take nothing but your books."

"Yes, you're right," I agree. "You'd think he'd throw in some Stephen King or Dean Koontz in there."

"He *is* a looker, isn't he?" Lucas says, sighing.

Next to the article is a picture of George McIntyr. He has full pouting lips, a straight nose, high cheekbones, and dark brown hair that falls into deep blue eyes. I stare at the picture for a moment, those eyes tugging at something deep inside of me. It's like I *know* those melancholy eyes, have loved them in a past life.

Realizing that Lucas is staring at me, I shake my head and shrug. I must be living in my newest book's world again. In it, a couple of soulmates find each other through many lifetimes, always by something new—one time by bumping into each other on the street, another through a psychic, yet another through a painting the woman has featured in an art show.

"I guess he *is* good looking, sort of," I mumble.

Lucas grabs two mugs and fills them with coffee, two sugars, light with cream for me, black with sugar for him. He brings them over to the little kitchen table and slips into the seat opposite from me, crossing his legs.

"It's all kind of cute, isn't it?" he says.

"In a stalkerish kind of way," I reply, "I guess."

He sighs dreamily. "Oh, how romantic, a stalker."

"There's nothing romantic about getting knifed in the middle of the night," I respond, laughing.

"Unless you're into that type of thing!" Giggling, Lucas reaches for the paper. "We have to frame this, girlfriend."

"I'm going to go write," I tell him with an eye roll.

Staring at the blank page of the chapter I'm supposed to be writing, I can't help but think of George McInyr. Not that I'd ever admit it to Lucas, but I *am* flattered in a strange way. My protagonist would take this as a sign. She'd seek out this George McIntyr and see what he was all about. In my book, it would turn out that he was her soulmate, her long-lost lover throughout the ages, and they would get on with whatever adventure I had planned for that particular section of the book.

After an hour of unsuccessfully attempting to get the chapter going, I close my laptop and pack it into my travel backpack. Inside of it is my on-the-go writing tool kit: pens, a writing journal, two books of writing prompts, a copy of the current Writer's Market book, and space for my laptop.

By the time I go downstairs to grab my car keys, Lucas has already left for work. He's a waiter and part time bartender. He doesn't have to work as much as he does—I own the house we live in - but he enjoys it. Putting on some sneakers, I scoop up my keys, and I'm out the door. Inside of my black Toyota Yaris hatchback, I don't think about where I want to go, I just start driving. Twenty minutes later, to my surprise, I arrive at the county jail.

The large building looms in front of me, seeming to laugh at my idiocy. The bricks are piled five stories high, making it one of tallest buildings in the area. Bars line every window, including the bottom floor and the double doors leading inside. Four long, wrap-around stone steps lead into the mouth of the station.

"What are you doing?" I mutter to myself, feeling dumb.

Knowing I can't just waltz into the jail and ask to see this man, I make up my mind to pay his bail. Figuring that someone must have posted it by now, I make that my condition to stop this silliness. Just having done this is ridiculous enough; having a police officer give me a look for posting my own stalker's bail will drive me over the edge so that I don't do anything else crazy.

With a deep breath, I walk into the facility.

Although the place is milling with police officers, a pretty police woman with short blonde hair and bright green eyes is the only person I see at the ample desk.

"How can I help you?" she asks in a voice much deeper than I had expected.

"Hi, I'm here to pay George McIntyr's bail," I respond, hoping she doesn't recognize me.

"Please wait one moment," she replies, typing something into a computer. "His bail is five-thousand dollars, so that'll be five-hundred dollars."

"That's it?" I ask. "And no one has paid it yet?"

"No ma'am," she replies. "Isn't that why you're here?"

"Uh, well, yes," I say quickly, "but I was a last resort."

She nods as if this tale makes sense. I pull out five one hundred dollar bills from my wallet and hand them over. She takes them and types something else into the computer.

"He'll be released in about a half hour, if you'd like to wait," she informs me.

I look around at the seedy people surrounding me. There's a man who looks as if the last time he's eaten was five years ago. He reeks of cigarettes and something else, a plastic undertone that I can't quite place. Another woman sits in the corner in handcuffs, her short red skirt barely covering her goodies, her shirt, nothing more than a crimson bra. There's also a muscular man mumbling to himself about white power, a swastika tattoo adorning one of his bulging biceps.

"I'd rather wait in the car," I say. "If you don't mind telling him the black Toyota Yaris."

"Yes ma'am," she says.

I return to my car and wait for the man with the sad blue eyes to walk through the door. Less than thirty minutes later, I spot him coming out of the double doors. He pauses, scanning the parking lot. I had moved the car back a few parking spaces, so that I could get a good look at him before he saw me. Seeing the car, he slowly makes his way to me. Several feet before he gets to me, he stops, as if unsure of what to do.

I get out of the car and close the distance between us. His eyes widen when he realizes who I am.

"Ms... Saph... ronite?" he stumbles through my name. "You? You p-p-paid my b-b-bail?"

Extending my hand, I give him a smile. "Hi, George. I hear you're my biggest fan. Please, call me Annabelle."

George's handshake is surprisingly firm.

"Thank you, Ms... Annabelle," he says, training those beautiful eyes on me. "But I'm sorry to say I can't repay you."

"Sure, you can," I reply. "Come out to lunch with me and tell me why you stole those books."

An eyebrow shoots into George's hair and his lips part, but only for an instant. I wave to my car and we both get in. We drive in silence for a minute, before I can't take it anymore.

"Do you like sushi?" I ask him.

"Yes, but again, I can't pay," he says, his voice low.

"Don't be silly," I say. "I'm taking you out; that means I'm paying."

George turns his head and watches me for a few minutes. "In that case, I'm much obliged."

I pull up to my favorite sushi restaurant, and we walk into an ambiance of warmth and Japanese tradition. There are Japanese kanji on the seats and geisha paintings hanging from the walls.

Turned down low is traditional Japanese music. After we are escorted to our seats and place our orders—California and vegetable rolls for me, spicy tuna and dragon rolls for George—I get to the matter at hand.

"So, George, please tell me," I say, "why did you steal my books?"

George's cheeks flush and he looks down. "I couldn't afford them."

"You could have borrowed them from the library," I suggest.

"I needed to own them," he responds.

"Why?"

"You won't believe me if I tell you."

"Try me."

George squirms in his seat. "They... called to me."

I stare at him. "Called to you?"

"I told you you wouldn't believe me."

"I didn't say that. I'm just trying to understand."

George lifts those drowning pools to gaze into my eyes. "Your writing speaks to something inside of my soul. I feel like we've known each other before this life. I thought if I could own your books, read them front to back, back to front, I would get the message. That freak-out about wanting to be your best friend was just a cover for the police. I was hoping if they thought I was nuts, the judge would go easier on me."

"Oh, so there's something wrong with being my best friend?" I tease.

"No, I mean, there's nothing..."

"I'm just kidding," I interject.

"Oh."

"The thing is," I say, "I think I know what you're talking about."

"You do?"

"Yes," I respond. "When I saw your picture in the paper, I felt like I had met you before, many times."

George nods. "That's exactly how I feel!"

"You know, in my next book, there's a couple that follow each other from one life to the next," I say, all of a sudden getting chills.

"It's like we're living the book." George announces what I'm thinking.

"That's not possible," I say. "Is it?"

George smiles for the first time since I've met him and my heart melts. "Why shouldn't it be?"

We suspend our conversation when the waiter comes with our meals. Once he's gone, I quickly dive back into it.

"Past lives, lovers following each other," I say, "all sounds sort of far-fetched, don't you think?"

George shrugs. "Yes, but you're a writer. Isn't it your job to make people believe in the far-fetched?"

The truth of this gives me pause. "I'm not sure I'm buying this, but *something* is going on."

George laughs. It's deep and soft all at once. "How about this, then: let me take you out for dinner and maybe we can get to know each other a little bit."

"I thought you didn't have any money."

"I don't—this week," he replies. "How does next Friday sound?"

Next Friday sounds like a year away, but I won't let him know that.

"Next Friday sounds amazing," I tell him.

****

For our six-month anniversary, I give George an advanced reader's copy of my newest book, "Lovers in Time."

"Read the dedication," I encourage enthusiastically.

George chuckles as he flips to the page. "To my biggest fan, my lover throughout the ages, my soulmate, my best friend, my husband-to-be, George."

Those perfect blue eyes that I fell in love with fill with tears as he embraces me.

"Thank you for believing in me," he says.

"*Thank you* for being a criminal," I reply, laughing.

Maze
Carla Sameth

I didn't expect to wake up at all. I don't know what I was thinking when I took all those Ativan and drank the wine. I didn't feel suicidal, but I sure wasn't happy with my life at the time and I just sort of lost track of how many pills I was taking. I always wondered how my daughter, Shoshana, took 80-100 Robitussin at a time. She explained once; she had a method, and she was a lot more organized and focused than I was last night. It just seemed for me that taking one pill, two, three, and then more, well, it wasn't enough. I felt more and more altered and not in the way I wanted to be, just pissed off that I wasn't going anywhere other than getting more agitated, really worked up and less confident that I could resolve anything or ever be happy and present again.

So I came home this time after I'd read through about twenty years of unhappiness in letters to my cousin from when we were first introduced as pen-pals, and I wrote her about all sorts of alcohol and drugs and searing words being shouted at me by mom, my dad, my siblings, and then me back at the world and at myself. No wonder I'd want to do a repeat performance losing track of the Ativan and the glass of wine. This time though, *se me pasó la mano,* it went too far. I wasn't feeling enough or I was feeling too much, so I just kept taking them.

I'm awake, but I am not sure where I left off last night. I know I didn't die, and I don't know why I know that, but I am certain, that I do exist. And I know I'm not asleep or dreaming. And I'm not in a hospital. But what the heck? I'm in the middle of a maze, and I felt like I was trapped last night in the maze of my mind but this is huge, and it's not my brain. It's not one of those Zen spirit-type female strong spiritual labyrinths, and forgive me if words fail me, but what do you think might happen to you if you woke up in the middle of a giant maze? I think I saw a scene like this in Harry Potter or maybe it was Alice in Wonderland. Where was that giant chess set? Damn, I cannot remember!

This maze is like an on-steroid version of the hedge maze in Descanso Gardens over in La Canada back when we lived in Southern California, where I remember my friend's three sons chasing my little girl and boy about like a scene of magical realism. Here in this maze, I can't think of anything which is a blessing. I had been thinking I was so desperate to quiet my mind, I sadly was ready to give up and try heroin, knowing it would turn me into an addict and be a shitty solution to offer up when my daughter, Shoshana, has struggled so hard to be sober. I think of heroin because one addict once told me that it is just like Demerol, which I've found to be the perfect antidote to a continuously anxious mind. Of course, I've only had Demerol prior to otherwise uncomfortable medical procedures, and once in the ER on the day of my wedding when I injured myself. It completely took my mind off of seating!

"You have one hour. Don't touch the walls."

I keep looking at what is written in front of me on the sign hanging from the ivy. I really believe that if I keep pinching myself or slapping my face I WILL wake up, but so far I seem to be awake and in some alternative reality. Was I kidnapped? Was I deposited in some insane asylum after someone found me blacked out, passed out? I was tired of worrying about money and if I'd ever publish my book and why I have doubted myself, my decisions, so many things for more than fifty years and how I might stop and love myself and love life without Demerol or heroin, without twisted and addictive relationships, without financial security. I have a strong, loving girlfriend, but as far as I can see she is not here either. I'm alone. I have to assume my daughter is safe; she's high ranking now in young people's AA and selling expensive shoes at Nordstrom, and my son is off studying Portuguese in Brazil, being chased by boys.

But I'm in this weird, green, giant maze and now, having sat and thought about all this, I have less than one hour. I am also clumsy, but I seem to be walking barefoot and more nimbly now, so perhaps I won't touch the walls, but why the hell can't I? Are they actually electric fences and maybe I am dreaming in a dream about another episode where some people were kidnapped? (Ah yes, it was a CSI episode or something I watched in my hotel room in Sidney.) Now I get it, how my mom can believe she was married to Booth in the show *Bones* or to Mr. Darcy from *Pride and Prejudice* and mix up her reality with TV or videos. Yes, she likes her bad boys! What we don't do with drugs, our brain does with dementia.

I take one step forward, and now I'm sort of cantering… like a horse I'm trotting, now galloping. I know I'm not a horse, or a centaur even, but I have this odd gait, and so far, I'm batting one for one, or whatever you say to mean I'm going through the maze without any dead ends.

DAMN! Almost did run into the wall. What might happen if I did? There are no obvious dangers, but since I was in my bedroom, in a pretty wasted state and I woke up here with no clear notion of how this transpired, maybe anything could happen. Though I've never liked to obey or comply with strict rules, I'm always looking to find what I need to do to get people to love me, pass the test, whatever to be "good" – yup. I am desperate to please, be a better student, "a worker amongst workers," and when I work out "a worker-outer amongst worker-outers," to be liked, be acknowledged, etc. etc. etc. and yet I'm so rebellious, so not coloring within the lines (I really can't). I'm an imperfect perfectionist. I had two elaborate weddings that many say were the best they'd ever attended and two of the worst marriages, I'm sure. I'm a mess of contradictions, and now I've hit another dead end.

Oh no, oh no, oh no – there are people running at me, and they look like they mean to handcuff me, not in a BDSM way, (whatever that is or means), but in a strait jacket punishing kind of way. No drug escape to the everything's okay land but rather, face the music, lock you up with sadistic and very low paid workers who just wish this country didn't push them into this highly unsatisfying, degrading and stinky work cleaning up and looking after crazy people. And their shit. Literally.

I have fifteen minutes now. I saw a flashing sign. I didn't touch the walls, but I am completely lost. I am overcome with a desire to lay down and sleep, and I can smell something much more pleasing ahead, it's a sort of sweet, gardenia smell, then a blend of cardamom and nutmeg, then jasmine, and things just look way better maybe twenty feet away. The air is warm, vaporous, sort of tropical and if I move slowly, languidly, I get there faster than my galloping about before. I believe I may have just been galloping in place, not going anywhere at all. The posse sent to fetch me is gone, disappeared down another part of the maze, and there is a hammock ahead. I climb in, I lay down, I rock back and forth. I feel a gentle, sweet breeze. I lie down and sleep.

Misrepresentation Murder
Sue Ann Whitston

Blood splattered the van's windshield and dashboard that was parked at the hospital visitor's lot. With the driver's window still open, dew sparkled on the upholstered front bench in the winter sun as the policemen fastened yellow tape around the vehicle. Other patrol officers performed the same ritual on a street where Detective Stephens stood on the sidewalk, studying the situation.

He scribbled in a spiral notebook, noting that there were no homes closer than a mile. What trees remained were scraggly and unkempt with debris scattered in the overgrown weeds.

Detective Stephens mumbled, "This is the perfect setting for teenage trysts or drug buys."

"What did you say, Detective?" a young police officer asked, holding an evidence bag.

"Oh. Sorry. I was just speaking out loud about this being a perfect place for teenage trysts and drug buys."

"It is, sir. And we've tried, but we can't catch the perps in the act."

"You're right about that, Officer Jenkins."

Detective Stephens watched the Accident-Investigation team measure tire tracks. His job here was about finished. He would drive to the hospital and examine the kid's van before talking to the survivors.

A second officer stepped over an old tire before saying, "Detective, we found one bullet wedged into the curb. Was there supposed to be more?"

"I'm not sure. I'm heading to the hospital and talk to the five survivors. The sixth was DOA at the hospital. And you've got a good eye, Officer Smith. Keep looking. What you found may not be part of this shooting. This is about the same place as an unsolved shooting three months ago. The officers could not find the third bullet. Seeing the trash here, I wasn't surprised."

"I will, sir!"

"Thank you," Detective Stephens answered, entered his vehicle, and drove the short distance to the hospital. Helen Dithers was on duty at the Information Desk and told the detective the five teens were in Emergency. She added, "Jonathan Phillips has been admitted with a concussion. Check with his physician to see if he can have visitors."

"Thanks, Helen," Detective Stephens returned. "I'll save him for last."

Detective Stephens met Parker Holmes first. The boy said the shooter was a tall black man wearing khaki pants, a blue shirt, and drove a black Mercedes. The man walked up to the open window and fired. Parker ducked, but the bullet struck Jillian Norris in the head. His foot hit the accelerator, hoping to get Jillian to Emergency to save her. Sharon Boone reiterated the same story. Charles Watson added the man wore orange sneakers. He was leaning against the window beside Sharon and heard two rifle shots. Denise Shaw did not see the shooter as she was beside Jonathan Phillips but heard two shots. She added Jonathan's head struck the back of the front seat when Parker hit the accelerator.

As Detective Stephens reached Jonathan's room, he heard the boy mumble, "Why did she do it?!"

"*She*?" Detective Stephens muttered. He saw the boy lapsed into unconsciousness. Confused because the other four said the shooter was male, he turned, headed to the nursing desk. To the nurse, he said, "Would you let me know when he is awake? I want to know who he is talking about."

"We can do that."

"Thank you."

Detective Stephens returned to the station, gave the findings to his Inspector, and wrote the report. The Inspector rapped knuckles on the table, jolting the Detective from enjoying a hot cup of coffee.

"Well, Stephens, I've read your report. Five teens and four say a male shooter. One muttered *she* when you passed his room. What is the discrepancy?"

"Since Jonathan Phillips has a concussion, I have to wait until he's conscious before I can question him. They said the shooter wore khaki pants. Two said he wore a blue shirt. One said the man wore orange sneakers."

"I assume the hospital will call you about Mr. Phillips?"

"Yes, sir."

"Good. We want this shooter ASAP. Have you talked to the victim's parents yet?"

"I am on my way now."

"Go, before the media gets there. Then you can finish your report."

After telephoning, Detective Stephens drove to the Norris home, dreading the conversation with elite society. Mrs. Norris answered the door. "You must be Detective Stephens. Won't you come in?"

The detective sat on the side chair, facing Mrs. Norris seated on the couch. "First," the detective began. "Let me express my condolences on your daughter's death."

"Thank you, detective. My husband would be here with me, but he had to arrange his employee's work schedule before we make funeral arrangements."

"What I need to know is whether your daughter had any enemies? Someone who may have followed the van to that secluded place?"

"Jillian has — had no enemies. Everyone loved her. She was a straight-A student. She was going to become a doctor, specializing in Pediatrics. She worked two part-time jobs and volunteered at the hospital."

To Detective Stephens, Mrs. Norris' remarks were no different than any other society mother encountered as a police detective. Their offspring were always superior, with high aspirations. Maybe Detective Stephens did not graduate from an exclusive high school, but he did graduate near the top of his class from a public high school and university. He passed the detective exam the first time. Not many of his peers counted that achievement.

Detective Stephens asked, "Did she know the kids in the van?"

"No!" Mrs. Norris was adamant. "I don't even know why she got in that van! She was supposed to be going to a movie with Sharon Boone."

Detective Stephens remained expressionless since Sharon Boone was one of the teens in the van. Remembering the words from the Inspector, *Follow the money*. He would pursue the money aspect as he rose. He thanked Mrs. Norris. He talked to the other parents, learning that their children have no enemies. Returning to the station, he finished the preliminary report.

During the evening news, Detective Stephens heard Mrs. Norris say that Jillian did not know anyone in the van nor that she did drugs. She pleaded for the audience to help find a tall black man wearing a blue shirt, khaki pants and orange athletic shoes, driving a black Mercedes.

****

Two weeks later, the telephone jangled. Detective Stephens picked up the receiver and said, "Detective Stephens, how may I help you?"

"Detective Stephens. This is Jonathan Phillips," the voice stated. "I would like to talk to you about the Jillian Norris murder."

"Are you still in the hospital?"

"Yes. I won't be released until this afternoon, and I want to get this off my chest."

"I'll be there in half an hour."

"Thank you, detective. And there is one other thing."

"What's that?"

"I want to refute whatever Jillian's mother is saying on the television about the teens in the van with her daughter."

Detective Stephens cradled the receiver, wondering what Jonathan would say that refute his friend's mother's statement when driving. Helen Dithers was again at the Information Desk. She directed him to the fifth floor. Detective Stephens rapped on the door casing.

"Detective Stephens!" Jonathan greeted. "Tell me, detective, how long has the case been open?"

"At least two weeks," Detective Stephens replied.

"And do you have any suspects?"

Detective Stephens consulted his notebook before he answered. "No. Your friends provide a vague description of a tall black man, wearing khaki pants, a blue shirt, and orange sneakers. We do know that a black Mercedes was seen speeding away on a surveillance video, matching their description."

"I heard that. My friends got one thing right: the clothing. But the driver was not black nor male."

Detective Stephens clicked his pen. "How do you know?"

"I remember the incident clearly, now. The shooter was female. It was Liberia Martin."

"I heard you mutter, 'Why did she do it?' You were the only one. So why did your friends finger a tall black man?

Jonathan smiled. "I can guess. I hope you can arrest her for murder."

"I hope we can. Maybe your friends will recant after knowing what you said. That's why I want your statement as you are the only one who said 'she'."

"Okay. Sharpen your pencil, and I will tell you."

Jonathan took a deep breath and a sip of water before beginning. "First, Liberia followed us to that secluded area to collect from Parker for the marijuana."

"Let me guess: he cheated her."

"He did. And this was not the first time. He likes to wrap a hundred-dollar bill around a wad of paper so it would appear to be five hundred dollars. Well, I saw the black Mercedes park behind the van. Liberia got out and walked up to the driver's window and demanded the rest of the money from Parker. Parker just laughed and said, 'Make me.' Of course, Liberia was furious. She stalked back to the car and returned with a handgun."

"Not a rifle? That's what your friends said. The evidence said otherwise."

"They were wrong. It was a handgun. Even a sawed-off shotgun does look like a handgun. My father has been teaching me to shoot for when we go deer hunting next fall. Anyway, she fired at Parker and missed. I don't know how she missed him at such close range. Maybe he ducked? But I saw Jillian's head pitch forward, and the blood splattered the windshield and dash. The bullet went into the back of her head. Parker hit the accelerator. I heard him say, 'Hang on, Jill, I'll get you to the hospital!' before I passed out from hitting my head. I knew she was dead."

"I'm sorry you lost a friend."

"Thank you, but I learned my lesson. I am not going out with those 'friends" anymore. Not one came to see me at the hospital."

"But other people might help you in the future."

"You are right. Maybe I'll become a patrol officer or a detective."

"You don't want to become a doctor?"

"No, I don't."

"Oh."

"Detective Stephens, you know there are three reasons teens get in a van."

"What are they?'

"Drugs, sex, or alcohol."

"No different than when I was a teenager."

Jonathan laughed. "One thing still bothers me. Why did Mrs. Norris tell the news media that Jillian would never get in that van because she did not know any of those teens? We went to the same school."

"We discounted that statement, thinking she was anxious with the unsolved murder of her daughter. With your statement, we can ask your old friends to recant and proceed with the arrest of Liberia Martin for murder."

My Only Brother
Jakub Wisniewski

Bones don't lie. Mouths lie, bones don't. They may lie under our feet, they may carry our tangled minds, but they would never lie to us: when their time comes, they just collapse, with all honesty and ennui. My bones are cold and that tells me I've been here for hours. Dew bit through my clothes, licking my skin, teasing my armpits with a virus-like interest. I get up, stretch my legs, look at the sky curbed by the moss green walls and take a breath deeper than the weeds I'm in. I'm in charge of this mess.

Because I wanted to be here. I let myself inside. They told me not to. They flung their warnings against my skull the way you toss a coin in a beggar's bowl, to lay off the burden, to feel better. I didn't listen because I was born deaf to alien mouths' wisdom. Because they don't know. They don't know the itching, the restlessness, the curiosity. If you look around the corner, you're the only one that sees what's there. You can hear others siccing their screams, like dogs, on you: don't look there! Like I'm Lot's wife or something. But what good is it to stand where they stand, to spend the time making amendments to the future, warning others about hot 'n' spicy dishes their tongues never touch.

I guess that's why I'm here. 'Cause I like looking around the corners. And that's about the only thing to do in here. You take a corridor, you go straight until you see a corner then you go faster and reach it and look what's behind it and suddenly you're in another corridor but you don't look back cause even if you do look back it's not behind you anymore, it's ahead of you. That's the way things gamble their meanings away, not asking us for permission. That's my hardboiled relativity lesson.

You could say that starting a career of a dopehead at the age of fourteen is a shitty thing to do. You could say that. But mum didn't say that 'cause she was busy working. And dad didn't say that 'cause he was busy dying. I found my own way through these things, through their absences and tumors, growing more and more distant, watching them become irrelevant details, black stripes on the flat, white surface of my saddish life, something you can dodge like puddles if you only have enough smack.

The walls of green are tall, much taller than me. There's a light above my head but it seems to be sourceless. A muddy reddish afterglow that saturates the ivy and makes it livelier, thicker, tighter. There's no way I could see through it, but I don't mind. I keep checking the corners.

What makes me concerned is that there's no smell in here. It got left outside, somehow.

I can't smell the green or the dew or my own feet. I can't smell a thing. I hope it doesn't mean I'm not here, or I'm dreaming or something. I've had enough of such trips. Fortunately, the fatigue is real. It keeps stinging my feet as I run around barefoot, brushing the grass with my toes. Bones don't lie. I don't have trouble breathing and my heart seems to be doing its job alright.

I'm not sure about the time. The sky hasn't changed a bit and it's still hanging where it should and every few minutes some dark shapes cross it like running stitches as if someone was trying to drill through the reddish blue from the other side of it. The shapes make no sound, they're hovering over the labyrinth with pride and indifference. Their beaks are hooked, their feathers black. Their wings are wider than any open arms I've ever seen and their hunger is lofty as if saying: we can wait, but we'll get our share.

I think I should follow the birds, so I keep walking, keep looking around the corners. The basic thing is not to be honest with yourself. Once you start being honest with yourself, really honest, honest as only death can be, the very same moment you're done. That's why I didn't put a single mirror in this maze, I made it with evergreen walls instead, with hedera cypria and hedera helix and they're feeding on the bricks, like some verdant pet parasites.

I touch my arms but there's not much to touch. A few tiny holes, a bit of skin and bones and some pulp in between. I seem less real than the maze. But I need to scratch my legs every few seconds, and that makes me feel palpable enough to follow the birds. I can almost hear their wings work. It seems to me I took more turns left than right. And I think I'm getting closer. Well, it's not that easy to build a maze and forget it completely.

Why don't I despair? You see, despair is not what it appears from the outside, it's actually a funny little thing. It's a liquid, you can dabble in it like a child, just for the fun of it. It's like any other drug. I mean it's not a controlled substance, but its substance is controllable. People like to despair 'cause being weak is a weapon as good as being strong.

Maybe the color of the sky is its final signal, an evening message, a farewell transmission. Maybe it glows red for the birds, to let them know about the feast. Maybe I need to hurry up to be there on time before the sky goes out like a tired candle.

But let's stay calm. The center of the maze cannot be far. I took the right turns. The birds called their kin, they crowd in the sky and come closer to the ground, their eyes glistening with gemlike pride. I try to stop the scratching; my leg skin needs a rest. That lets me walk faster. But let's not get nervous.

I just hope no one stops me before I get to the center. I imagine them trying, calling for help, for someone to save me, to wake up my weightless body with doctors and nurses and their cold, hopeless trade. I don't blame them. They don't blame me. It's all good. They may even think I'm here by accident, they may want to believe it. That's alright with me, as long as they don't stop me from reaching the center.

I think the ivy starts changing its color. It's yellower, thinner, drained. Bricks start showing through. I must be close.

And then the smell comes. Sweet, bitter, sour, I don't really know, some salty spume, sizzling shipworms, shrunken shackles binding my senses till they get all mixed up, smells turn into words, sounds into throbs, ivy into bricks. The maze gets all rocklike, it's colder and darker, it's like a cave with too many ways in. Now I need to rush.

Corridors get shorter, the walls are all bricks with no green on them. There's still grass under my feet. I forget about the itching and stop touching my legs. My feet get more power, they work on their own, I forget about them and focus on finding the way. I don't look up, but I'm sure new birds joined in. There's no sun to cast their shadows down here but I can feel their winged hunger unfurled like sails against the air. They know there's no time.

I take two turns left, one right and another one left, and I look ahead and stop. My heart keeps on running. The corridor in front of me is different. It's longer and the walls get narrower. It's actually so long that I can't see its end. There seem to be no turns left or right. I take a deep breath and look up at the birds: they all seem to be drawn in the same direction, like numb mammal moths drawn to some source of light I'm unable to see.

I start walking again, at first slowly, but my gait has its own rules, it hastens my feet and gets sucked up into the run. My eyes get fixed on the corridor's end, and it doesn't seem to get closer, it forms a scaled-down horizon, a running rabbit I cannot catch. Now that I really started running, I feel tired. Weariness is breathing down my neck, it's chasing me for fun like some unborn little brother I never wanted to play with. My lungs get crazy. My feet kick the grass. My jaws stick together like two scared kids. The itching goes away or my mind forgets it.

A minute later, the corridor's ending seems to get closer. It grows, like a grin or a newly opened church. I reject the tiredness, but my body accepts it. My thighs are trembling. It's been ages since the last time I did any kind of physical activity, isn't it funny I'm doing it now? Thoughts swarm in my head, thoughts of all kinds, thoughts of review and regret. Thoughts of the end. Well, it seems I've finally come to accept my decision to come here. I've always found it hard to come to terms with my own choices. They sort of lived on their own, somewhere next to me, like a snippy neighbor telling me what to do.

Because I came here to end it all. I built the maze lying on the sidewalk, my head on the curb, my back on the concrete, my hands hidden underneath as if ashamed of their owner. I took all this shame, I took all my fear, all these years of dope, my teachers' disgust, my mother's helplessness. I took the way I felt homesick when I missed my dead father. I took all these things and much more than that, I took it all to the corner of Dix Street and Middle, next to the barber shop and I sold them for a golden shot. I bought a brand-new needle, first time in two weeks. I died on Dix Street, but I still felt them trying, trying to help me, trying to wake me, so I built the maze to find myself in it and get it over with.

And here I am. I stop running. The longest corridor is over. I look around the final corner and I'm right at the center. It's like a meadow surrounded by brick walls, the grass is cut neatly like in a city park. Birds flying in circles. Birds over my head.

My body lies right in the middle. I come closer to have the last look. I am pale and thin. Bones don't lie. I'm almost a boy, I didn't even know I looked so young. My pants are all dirty. Blood on my forearm. The eyes are open. I touch them. I close them. I am my only brother.

Nightmares at Nara Dreamland
Mark Hudson

(Nara Dreamland was a Japanese amusement park built in 1961, to try and mimic the success of the American Disney theme parks. It was built by a Japanese businessman, who apparently consulted Walt Disney, but could not come to an appropriate financial agreement to use Disney characters. Nonetheless, they used the Disney parks as an example to build their amusement park, whose doors closed in 2006. Since then, the amusement park remains there abandoned, in disrepair, with a crumbling castle, vegetation growing over the rides, and as someone who went there said, it seems "eerily untouched." In Japan, it is "forbidden to go there," and it is surrounded by barbed wire, and it is occasionally patrolled by security guards, surrounded by fences, spikes, and barbed wires. If you get caught on the premises, you can get a fine of 100,000 yen, or 950 Euros. Yet thrill seekers venture there to take photos of the abandoned amusement park, and some get away with it. I suppose on Halloween, it would be the perfect scene for a haunted theme park story...)

Jonas James was an American photographer, taking pictures in Japan, and he had been legally permitted to do so. He was there with his wife, Beatriz, and his teenage kids Elroy and Amanda, both amateur photographers in their own right. They were staying not too far from Nara Dreamland, an abandoned amusement park they saw on a program advertised on television.

The television warned people not to go there, which gave Elroy and Amanda the brilliant idea to sneak in and take photos.

So on October 31, 2016, Jonas James was sawing logs in the hotel room, and Elroy and Amanda snuck out, taking their rental car, and driving off to Nara to see what they could see.

When they got there, the gate was closed. But when they walked up, the gate eerily swung open, as if it was expecting them. They walked in, cameras poised. They snapped pictures of Aska, the wooden roller coaster, the screw coaster, the steel roller coaster, the double corkscrew, the Bobsleigh, the Jungle cruise, and outside, they were greeted by the haunting sounds of bullfrogs in the distance.

Suddenly, to their shock, the whole amusement park seemingly came to life, all the lights went on, all the rides were working as if ghosts had turned everything on.

"Oh, it's beautiful!" said Amanda. "Should we ride the rides?"

"I don't think so, Amanda," Elroy replied. "I think it's a trick, and security was alerted. I think we need to get out of here. We got the photos we wanted, let's scat."

Suddenly, the front doors closed with a clang! A Japanese robot, the legendary Mascot 6-22, the old-wives tale about the killer robot who haunted the park, guarding and protecting the park with the potential to kill, appeared; so apparently, the rumor was true!

"Intruder alert! Intruder alert!" Mascot 6-22 shouted.

"Shoot! We need to leave!" stammered Amanda.

Mascot 6-22 began wandering around, looking for the perpetrators, the trespassers, and spotted them quick. He began to spew forth electric bursts in the direction of the two trespassers.

"Divert him, Amanda, and I'll creep on him, and unplug him, it's our only choice!"

So Amanda ran towards the exit and Elroy snuck behind the robot's control panel, and being computer-savvy, knew how to deactivate the robot.

"Does not compute. Computer reactivating destruction…." and the computer turned off.

Elroy quickly joined his sister at the front of the park, where sirens were going off. They hid by the entrance, and a bunch of Japanese military police came through the entrance, at which point, they promptly snuck out, undetected.

They crept out to their dad's rental car, hidden in the bushes, and made it back to the hotel room safely.

The next day, they downloaded the photos they took on their laptops and took a look. In each photo, there was no doubt about it, ghosts were captured on film in the background in each and every photo!

Amanda looked at her brother and said, "Wow! I'm scared!"

Elroy put his arm around his sis and said, "But sister dear, it is All Saints Day. The evil spirits are done roaming the Earth."

They looked at the photos one more time, and the ghosts were no longer in the photos.

Amanda looked at her brother. "Now, you saw ghosts in those photos like I did? I'm not just imagining things?"

"No, I saw it too. And we both saw Nara at night. But who back in the states will believe us? No one. It's like the old American commercial where they used to say, 'Ancient Chinese secret', only, in this case, it's Japanese!"

Non-Virtual Reality
Mark Hudson

I was sitting in Hot Dog Island, a restaurant in Evanston that hasn't changed since the seventies. It is situated in the middle of the intersection, right near the world-famous Sarki's restaurant, just two blocks away. I was having an Italian Sausage sandwich and three New Trier students came in wearing North Face jackets and sporting acne and braces.

The two kids were boasting about their X-Boxes, and the fancy video game equipment they had. Hot Dog Island has always had pinball machines since the seventies; they've not changed one iota.

The teenagers were teasing their one friend, because he didn't have as cool video games as they did.

"Hey, look, Frederick, there's a pinball game, that's more your speed!"

I glanced over at the pinball game. It was called *The Wizard of Oz* and contained cartoons of the characters from the *Wizard of Oz*!

"Hey, you kids don't know what you're talking about! Pinball games are better than video games! Haven't you ever seen the *Wizard of Oz*?"

"Oh, that's just a kid's movie!" they chuckled."

"No, it's not; it had a message about socialism and politics in it, and if you think Harry Potter was blacklisted by librarians and parents, you should know that *Wizard of Oz* got bad reviews when it came out, and parents and librarians thought it was trash!"

"Really?" Now they were intrigued.

"Tell you what, you young video game aficionados, I bet I can beat you at this pinball game! If I beat you, all three of you have to buy me a cheese fry!"

So I put in a quarter, and we all found ourselves right inside the machine. One teenager was the tin man, one was the cowardly lion, and one was Dorothy! Wasn't someone missing?

"Who am I?" I said.

"You're Toto!" they exclaimed.

I looked in some water, and sure enough, I was a dog!

"But there's a character missing? Who is it?"

Suddenly a witch flew by on a broom. "Boys! Get back to class!"

"It's our homeroom teacher! Run!"

We followed the yellow brick road, and we heard the song *Pinball Wizard*. Then we came to a castle, where a hologram was singing *Pinball Wizard*.

We opened the curtain, and there was Elton John, all timid and mild-mannered.

"How do we get home?" we asked.

"Click your heels and say there is no place like home!"

So we did!

"Mister, mister, are you okay? You bumped your head on the video game."

"Where am I?"

"You wandered into the video arcade, and you bumped your head, and passed out!"

I looked up. I was slumped in front of a video game called the *Warriors* which had cartoon scenes drawn on it by the seventies movie of the same name by Walter Hill.

As I walked out of the arcade, I heard the theme song, *In the City* by the Eagles playing, and I thought, man, do I have a migraine!

On the Exotic Beach Afterwards
A.C. Josepha

Yvette sat on the balcony and sipped her wine. The ocean was her constant companion these days, the sound of the ocean replaced the soundtrack that had been in the background of her life for thirty-five years; the sometimes faint, but never-ending roar of traffic. No matter where your perch was in Los Angeles county, the sound was inescapable. Even along the coast of Malibu, you could be looking out at the surfers as they expectantly gazed at the horizon in their slick black suits, you could hear the waves, see the waves roll right up to your back deck, but then behind you was the incessant roll of tires on Pacific Coast Highway, a constant.

Sunset had always been her favorite time of day, no matter where in the world she was; watching a slant of light in shades of gold change to blues, to grays, and then darkness.

Michael came out and stood staring at his phone. "Did you hear about the earthquake?"

"Where?"

"Not far from here."

"You love to say everything's close here." She waved the back side of her hand at him. He stopped looking at his phone and leaned against the balcony rail.

"It doesn't matter you know," he said.

"Of course it matters, we're in a third world country without retrofitted buildings."

"I'm not talking about the earthquake," he said, looking her in the eye with a grave expression.

"Oh, that—yes—that matters very much to me."

"No one will remember it two hundred years from now. No one even knows what you did, except for me."

"Oh, come on Mike, if you looked at life that way you'd never be motivated; you'd have no shame, you'd have no morals at all." She sighed heavily, put her wineglass down and held her forehead in both hands as though she was in pain.

In silence, they stared at the sunset, watched it cast shadows against the sand and waves, deeming the water silver and the sand dull gray. A wisp of incense blew toward them from somewhere on the beach below.

The water pulled back and back and back until it was like a gaping mouth a mile out.

"Where did you say that earthquake was?"

Precious Time
Lisa Scuderi-Burkimsher

Rummaging through an old tub of clothes, I came across my favorite childhood blue blouse. I remembered wearing it my first day of seventh-grade. I thought I was so cool. I walked into school all smiles, flipped my hair behind my neck and slid into my chair. Most of my friends chortled, but I didn't care. In between classes, I strolled the hallway, swinging my arms, proud of my blouse. My father bought me that blouse, and that's why it had been special to me. My mom and dad were divorced, and that was my weekend with him. My dad always made sure he spent quality time with me on those weekends. Most dads didn't like to shop, but my dad never minded when I asked to go to the mall. That's where he bought me the blue blouse. Remembering that moment, I put the blouse close to my chest, and in an instant, I had been transported back to the mall.

Blinking several times, my father, Tom, appeared wearing the same silly striped green button-down shirt and jeans, tapping his foot in tune with the instrumental music playing over the speakers. "So, Belle, what store do you want to shop in?"

I pointed to the young girl's boutique. "Uh, there," I answered, flabbergasted.

"Okay, let's go."

I couldn't believe I had been transported back in time, and the mall crowded with shoppers for the back to school sales. Crossing over to the boutique, a young boy, Timmy, who I went to school with, waved and yelled hello. *How old did I look?* When we went into the boutique, I went to the mirror, and my hair was short with bangs, and I wore blue jeans and a white sweat shirt. The same outfit I had on the actual day. I was thirteen-years-old again.

The Grey Wolfe Den Anthology

My stomach churned. I looked thirteen, but didn't feel it. I had adult instincts. My dad asked me if I wanted a soft pretzel and I told him no, because it would ruin my appetite for dinner. He leaned his head back, chuckled and said he'd like one and would be right back.

"Go ahead and pick out what you want and try it on. When I get back, we'll pay for it."

There it hung on the rack; the pretty, soft-colored blue blouse. I touched the material, and it was as I remembered it, silky and smooth. I found my size and went into the dressing room. I didn't try it on because I knew from past experience it would fit. I went through the motions, and after what had been a reasonable amount of time, I came out of the dressing room with the blouse. Whatever adult feelings I had were gone when I saw my dad standing at the counter wearing mustard on his chin. I smiled and brought the blouse to him.

"Belle, this is a nice choice. I bet it looks lovely on you."

"It fits good, but it's expensive."

My dad rubbed my cheek, his hand sticky from the mustard. "You're worth it, Sweetie."

As we left the mall, my dad took my hand and said he'd promise to take me shopping again.

When I opened the car door, a swirl of white lights appeared, and dizziness came over me. I remembered falling, but not hitting the ground, awaking in the attic with the blouse in my hands, clutched against my chest as before.

I touched every inch of my body and knew I was twenty-nine again. To make certain, I looked in the broken mirror in the corner of the attic. *Definitely twenty-nine.*

"Wow, what a dream I had." I never realized how much I missed my dad until then. As I folded the blouse, I noticed a mustard stain that had not been there before. I thought back, and on the way to the car, my dad spilled mustard on the bag with the blouse, and some must've gotten inside. That didn't happen the actual time he took me to the store. I wondered if I had gone insane, or if my dream was actually a reality?

Rendezvous Beyond Nether
Debansree Banejee

The last thing I remember was crashing into the giant oak. It was overbearing and impractical for someone so inebriated and angry to be driving his Lincoln convertible, going at a hundred and fifty miles per hour. I did not know what had made me so angry; maybe it was Michelle's infidelity, maybe it was my gradually trickling down list of clients, or maybe it had something to do with my dwindling reputation as a highly volatile attorney-at-law. But most likely, none of these was the actual reason...

It must have been my own self-deprecating sarcasm that had chased me for the past year, never letting me sleep, eat, think, or live with the joyful abandonment of 'not knowing'. Why did Pa have to commit suicide at seventy? Why couldn't he keep up with the pretense that he was enjoying his septuagenarian existence, caring for an invalid wife and craving for the company of a successful son who never turned up to ask after him?

I would never understand that his departure would jar me as much as it did then; it had been something I simply never gave a thought to. I had been so busy keeping up with my practice that I didn't have enough opportunity to look into the mirror and notice my gradually graying sideburns. Nor did I ever find enough time to ask how Pa managed to care for Mom during her 'worse' periods. The Alzheimer's had gnawed away most of her memories, leaving big holes in her world as she knew it. Sometimes frustration rode her so much that she turned violent at everyone around her, and Pa had to look after her in spite of his arthritis. Of course, the servants were there; I hadn't been negligent in as far as servants were concerned, but they hardly knew how to share someone's mental burdens. Pa's last note said as much...

Hence, I did dream of Pa one day, as if we had been walking in a watercolor-perfect landscape, laughing at each other's jokes, something we had never done since I tasted the salt of success. But something snapped inside me right then, and the next moment I knew, Alexander Lee Cobb, the famous attorney-at-law, was crying. It was the onslaught of my severe depression anxiety disorder that left me more or less dysfunctional.

****

I had the sudden, swooping feeling of having sprouted strong soaring wings; it was a sensation so brilliant and liberating that I instantly forgot all the lousy feelings I had harbored inside me for one year now. Neither did the shrink alleviate a bit of my suffering, nor did his prescribed medicines do that. While I had a feeling that all the mumbo jumbo about chakra healing might help me, meditation was too trying for me. I simply never had the perseverance for that. Nonetheless, the strange Eastern philosophies had certainly left some impact upon my mind of late, but not strong enough to stop me crashing into a tree after drunk driving.

I opened my eyes and was startled to see rolling valleys below me, lush meadows with brilliant blue streams streaking across all the greenery. All the flowers that grew along the slopes gave an ethereal and watercolor-like beauty to the scene below me. *Where was I*, the thought struck me, but the beauty unfolding in front of me was too overwhelming to leave enough reason in me.

At precisely the same moment as I decide to venture into the painting myself, a voice inside my head tells me that it's all mine. *Mine?* I wonder... *Am I imagining this?* No! I was fully awake because I could feel the rush of a gentle breeze against my skin and smell the scent of flowers wafting through the entire area. *What do I want now*, I ask myself? I had to search for someone who could show me around and tell me what I was doing here. Someone who could tell me where I was...

I began looking for someone who could do all that, but I was evidently all alone. It didn't bother me one bit to think of my absolute solitude because I had lots of new places to venture to. I embarked upon my discovery of everything I saw around me; the landscape was an unending stretch of beauty. After an unknown period of time, I had the first qualms of panic. Was I really alone here? No, I couldn't be, and as soon as such desperation crossed my mind, I could almost hear the meditation instructor speaking.

There's no birth or death for a soul; it just changes the outer covering that we call our body. We are so conditioned in our various births that we lose the insight into understanding the fundamentals of our existence and start believing that the body is who I am. Meditation teaches us to open our third eye that looks past the experiences we assimilate during our current birth; it helps us heal, and understand that there's no reason to lament upon the loss of our loved ones. They are still there, having only shed their earthly bodies. They never leave us...

Meditation helps us reconnect with our only friend, the Supreme Master, who is our creator and benefactor. Welcome him into your lives by starting to meditate every day.

****

Was I dead? Was this purgatory? Would I be eternally condemned to be trapped within this lifeless imitation of life? My desperation turned into outright fear now, and the only thing I wished for was to be relieved of this desolation by someone who could show me some sense of where and how I was.

I suddenly heard some movement behind me; it was a strange-looking, handsome young man with a beard and long hair. He looked familiar. Everything seemed to be addled up in my brain.

"Jesus!" I exclaimed at length.

"Yes, it's me," he said, and I immediately felt a warmth spreading through my entire being.

"Where are the others?" I asked.

"The others?" he smiled.

"Yes... the others," I managed to mumble, getting even more perplexed.

"You want others to be there?" he asked.

"Does it matter?" I answered.

"As a matter of fact, it certainly does, because there aren't others, but there can be others if you wish. I have a feeling that you want your Pa and your dead golden retriever Maggie to be here. So be it!" Jesus spoke very softly, and as soon as he had spoken, I was dumbstruck to see Pa walking towards me, with Maggie on her red leash, like the olden days.

"May I ask you something?" I asked.

"Yes, you may. I am all yours today," Jesus said.

"Can you tell me how long Mom has?"

This time his smile spread even further, and he said, "I understand that you're anxious to see her here too, free from all her pain. The good news is that you can do that RIGHT NOW."

Lo and behold! Mom stood before me in her knitted maroon cardigan. I was all smiles, but something nagged behind my mind.

"Lord, is she dead already? Otherwise, how did you manage to bring her here?"

He smiled again and answered, "She's here because you're here. It seems you haven't understood the full depth of things till now."

I was at a loss for words and must have looked really befuddled, for Jesus continued.

"You see, there is no one else here or there or anywhere in the universe... it's just you and me. It's you who has gone there, sometimes as a blade of grass and sometimes as an orca. Do you realize that you have this immense capacity to be born as your own child? Or as uncountable things, however microscopic they may be, or however large... and all simultaneously. You never lost your Pa because you were him, or Gandhi or Socrates or Einstein. You are every single bit of energy in the universe because I created you in my wake. You were to be the masterpiece I had created; my own inspiration, my partner... but look what you've done. You've forgotten everything and are now in the process of killing fragments of yourself in my name. Ironically, you can't even die as long as a single grain of sand exists, as long as I exist. Come to me, because you are me and I am you."

****

The swoosh of my own heartbeat that made all the machines beep and wheeze was the first thing I felt after returning. I was in an Operation Theatre, surrounded by grim-faced doctors. Evidently, they didn't understand that I was back inside me again, because I didn't bother to open my eyes. I could see everything clearly; I no longer needed my eyes to see anything because I had seen myself.

Schneider's Last Stand
Matt McGee

Schneider was driving home slowly through thick, foggy night. The mist seemed to come from two directions; it lifted up off the asphalt and billowed in swirls from every angle in the darkness. He rolled down the main road that led through the heart of his city, away from the fast food restaurant he'd been in almost an hour.

The date had been a last minute, late-night idea. Schneider was new to this online thing, and frankly, *Plenty of Fish* kind of repulsed him. But someone had talked him into it, and it beat sitting home. Now as he slid along through the fog, one sentence bounced over and over in his head like a skipping CD:

I can't believe it was her.

Maybe the whole date had been a dream. He replayed the whole hour over and over in his head. He didn't really see the fog anymore. It was in that glassy-eyed moment when, from out of the darkness, the old white Mazda pickup appeared. It stood parked beside the road with moisture streaking down its sheet metal, dripping through the original rally stripes some owner had worked hard to preserve. It was just like the model Erin had owned, and *For Sale* sign hung in its cabin window. Schneider went bug-eyed for one haunted moment.

He didn't believe in much but he believed in signs.

Schneider put a key in the same front door lock he'd been opening for decades. He didn't consider himself the type who was stuck in the past, but he also wouldn't deny being stuck where rent was cheap. His life had settled into comfortable routine and his neighbors changed over enough that no one really noticed his status as the old salt of the townhome complex. Those that did just

The Grey Wolfe Den Anthology

assumed he owned his own place.

The two front rooms of his townhome are lined with furniture he's owned but rarely sits on. Shelves hold up books he's read but never revisits. A DVD player and a stack of discs stand ready, but he's never home to watch them. He'll clean the house whenever a woman enters his life, which isn't often, and obviously there are no real plants or pets.

At the end of the hallway is a small master bedroom, a bachelor cave, and at the end of every night his drive home ends this way; Schneider taxis along the runway of his hallways, down those final fifteen feet of graying pile carpet to a bed where dreaming is allowed any time. He wouldn't admit it but, lately, those dreams have received a little help from the pharmacy. The $2 bottle of Ambien prolongs the night's rest without waking or rustling at the slightest sound.

Schneider stripped then folded his top clothes back into their assigned drawers. This was a well-established bachelor trick; socks and underwear go in the hamper. Anything not worn more than 10 hours or slept in gets tucked into drawers or re-hung to be aired and reused. Some people read *Bachelorhood-for-Dummies* and crave the single life and others groove into it after being dropped into its tide unexpectedly.

Schneider's single life came unexpected. Some would call it cursed. As the fog wrapped around the condo, and the sheets that smelled like only him wrapped up his shoulders, he thought now again of the Mazda, a reminder of all the things that have chased him to bed.

It happened during his young dating life, the mistakes of which most people should be forgiven for on the basis of age alone. He was delivering pizza for a local Mom & Pop shop. He had a wickedly fast car and a girlfriend he hadn't meant to meet.

Erin's parents had bought her new white '87 Mazda B2000. As Schneider drifted toward Ambien-free sleep he pictured one like it, just like it, parked up the street for sale. Maybe it was a time capsule capable of taking him back long enough to apologize. As his eyes drifted closed, he heard once again the question she'd asked tonight:

"If there were one person you could fall asleep and wake up as tomorrow," she'd asked over their *Plenty of Fish* dinner, "who would it be?"

For a serial dater, she was pretty. Smart, not smarmy. Schneider almost couldn't believe he'd been allowed to go out with this woman. Way out of his league. He felt the eyes on them the moment the two of them walked into the fast food joint. She'd made her way a few steps up the grooming ladder, past the rung he'd been standing on since the mid-90's. Sooner or later those preserved clothes would come back into style.

Schneider wasn't a big believer in technology but he'd been talked into trying online dating. The hookup was easy. She looked cute, and she'd contacted him first. That blew his mind. He agreed to meet her at the fast food joint. They both worked nights. *What the hell.*

She had a vaguely familiar tone. But by this age a lot of people start to look and sound like other people in the catalogue of the mind. He'd given his real name. *Schneider*, he'd said, as if presenting a badge. Telling the truth just felt better. Then she asked him a genuine question over a casual dinner of fried food in the middle of the night.

"If I could fall asleep tonight," he repeated, "and wake up as a different person?"

"Yes."

Schneider shrugged. He couldn't have once fathomed exposing something so deeply personal, so tragic, and so long ago to a total stranger. But now, the words were about to roll out of his mouth.

And that's when she smiled. An adorable mole stretched over the left corner of her mouth. And as Schneider stared at it, not realizing he was staring quite so long or so hard, everything came rushing back.

Erin.

The Erin.

The Erin he'd hurt thirty years ago. A pretty soccer player, they were both fresh out of high school and, enjoying their Gap Year. He delivered pizzas in a fast car. She'd throw a bag of balls into her little white Mazda and head off to practice.

Their relationship had started deliciously awkward. A match-making, mutual girlfriend invited him to meet her. Erin, not knowing Schneider was coming, swung open the front door expecting only the girlfriend, a teammate who'd already seen everything in the locker room. So when she flung open the door completely naked, Schneider was shocked at the sight of a strange woman's bare, soccer-firmed buttocks. They turned, flashing, running the other direction. It was the worst tease he'd ever endured.

The embarrassment became their bond. The ice wasn't just broken it was smashed completely. They started dated while he delivered for the Mom & Pop. A week into their relationship, he found a better paying job with a national chain.

And with the ascendancy up the income ladder came a chance to meet new, attractive coworkers. One of them hit on him the first night. By morning they were an item. It wasn't until they were into their third day of heavy dating, making out every chance since meeting, that Schneider's phone rang.

It was Erin. The Erin.

He was only nineteen and had his first senior moment. How do you forget you're dating someone? Distraction. A pretty little rich girl with the body of a cheerleader and a north side address in her parent's spare room. But now, there on the phone, Erin.

She had just been wondering why he'd stopped calling.

Now, through the miracle of online dating, they'd somehow swum slowly back to each other.

She'd already led him through an iPhone gallery of her grown kids. "Never had any," he admitted. And she said the words everyone their age recites—especially after being torn limb from limb through childbirth, stretched thru the rearing years, and in their mid-life crisis when they meet someone who skipped the whole process:

"You were smart."

Schneider never really believes the people who say this. He'd long suspected he would make a great father but knows he never met and settled on the right woman. All of his great romantic what-ifs fell apart for various reasons, all of which were followed by the thought *I wonder what ever happened to Erin?*

He'd Googled her, searched her out on Facebook. But despite the iPhone, apparently, she didn't care for technology either.

The date ended in a friendly enough way. He'd answered her question with some lame reply about wanting to be Mark Twain so that way he could know how to write a really great novel way before the advent of typewriters. She had nodded. He asked her the same question. He couldn't remember what her answer had been.

Now as the blankets wrapped around his naked torso and the fog wrapped the walls of the townhome, he imagined this was a bit what it must look like to be an insect on a table as two human hands slowly cupped around it. They could smash. They could gently lift and return him to a natural habitat. It was all up to the big hands.

Schneider fumbled his fingers across his nightstand to his cell phone. The number he'd exchanged forty-five minutes earlier was at the top of the call list. He pressed the green dial button.

"Hello?"

"I'm surprised you picked up."

"Me too. I saw it was your number, and thought…"

"…And thought 'oh shit, he's a stalker.'"

Erin laughed. "Well not exactly. I was thinking more along the line of booty call."

"Erin," his said directly, "if I could fall asleep tonight and wake up as one other person tomorrow…?"

"Yes?"

"I'd wake up as nineteen-year-old me. And I would call up a beautiful girl who drove a white Mazda pickup, one that played soccer…"

Erin didn't speak.

"… and answered the door butt naked the first time I saw her."

"I knew it was you."

"Really?"

"Actually, I wasn't sure. But how many Schneiders are there? And I didn't know how to ask of course. Oh my God, how are you?"

Schneider continued. "If I could wake up tomorrow as nineteen-year-old me, I'd slap him upside the head and say 'never, *ever* treat someone that way because it follows you the rest of your life. And someday you'll be lying in bed thinking to yourself 'you missed out on a pretty wonderful person.'"

There was a moment of silence. Then, with a sigh of relief, she just said:

"Thank you."

"I'm lucky I got to say that."

"I'm lucky I got to hear it."

"You're not going to believe this, but every time I've passed a late 80's Mazda pickup on the road I turn to see if you're driving it."

"Myrtle! Oh my God, my old truck. I loved her. She was so good to me. I drove her all through college. Then she just gave out on me one night leaving the Bay Area. She'd taken me as far as she could. I sold her for scrap. I took the money and put a down payment on a new car that fit my new career."

"I passed one tonight on my way home," he said.

"Did you look to see if I was driving it?"

"Yeah," Schneider said. "And it was for sale."

"Really."

"I'm thinking I should go put a bid on it. You know, for our second date."

She didn't hesitate, and her tone was sincere. "Second date, yes. Truck, no. I'm not that person anymore."

He processed that a moment. Then he said, "neither am I."

"Good. Because it took me a while to get over being ignored like that."

There was nothing he could say.

After a few moments she added, "sorry."

"No. I'm sorry. I've been sorry a long time." Another pause. "I always wondered if the reason I'd been single this long was because I screwed up the right one."

"I don't think karma goes on that long. Unless you're a Cubs fan."

He laughed. "In that case we've got a chance!"

"Agreed."

"So," he said, "when I wake up tomorrow, I'm going to do what I should've done twenty-nine years ago."

"You're going to call?"

"I'm lying in a room full of things I've traveled the world to collect, and worked hard for decades to keep a roof over my head. And yet when I wake up tomorrow I already know that all that's going to matter to me is if you'll answer the phone."

"I'm going to answer."

They said their good nights and, in the morning they began calling, texting, occasionally writing long e-mails just for fun. On her birthday, he sent her a card in the mail because no one does that anymore. But it was a reminder of a time they'd lived through.

And after that foggy night he never saw the Mazda pickup beside the road again. He assumed the owner had sold it, but he liked to think it was a ghost, one that had been set free now to haunt someone else.

Sentient Children
Shalom Galve Aranas

I skinned my knees playing skip rope. We sucked flower sap by pulling the inner stem from the outer stem of a flower. It tasted sweet. Hopscotch was easy. I knew how to balance my body and was an obvious choice for the cheer dancing team. I loved after class activities. We, the big girls, were in their elements and could boss anyone around. I wouldn't go home yet. I told my father I'd go home late because of a classically invented varsity practice excuse so he'd wait in our company office and wait for me to finish before fetching me. He held a certain pride that I was doing something worthwhile and might even get an athletic scholarship in college. Now in high school, my parents were very hopeful. *Pathetic*, I thought. Anyway, I'd get by once they knew I was going to be a cheer dancer.

Finally, we played the usual hypnosis while chewing mint gums. I would slap the palm of my classmate, and she would close her eyes while placing her palm above mine, without touching, just slightly grazing. And there it was. Undeniable. The magnet buffering between our stupid, sweaty palms. I would leave her, eyes closed, palms still floating on air.

Then I coaxed the palms to rise with my own hands. After a moment, the hands rose, higher, higher, higher even than her head. It was always exhilarating and mysterious, as though we had a connection with the stars.

****

When it was my turn, I said; let's try something else."

We ran to the school field, which was very green beneath our heels. I lay down on the grass, unmindful of the pointed tips that penetrated through the back of my blouse. I wanted my whole body to float. They said it couldn't happen. I told Genevieve to do it, or I'd tell everyone she wasn't a virgin anymore. Genevieve tried not to look affected, but her face screwed up and really seemed close to tears.

Without waiting for her to move or reply, I closed my eyes and imagined I was going there, to that place where our hands go when we let it go and tell it to go up by itself. It was that place where we didn't know whether we spoke with God or the devil. We suspected the devil, of course. But it was such a harmless little game we've always played without anyone getting hurt. Why should it be the devil?

Everything became very quiet. It was an unusual kind of quiet. As though everyone had abandoned me.

I felt I was floating higher and higher until I reached a certain level where I had gone past people. I had to open my eyes. I was nowhere I could recognize. I moved from my levitation, to stand on black soil. It was a different world, and yet I could still hear the choir practice from a distance, as though I could choose to go back, to school.

I stood up and looked at the new world before me. A voice booms out; "This is yours now. Craft it well."

****

I decided it would have two moons. Each to light the other in perfect symbiosis. I didn't want a sun. I want everything to be dark.

And there were people with black lips and clammy grey skin walking beneath promontory where I stood watching mankind lose hope. They walked sluggishly with circles beneath their eyes.

I wondered why I would want my world to be bleak and dark. What was wrong with me? I needed to talk to someone, someone wiser, someone who understood me better than I knew myself. I created a man.

He was an astronaut who came from the moon. He loved moons and came back to my world, the dark Earth, to help sort me out. But he begged to go back to the moon as soon as he could because that is where he lived.

"Alright," I promised. "Why do I like this world, as though I wanted death?"

The astronaut clapped his hands, and thick velvet curtains appeared before us, between the River Styx and the River Styron. I saw myself playing astronaut with my very young brother. He wanted to wear the helmet. I said no, he couldn't because Mom said he *shouldn't*.

I pulled off the helmet and tossed it aside. I was tired of playing astronaut. I fell asleep on the bed and left my brother to play by himself. It must have been a while because I woke with the moonlight streaming on my face like a white, pallid river.

William, my younger brother, was gasping for air. I pulled the helmet off of his head. He was breathing normally after some time. But I don't think he ever breathed normally after that. I never told Mom.

****

It was just something I couldn't tell anyone, least of all my mom. He went on with life, but he had learning disabilities, ADHD, asthma attacks, and a whole bunch of other problems. Sometimes I'd practice not breathing to see how my little brother actually felt. What his world was like. And it was so much like the dark world I created. I couldn't tell my mom.

But I could tell my dad.

I dreamt one night about the astronaut I created. He took off his helmet and it was my dad.

The next day, I talked to my dad about what happened to my brother during playtime. My father listened to me. After some time listening, he told me something I never knew. When my brother was born, the umbilical cord was wrapped about his neck. It was a delicate pregnancy and he was sorry I was not told about it. They were certain it could not have been from the toy helmet of an astronaut.

Dad brought me home to a world where there were stars, a moon and a sun to brighten my day. After Mom knew how I felt all these years, she made a nice breakfast for all of us: my brother, my dad, and I. We ate a hearty breakfast at a table where the sun shone about us. I looked outside to our garden with all the birds and stirring bees among the shrubs and flowers. White clouds scudded in the bright blue sky and I was happy. I felt happy. I was home.

These days I bring my brother to therapy and little by little he is getting better. Next year he's going from Special Education to mainstream high school. Whenever he is asked what he wants to be when he graduates, he says an astronaut.

Size Doesn't Matter
J. Forrest Wellman

Size doesn't matter when it comes to a toothache. All teeth are created equal. The tooth throbs with every heartbeat, and for some reason, we want to touch it with our finger or tongue as if this is going to help.

When I was about twenty, I had an agonizing toothache. It was my upper right wisdom tooth. I had suffered most of the day and had put off going to the dentist all day, hoping it would somehow get better. Needless to say, it didn't. It only got worse. By the time I decided to do something about it, the dentist had already closed for the day. I was delirious with pain and had to have some relief. I had become desperate.

I remembered a story my uncle used to tell about pulling several of his own teeth with a pair of pliers. He said he just pulled and twisted and it popped right out. I thought about it for a while and being the smartest person I knew, like most young men, I quickly concluded it was a good idea to pull my own tooth. It was already killing me, and I couldn't see how it could hurt anymore.

I went to my truck and got a pair of small needle nose vice grip pliers from my toolbox. I figured these would work best because they were small enough to fit in my mouth and I could adjust them to lock securely onto my tooth. I went to the bathroom and stood in front of the mirror and opened my mouth as wide as I could so I could see that cruel wisdom tooth. I eased the pliers onto the tooth and adjusted them to fit and locked them. When I saw myself in the mirror with the pliers hanging out of my mouth, I started to think I might be making a big mistake. I'm sure the first man to ever jump out of a plane with a parachute felt the same way. But I had convinced myself that if my uncle could pull several teeth, then I could at least pull one tooth.

I reassured myself by telling myself it would be over in a flash and my excruciating pain would be gone. I then turned and placed my forehead against the wall so my head wouldn't move when I was ready to pull down and twist the tooth with the pliers. Just like my uncle.

My forehead still against the wall, I spread my legs for balance. I closed my eyes and placed both hands on the pliers and gave a big jerk. My pain went off the charts. I didn't have time for the twist because the big jerk stopped me from doing anything other than release a scream that was equal to a train whistle blowing. I yelled out something that was supposed to be swear words, but it sounded like I said {other other} because my brain had gone into Safe Mode. It had malfunctioned due to the mind numbing and sustained pain it was receiving. The pliers hanging out of my mouth didn't help things either.

I felt like I was going to pass out. My forehead slid down the wall as my legs collapsed beneath me. I fell to my knees on the bathroom floor. With my trembling hands, I removed the pliers from the unyielding tooth.

The agony was unmanageable. I had never experienced pain of this magnitude before or since. With this much pain coursing through my body, my malfunctioning brain concluded we had died and released all my bodily fluids. I broke into a cold sweat, and my nose was running like a raging river. Tears flowed down my face as I got up and staggered over to the commode, just in the nick of time. After a few minutes, I was able to compose myself enough to get the phone and call the dentist. He agreed have me come into his office, but I would have to pay an after-hours fee. I didn't care about the cost, money meant nothing to me at this point. I would have given up a kidney to stop this pain, both of them if need be.

Then I got lucky. I saw my mother's Bible on the end table next to the couch and remembered the purple prayer cloth she kept inside. It was a small piece of silk that had the words prayer cloth embroidered on it. When I was younger, she would place it on my head when I had a fever or on my belly if I had a stomachache. So I figured it might have some toothache suppressing qualities as well. I snatched it from her Bible as I bolted out the door.

I held it to the right side of my face so it could go to work on the hellish pain. I got in my truck and realized I was going to have trouble holding the prayer cloth to my face and drive because my truck was a standard shift. I solved this dilemma by cramming the prayer cloth in my mouth right on the tooth. I figured this would work better anyway because it would be right on the evil tooth. I couldn't get it all in my mouth, so that left about three inches hanging out. If someone had seen me like this, they might have concluded I was eating an expensive blouse. Again, I was in excessive pain didn't care, and also remember, I was twenty and still knew everything.

I pulled out of the driveway, slinging gravel from my tires as I hurried to the dentist office. The prayer cloth must have started working because I screamed less and less between prayers as I drove like a maniac. After what seem like forever, I roared into the parking lot at the dentist office, but he hadn't arrived yet. I sat and watched each car as they came by, hoping to see a turn signal come on. I also prayed for the dentist to drive faster. He finally got there, and I followed him into his office like a stray dog. I got in the chair and eagerly waited for my much-anticipated shot of Novocain. He gave me the shot, and within minutes, my painful ordeal was over. He pulled the wicked tooth.

From that day on, I became a firm believer in good oral hygiene and left the dental work to the professionals. I also know why they are called wisdom teeth, because when I gave my tooth the big jerk, I instantly realized this stunt was "stupit" as my New Jersey mother-in-law would say.

That One Winter Night
Robbie White

"Nice touch," my friend Jillian says to me. Her voice is filled with perfected sarcasm.

"What touch?" I ask with equally perfect innocence.

"Rides powering up when the park is closed for the season. And they power up at exactly the moment we are skulking around the boardwalk."

"Um, I had nothing to do with this."

"This was your idea."

We walk on in silence. After a few minutes, I get nervous and start to babble, "You know the first Ferris wheel was made in the late nineteenth century for some expo in Chicago. It was more than two hundred and sixty feet high. The guy who built it wanted it to be better than the Eiffel Tower in Paris. Ha. Epic fail."

Jillian stops walking and rolls her eyes at me. "You are a nerd."

I stop talking, and we resume our exploration.

On a hot summer night, the boardwalk would be filled with people longing to answer the call of hawkers who lure them in with singsong voices. There would be antique carnival music playing on the tinny loud speakers. The rides would have their own hawkers, but the machine sounds would blend into the mashup created by the people, hawkers, music, and games.

In the middle of winter, there is nothing but the wind. The only sounds are the ghostly machine noises of the antique Ferris wheel, the clanking of swing chains, the screech of the wooden coaster. All are mixed with the icy wind. It is extremely creepy.

The lights didn't come on when the rides started up, so the park is still cloaked in shadows. The little shops and cafes are boarded up against the snow and cold which makes them even creepier.

There has always been a huge tree in the center of the boardwalk square. Tonight, it is blowing madly in the wind. I can hear the gentle rumble of the Ferris Wheel relentlessly turning in its pointless circle. This place is so old that some rides are not even electric. There is a whole section of wooden swings shaped like canoes, long boats, and cars that are intended to be powered by several children at a time, working together to pump the swing higher and higher.

They are swaying in the wind, adding their bitter, wooden creaking to the night. The quaint little roller coaster, a real wooden contraption, is hauling a set of cars up the highest peak. The clicking of the chains screeches in the cold without proper lubrication. There is a feverish rising of noise as the little line of coaster cars is allowed to free fall down the slope up into the loop.

We grew up with this old amusement park. Our grandparents came here wearing long skirts and saddle shoes. Their dates wore crisp jeans and dress shirts if they were good boys; leather jackets and t-shirts if they were not. They "courted" here when Saturday night was date night. This was considered an elegant evening out. They might have even visited the drug store's soda shop for a milkshake afterward.

Our parents spent summers coming here to drink from flasks and make out on the Ferris Wheel. They wore cutoffs and tank tops instead of the elegant outfits of their parents' generation.

In those days, the owner built the bandshell and had live music on weekend afternoons. My parents tell stories of drinking cold beer and getting sunburned in the hot summer sun listening to the local bands.

We came here as kids for birthday parties. The bandshell is no longer in use. The park is just this boardwalk with games, the old coaster, Ferris Wheel, and a really great playground.

"Do you smell popcorn?" Jillian asks me suddenly.

"Yeah, actually, I do."

Even in the shadows, I see the steam from a little popcorn kiosk. Its protective tarp is a lump of dark shadow on the ground. The little white cardboard boxes of buttery hot popcorn sit on the windowsill, enticing us to come closer.

I look at Jillian, "You hungry,?"

Her eyes are huge as they stare at the cheery site of popcorn. There are no lights except for a pair of candles on the sill of the popcorn kiosk.

"Maybe we should go," I suggest laying a mittened hand on her arm.

"Yeah, maybe," Then she smiles at me, "But then again... maybe we should see what's going on?"

She is moving toward the candles and popcorn before I answer.

A few hours ago, we were sharing a pizza, bitching about how boring this winter has become since we don't have football playoffs. We were picking at the last piece, sucking at empty straws, when suddenly I had an idea.

"You know, the old amusement park Joe worked at last summer?" I asked Jillian, referring to my older brother's summer job as a carnival hawker.

"Oh, don't remind me how adorable he was wearing that vintage carny costume." She leaned her head back against the vinyl seat of the Pizza Hut booth.

"I was thinking it would be cool to see what it looks like in the snow."

Her head popped up, and her eyes sparked. And now, here we are walking toward something that cannot be good in the dark and cold. Our boots crunch on the snowy path. She reaches out for the popcorn, a dark figure steps out from the shadows. I gasp. Jillian doesn't even flinch. She continues to reach for the popcorn, confidently cupping the box in her gloved hands, raising her eyes to the dark figure.

I step back and am shocked to find my way blocked by a tall warm body. I gasp again and spin around.

I look way up into the laughing eyes of my best friend, Steven. He starts laughing, and I remember that he used to work at the carnival with Joe. He probably still has a key. He probably heard us talking at the Pizza Hut. He probably followed us here.

I punch him in the arm, which only makes him laugh harder. Behind me, I hear Jillian's voice softly talking and turn to see her embraced by my brother Joe. Well, that explains that.

* * * *

Red lights flash in the fog as each flash freezes the scene in a macabre winter wonderland. Two fire engines flank the entrance to the abandoned park. Inside the park itself, an ambulance sits busily, surrounded by paramedics.

For one hysterical moment, I see it all like a children's storybook page. From above, the amusement park is drawn carelessly cheerful in the snowy landscape. The little kiosks that in summer will sell popcorn, balloons, cotton candy, and caramel apples in summer are covered in tarps, lighter shapes in the dark night, surrounded by happy piles of perfect cartoon snow. In the storybook version of this night, the boardwalk and paths are covered with many inches of artfully drifted snow. The little cartoon firefighters are clever animals dressed in protective gear running to the rescue with bright eyes and happy smiles. Maybe the paramedics would be depicted as a pair of foxes with cases full of instruments working on the accident-prone cat wearing suspenders. Everyone would be having hot cocoa in Mrs. Cat's kitchen before the pages turned. I doubt we will be that lucky tonight. Nobody here is smiling.

I sit on the side of a fire engine wrapped in a grey emergency blanket. I can't stop shaking. A fireman brings me a cup of something hot. Do they carry hot drinks on the engines or did someone make a run to the nearest convenience store? I hold the hot paper cup as I stare unblinkingly at the ambulance. I can't see the scene beyond, but I know my best friend is still being freed from the wreckage of the old coaster. I hear some urgent commands and see a suited-up paramedic run to the back of the ambulance for another piece of equipment. In the distance, I hear the helicopter they dispatched to take Jillian to the trauma center, if she lives long enough to be freed and transported.

The head fireman stands in front of me, "How are you?"

"Cold. Scared."

"Good. You should be. She's not in a good place right now." He squats on the snowy ground to meet my eyes, "Care to tell me how this happened?"

I look at his eyes, full of concern. The dark blue seems utterly lacking in condemnation at the moment. I sigh and lean back against the solid bulk of the red engine. "I don't want to tell you, but I know it's the right thing to do."

"Good answer."

So, I told him, "Earlier tonight, we were sharing a pizza, bitching about how boring this winter has become since we don't have football playoffs. We were picking at the last piece, sucking at empty straws when suddenly I had an idea." I looked up into the cloudy night sky wishing it would snow.

"That's when I said, 'You know, the old amusement park Joe worked at last summer? I was thinking it would be cool to see what it looks like in the snow.' Jillian thought it was a good idea." I shrugged and adjusted my grip on the hot cup. "The guys were here already. Steven and Joe. You probably already know that Joe is my brother. Steven is his best friend." This fireman was an excellent listener. He just squatted there in half a foot of snow waiting on an idiot teenager to spill the details of how a series of idiotic decisions lead to this disaster.

The ambulance carrying Steven and Joe was already speeding to the trauma center. They were lucky. Joe had a dislocated shoulder which one muscled fireman had reset with an extreme amount of yelling from Joe before the pain meds kicked in. Steven had some cuts that needed stitches, and possibly a concussion. Jillian had been caught between the cars when the old chains had frozen as we were free falling on the antique roller coaster. I was lucky to have been thrown entirely clear of the crash. I may also have a concussion since I woke up in the middle of a snow pile covering a fluffy shrub. The "woke up" part tells me I was not conscious.

"We were pretty stupid, all of us. The guys had overheard and followed us out here. God, I am an idiot. We all are." I finally started to cry. I wipe the tears and take a deep breath so I can finish. "Joe and Steven worked here for the past couple of summers. I think they still have keys or something. They know how everything works, it should have been safe. But now that I think of it, nobody has done maintenance or checked out the machines for cold weather running. We all should know better."

"We are all stupid sometimes." He glanced over his shoulder toward the ambulance, "My people will do all they can to help her. I can't promise anything, but she is still alive. She may lose the leg, and she's in for a long recovery if we get her out of here. One more thing, was anyone drinking or doing drugs? It's important, not for prosecution but for her medical care." He stared hard at me expecting the truth.

"We all had some vodka after we got here. I didn't see anyone do drugs. I didn't do any drugs, just a few swallows of vodka. Neither did Jillian."

"Okay. Thank you. Now, take it easy. The police are on their way." He stood up and finished me off by informing me, "Your parents just pulled up."

The Abandoned Amusement Park
Kimberly A. Wisener

My friend and I were visiting a beach when we came across an abandoned amusement park sitting on a pier. The park was damaged years ago by a tropical storm and was never repaired and reopened. On the pier, it looked a little eerie. Tattered and faded flags still wave in the wind. It's easy to imagine how busy it once was with vendors and tourists crowding the pier.

As we walk closer, we can see that the gate is not secure and we both agree we would like a closer look. We scramble through the opening in the gate and start walking slowly down the pier. The first ride to our right is the carousel. Many of the horses and carriages are damaged from the weather and elements.

We continue walking and find the bumper cars on our left. Just as we get to the entry gate for the ride, the whole atmosphere of the place changes. The lights begin to flicker, and the rides begin to come on. You can hear the electricity snapping on the bumper cars. The carousel music is blasting through the speakers.

My friend and I realize we really should not be here and turn to run back toward the gate. As we get near, we see that there is no longer an opening in the gate and it is impossible to climb over. We desperately want to leave but can't see a way out. We try our phones, and neither of them will work. Looking back down the main street of the amusement park, we can see a clear path all the way down to the end of the pier where the open-air stage once was. We decide to venture down the path toward the end of the pier.

We pass many of the concession stands and carnival game booths that have been boarded up. You could almost smell popcorn and cotton candy and hear the vendors calling out trying to entice you to stop. My friend and I are both clinging to each other as we walk farther down. There is a lot of debris and trash to step over. The Fun House is on the left. I quickly hurry us by it as it is one of my least favorite things at an amusement park. At a normal park, I would have to crawl out of it. Being here, I think I would have a panic attack and die if I entered it. I am trying to understand what is happening and why an obviously abandoned place would have power and come alive just as we walked on the pier.

The Ferris Wheel sits next to the stage. You can tell that it was once magnificent, with lots of tiny pieces of glass all over it, making it shine in the sunlight. Its continuous turning is at odds with how a Ferris Wheel ride generally is, with many stops and starts as riders climb on and off. As we walk to the stage area, we both begin to breathe a little better as now we have a better view of the water and the rest of the world. There has to be a way out, and we will have to find it.

It is really thought provoking that when the pier was open, there was only one entrance and exit. Imagine if they had had to quickly evacuate, what kind of chaos would have ensued. There is not a possibility of jumping into the water as the waves would dash you up against the pillars that hold the pier up. The only way out is to go back to the gate, which means walking back down the pier.

As we head back, we notice other pieces to the park. There are several kiddie rides and a wooden roller coaster. It is so freaky seeing the empty cars moving down the tracks. The sign on the ride says, "Face your fears", and we feel like we are. Just as we get back to the carousel, everything stops just as quickly as it had begun. It is terrifyingly quiet now! We look at each other and walk a little faster.

At the entrance, we now take more time to look at the gate and also outside of the gate. Down below the pier, there is a truck. We both call out, and a man appears. He seems to have been fishing nearby. We tell him that we are stuck inside and need help. He climbs up the steps to the seawall and walks to the pier. He assesses the situation and walks back to his truck for a crow bar. He pries the gate open enough that we could slide through.

We thank him for his help and tell him quickly about what happened to us on the pier. He looks at us strangely and then calmly says that what we are saying is not possible and points to the power boxes and cables, which he said were disconnected immediately after the storm, and the power was never restored. My friend and I are confused by this, but at least we have each other to confirm what we did or did not see. Some things just cannot be explained, and this thought is enough for us to know that we definitely would not enter an abandoned amusement park again.

The Captain
Irish Goat

The Captain looked out across the waves. *Nothing.*

It had been weeks since he'd seen another human. Days since he caught his last meal. It wouldn't be long now. He could feel his death approaching.

His anger rose again. He could taste the bile frothing in his gullet. *Willie.* His first mate, and that mutinous crew of ungrateful swine. He'd made them all rich; him, the Captain —not that bastard son of a whore. *And what did they do to show their gratitude?* They stole the loot, killed the loyal ones, and marooned him out on this accursed island alone.

And why? Because they were yellow. Cowards, the lot. He'd been commissioned to ply the waves for a new route to the Indies. Riches and wealth were made along the way, but then...

Then the storm in that Godless Triangle. The crew begged to return home, but the gold had been taken. King Henry had demanded a new trading lane. He had to go through the Triangle.

The skies went dark, and the men turned green. Few had suffered this kind of tempest. A 'huracan,' those Taino natives called it. Some Carib god of wrath or some such mummery. But the crew believed, and that was enough. They waited until the storm passed, and then they struck.

Willie. He'd come to him as a deserter from the King's Own. They made two travels to the Canaries, seven raids off the coast of Africa, and led the *Indigo* to two victorious sea battles. For all his unsavory characteristics, Willie had always served him well.

It was the girl that poisoned his loyalties. The Captain laughed at the irony. With all that King Neptune had thrown at him in his four decades at sea, his death had been meted by the ivory breasts of a seaport slut.

That humping jezebel had Willie in her power before the corset slid off her ivory form. Had him boarding her, each night dropping golden booty down her buttoned undergarments. The captain had warned him about her. But her sex-craft was strong, and by the time the *Indigo* left port, Willie had begun his plan.

Mutterings were uttered in the windy corners of the poop. Eyes began shifting on watch. *And then. Yes, then...* The minute the crew lost heart in the storm, when the fear of the Triangle had reached its apex, Willie acted. The time was ripe. The knives were loosed. The blood was spilled. Young Conley, his charge for four years, watched as his own bowels slipped out from his belly. Jenkins simply dove into the waves to escape the blades. Kravitz and Smythe were killed on deck. All three bodies were unceremoniously dumped into the sea en route to the nameless island. The Captain's new home.

Willie. The Captain didn't care that he'd die on this worthless island. He just didn't want to do it before Willie got what was coming to him. He knew how fate worked on the high seas, and was certain Willie's comeuppance was at hand. But he'd love to witness the fall. *Oh, to hear the rope's song as it snapped the brute's neck. That long creaking pull of sinew, followed by the splash of involuntary bowels released upon the planks.* The dance of death was seeking his partner, and Willie needed to have his turn.

The Captain smiled, but winced as his salt-cracked lips split. *Nothing naval came easy, but there was always a way.* Escape from an island always seem impossible, but lesser men had won their freedom. And the Captain came from a long line of mariners. A lineage like that formed the basis of a caste that couldn't simply be marooned. You could kill them outright—as Willie should have done—but don't think leaving them on an island was an inevitable death sentence.

He had beaten the odds so far. He found water, fruit and a cavern that offered some shelter. He was doing alright until he got sick. *The fever.* He couldn't hold down the food anymore, and he had been shivering for five days. He was weakening. If he couldn't get the fever to break, he'd be dead in a matter of hours. *And Willie will have won.*

Third Mate Corbett had left him with a loaded flintlock. He had a single pistol shot. Luckily, he had kept the powder dry. He stored it in the cave where he slept. If all else failed, he thought, *there was always that way off the island*. But as long as there was any hope, he'd wait it out.

He looked out again at the endless horizon. The waves were beautiful. *Beautiful, and endless.* The horizon held nothing. *Nothing at all.*

Another day passed. The *Indigo* approached from the opposite side of the island and was coming into the shallows of the cove. Willie had been killed and the crew had voted to rescue the Captain. The morning mist thinned slightly as the sun rose before them. All eyes scanned the shore. As they put out the anchor, they heard the echo of a pistol's shot from the jungle interior.

Corbett saluted the land, assumed command, and hoisted anchor. They would not try the Triangle a second time. The *Indigo* sailed for home.

The Coral Pink Skirt
Sue Ann Whitston

I opened the cedar chest. Stale air mixed with the cedar. I was looking for the pale blue linen tablecloth with the silver embroidery. Mom placed the tablecloth and eight matching napkins here before her death five years ago.

With the family dinner approaching to mark her passing, the plastic tablecloth would not be as nice as the linen tablecloth. I sighed, "The tablecloth is not on top."

What was on top were the white sheets and pillowcases with elaborate tatting made by my grandmother that were supposed to adorn my bridal bed. Next, were the white terry towels with more tatting for the bathroom. Then, the satin pajamas with blue tatting. I could see an edge of the pale blue tablecloth under a green blanket and the coral pink skirt.

I placed the blanket on top of the sheets, pillowcases, towels, and satin pajamas. I bent to pick up the skirt. As I resumed an upright position, I was in the fabric shop, clutching a bolt of the coral pink material and studying the skirt pattern for yardage needed. Still clutching the bolt.

I held two pink zippers against the material and squinted. The one closest in value I held with the two thread spools and placed the other zipper back in the rack. Then, I added a pink plastic box with straight pins, sewing shears, a pin cushion, a placket with hooks and eyes, sewing needles, and bias tape. These were the materials needed to construct my first skirt in Mrs. Fellows' Home Economics class.

Now I was in the Home Economics Room with the pinned material laid on the stainless-steel counter used by the Cooking

Class. I checked the measurements from the folded edge to the bold arrow and the double-headed arrows to the edge of the fabric. The same numbers. I studied the pin placement. Definitely between the thick cutting line and the stitching line, but closer to the cutting line. I placed pins at the notches, the top of each at the cutting line. Mrs. Fellows came. She checked the measurements and the pin placements before extracting a ball point pen from her skirt pocket to initial all tissue pieces.

The scene faded and I was bent over the test on the sewing machine, matching numbers to the diagram. Successfully completed, the next step was to wind the bobbin with the coral pink thread.

I was waiting for the machine assigned me. A classmate said, "Come use the portable, Sue. No one is using it today."

I sat at the machine to sew my sample stitches Mrs. Fellows required for our notebooks. I pressed my foot on the floor pedal and moved gently and slow.

"Go faster, Sue! You'll get those samples done quicker!"

That is when the thread jammed. They panicked and fled when the bell rang, signaling class change for Math. Mrs. Fellows rescued me from Math and explained how she saved my work. She explained what I should have done. As a result, I did not sit at one of the portables for a long time. When I did, I sewed slowly.

After the sample stitches, the real construction for the skirt began. I pressed a quarter inch fold on the raw edges of the facings. I stitched close to the edges, sewed darts, the side seams. The back seam was set for twenty-two stitches per inch until I reached the marker for the zipper placement and switched to a basting stitch. I pinned the zipper in place and had Mrs. Fellows check. She approved, and I got one of the zipper feet from the closet.

I sewed the placket apprehensively. With a seam ripper, I pulled out the basting thread. When the zipper opened, I sighed.

The facings were next. Pinned to the top, sewn on the machine, Mrs. Fellows showed me how to grade the inner seams to lie flatter before I finished the task. Time to use one of my sewing needles and learn the hem stitch.

The hem was the last task. Standing on the table with stocking feet, the teacher used a yard stick to measure the hemline. When she wanted me to turn, she tapped my thigh with the yard stick. Keeping the pins in place, I measured three inches, folded a quarter-inch on the raw edge and stitched as I had done on the facings. I used the hem stitch again, this time at home.

The final piece was placing the hook and eye at the top of the zipper. Mrs. Fellows showed me the buttonhole stitch. I followed her instructions. She showed me an easy way to keep the hook from moving away from the fabric, a way to anchor it.

To this day, I liked the way her technique held the fastener in place. Time to don the finished apparel and go to Math. I wore the skirt again, proud of the accomplishment until I grew and the skirt was placed in the cedar chest with other keepsakes,

I returned to the present, fingering the coral pink skirt. This was the first garment created with my own hands and graded by a teacher. The first garment led to a sleeveless jumper with Mrs. Fellows before moving to junior high where I made a light green skirt and a blouse. The short-sleeved blouse had a white background with green dots. The difficulty was sewing the sleeves. A third teacher showed the class an easier method, one which required two rows of basting stitches and proved easier to pin to the armholes. There was a pair of culottes, shorts, a robe and a skirt with a matching vest.

After sewing Barbie Doll clothes for dolls given to Toys for

Tots, I started knitting and crocheting. I made some to sell at a November Arts and Crafts Show, not expecting to sell any that year.

A woman stopped and fingered a knitted Barbie sweater, saying, "It's getting cold out. Barbie needs a sweater."

"Thank you," I replied, handing her a brown bag with her purchase. And I aim to continue.

The Labyrinth
Sue Ann Whitston

I stretched my arms and said, "That's odd. Where's the extra pillow?"

I opened my eyes. I looked at a cobalt sky and not a white ceiling. Something jabbed into my back.

"That's not my mattress or the blanket," I heard my voice say. Twisting my arm behind my back, I extracted a clump of dirt. Dirt? "This is not my bed," I muttered and sat up.

I was sitting in a ten-foot circle with ivy walls. Straight ahead, there was a sign next to a gap in the wall. The center of a maze? I rose to read the sign:

You have one hour. Don't touch the ivy.

"Don't touch the ivy. Good advice as I can see the ivy has three sharp leaves with long thorns. They look like a cross between Gorse in Scotland and poison ivy. So, if I only have an hour, I'd better get moving."

I followed the dirt path between the ivy walls for thirty steps. The path turned right, and I walked sixty steps. Now, the path slanted left and scurried ninety steps to a trench.

I remembered the sign and muttered, "How do you get across this trench? It looks about five feet across and five feet deep. There is nothing I can grab to swing my body over without touching the ivy. I see a narrow edge, but it isn't big enough to walk on."

Suddenly, a staircase materialized, descending from one side and ascending to the other. I did not hesitate and scampered down the steps and back up.   As I paused and looked behind, the stairs disappeared.

Ninety more steps before the path slanted left again. I looked at the pedometer when I reached the next intersection.

"Ninety," I said. "Now the path turns right. Keep going! The clock is still ticking, and I didn't look at my watch to note when I started!"

Sixty steps to another left turn and another sixty steps to two trenches, separated by a small bridge. This time wide enough to cross. After placing the second foot on the bridge, I hesitated. I thought the bridge would collapse. When it did not, I moved quicker, remembering how the stairs disappeared soon after my crossing. After I reached the other side, I bent and read the pedometer.

"This is spooky," I heard my voice say. "First steps appear to aid me over a trench. Now a bridge. What next?"

Seventy steps and a left turn. It looked like the path tapered. "Nah, it's just the perspective playing tricks with my mind."

Three hundred steps later, the path narrowed. I turned sideways, eased through the gap, and sighed.

I have not touched the walls!

The path widened as it twisted right and left. I glanced at the pedometer: three hundred steps. Realizing I would be turning left, I knew what this maze was all about.

"I see a common denominator!" I screeched. "I started with thirty steps. Then sixty and ninety. Ninety and sixty. One hundred and thirty steps between the three hundred steps. I twisted for three hundred more steps. There is a pattern as the numbers are either threes, sixes, and nines. Using this theory, this path should have thirty steps."

I walked thirty steps, and a voice said, "Congratulations! You solved the puzzle in fifty-nine minutes."

The ivy walls opened onto my bedroom. I saw more mathematical patterns during the rest of the day.

The Mad World of Writing
Lisa Scuderi-Burkimsher

Barbara walked into the mental health facility to visit her husband, Donald. She saw the nurse Susy at the front desk and handed her a box of chocolates. "Hello, Susy."

"Hello and thank you, Mrs. Smith. You're always so kind bringing treats. I'm surprised I haven't gained twenty-pounds already." Susy shoved a chocolate caramel in her mouth and licked her fingers. "Boy, that tastes really good."

"I'm glad you enjoy them. How's Donald today?" Barbara asked.

"Oh, Doctor Michaels said he's improving. He hasn't heard any voices for a few weeks now," Susy answered and then took another chocolate out of the box, leaving the empty wrapper on the counter. "See you on the way out, and thank you again for the chocolates."

Although Susy was not the neatest person, she took great care of Donald. She read to him, cleaned his sheets, and most of all spoke to him even when he was off somewhere else in his mind. The doctor told Barbara he suffered from hallucinations. Barbara knew that there were mental illnesses on his side of the family, but Donald refused to speak of it. She never considered the fact that Donald would inherit the gene, and now feared the worst for her daughter.

"Hello, Donald." Barbara placed *The Great Gatsby*, on her lap. "I know how much you like this book." She read a chapter to him every time she visited. She sensed it gave him some comfort. Sometimes he would gently touch her hand in thanks without a word. He rarely spoke since the incident. She did not know if it was his way of blocking it out or just ignoring what happened. Occasionally, he would talk out loud to the empty room, and the doctor said it was common with his condition. The doctor had him on strong medication which made him sleepy, but kept him calm most of the time. Bouts of hallucinations were bound to happen. Not every medication was fool-proof. "Donald, did I tell you Breanna received excellent marks on her report card? Well, she did. Her favorite subject is English, and she loves to read. I can't tell you how many times she read *Jane Eyre*. Fourteen-years-old and she's very intelligent. She wants to come see you, but I told her it's too soon. Maybe in another month when your medication is working better. I tell you, I know Breanna is going to be great. I have a feeling she will make an amazing writer. It would be nice to have another writer in the family like you. How many books have you sold? Twenty-four. Not bad, Donald. Not bad at all. Well, I must go home now. Breanna will be getting off the school bus soon, and I want to be there. I'll come again in a few days."

"Bye, Mrs. Smith." Susy waved.

Barbara noticed the box of chocolate was empty. She did not know where that woman put it. She was as thin as a rail. Barbara waved goodbye. "See you in a few days, Susy. Ask Doctor Michaels when he thinks I can bring Breanna."

On the drive home, Barbara thought about that horrible day. It happened almost six-months-ago, but seemed like yesterday. She walked into Donald's study, and he held a stapler in his hand. But he was not just holding it, he yelled at it and pressed it so hard he stapled his palm. He did not even feel pain immediately. She would never forget.

"Who are you to tell me my story stinks? I've had bestsellers, tons of bestsellers." He threw the stapler at the computer, and it bounced off onto the desk, but not without leaving a scratch on the monitor.

It was not just the stapler, he yelled at his pen too. "You, stupid red pen. I know how to write. You just shut up and go back in your box." He shoved it back in its box and then threw his computer across the room. It was then that Barbara knew why he was so tense and not himself when she was around him. She thanked God Breanna had been at school when that happened. Children were very observant, especially teenagers, and she knew if Breanna witnessed her father's meltdown, it would have destroyed her. She adored her father and wanted to be a writer just like him.

Months passed, and finally, Doctor Michaels gave the okay for Barbara to bring Breanna for a visit. Barbara knew that would cheer Donald.

Barbara studied Breanna's wardrobe. She wore her best blue dress and gold earrings, a present from them for her thirteenth birthday. "You're visiting your father, not going to a dance."

"You're right. It's too much. But I'm keeping the earrings on. You and dad gave them to me."

"Of course, they look beautiful on you. Your outfit is a bit over the top, though. Jeans and a nice sweater will do, Sweetie." Barbara pushed Breanna's long hair behind her ear and kissed her cheek. "You resemble your father."

On the drive over, Barbara and Breanna remained silent. Barbara knew Breanna had questions and would ask Donald. She was not worried. He did not remember anything that happened. The doctor said he blocked it out and maybe in time he would remember. Barbara preferred he did not. She hated seeing him in that place and wanted her husband back home. Doctor Michaels said by year's end, he would hopefully be released. Donald talked now and had not hallucinated in three-months. He thought he was there for suffering a severe anxiety attack and needed rest. Which was not a complete lie. He did suffer from anxiety. In any event, the visit would do them both good. Breanna had been asking about her father often and missed him. Barbara pulled into the parking lot and turned off the ignition. She sat for a moment until Breanna opened the car door.

"Come on, Mom, I want to get inside and see Dad." She shut the door behind her and hurried in front of her mother.

"Hey, the place isn't going anywhere. You don't have to run like you're in a marathon." Breanna stood in the lobby tapping her foot. "Heck, I don't know where you get your energy, Breanna?"

"Forget that, let's get going."

Susy was at the nurse's desk. "Is this your daughter, Breanna?" Susy asked looking over the desk, expecting chocolates.

"Yes, this is my beautiful daughter, Breanna." She pulled out a box of chocolates from her tote bag. "Here you go, Susy. Did you think I forgot?"

"No, of course not. You never forget. You're such a nice person. Did you know your mother brings us nurses a box of chocolates every time she comes to visit your father?" Susy already had the box opened and chomped on a piece of chocolate caramel.

Barbara thought to herself. *For us nurses? Susy eats the whole box. She never shares with any of the other nurses.*

"No, I didn't. Mom, can we go see Dad now." Breanna tugged Barbara's jacket.

"We'll catch up some other time, Susy. Breanna is anxious to see her dad."

"Okay, thanks again for bringing the chocolate." She waved and continued eating.

"Hi, Dad!" Breanna rushed her arms around his waist. "I'm so happy to see you! I brought you my favorite book, *Jane Eyre*. I've read it so many times. I know *The Great Gatsby* is your favorite novel, but I thought for a change you would like to read this."

"She couldn't wait to give it to you, Donald," Barbara said with enthusiasm.

He took the book from Breanna's hands and held it close to his face. "Ah, *Jane Eyre*, another classic. I've read this book many times too. Thank you, Sweetie. I'll start reading it after our visit."

"Mom bought me an e-reader now, and I know you always preferred actual books, so I wanted you to have this." Then she went straight to the questions. "Dad, why are you here? I know writing must be stressful, but was it that bad? Couldn't you rest at home? Mom and I would take care of you."

"Sweetie, you shouldn't bother your father. He'll be home soon, the doctor said." Barbara stirred in her seat.

"It's okay, Barbara, I don't mind our daughter asking. She should know. Breanna, Sweetie, you're a good girl, but, you know, everyone is built differently. I had a great streak going, and then I over did it. I stayed up too late, I went without sleep for days to get a novel finished on time, and I just collapsed. I'm feeling better with the medication, and Doctor Michaels said I'm doing well. I'm especially feeling much better now that you've come to visit." He touched her earring. "I see you're wearing the earrings your mother and I gave you. They've always looked lovely on you."

"I love these earrings. I wear them a lot." Breanna pushed her hair back behind her ears. "I can't wait until you are home. Mom and I are sad without you, and we miss you so much." Her eyes began to water, and she changed the subject. "Did I tell you I got a hundred-percent on my essay? We had to write about our favorite past president. I chose Abraham Lincoln. Darn, I should've brought it with me so you could read it."

"Next time, Sweetie, and I look forward to it."

"We better get going, Breanna. I'll see you tomorrow, Donald." Donald gave Barbara a warm smile, and for the first time in months, she recognized her husband.

Breanna stood. "Aw, has it been an hour already? It went too fast."

"I'm afraid so, Sweetie."

"You go home now with your mother, and I'll see you next time. Barbara, make sure she brings her essay."

"Yes, she did wonderfully on her Lincoln essay. I'll make sure we have it next visit." Barbara kissed Donald and took Breanna by the crook of her arm.

"Mom, is Dad really here for just stress? It seems odd to me that he would be in here so long for stress," Breanna asked, baffled.

"You, know, Breanna, your father had a demanding schedule, and he just couldn't handle it. He had deadline pressures and sometimes things just take their toll on people. The main thing is he's feeling better, and he will be home soon. You know what I'm going to do when we get home? I'm going to make myself a hot cup of coffee with the percolator. Don't ever get those fancy coffee makers, Breanna. They don't make a good cup of coffee." Barbara hoped changing the subject would distract Breanna.

Breanna, still unsure of what to believe, decided to let it go.

Donald came home by the end of the year and seemed like his old self again. He never remembered the incident with the office supplies and Barbara never brought it up.

Breanna, thrilled that her father was back, never asked any more questions since that day in the car, and Barbara was the only one besides the doctor and staff that knew what really happened. Doctor Michaels didn't feel the need to resurface the memory when Donald was doing so well. And so Barbara, Donald, and Breanna went about their lives as usual.

****

Every time Breanna Smith typed a sentence on her laptop, she backspaced and deleted it. She banged her hand on the desk and cursed. She had her protagonist and surrounding characters, but she could not put them together. She was exhausted from so many late nights. She spent her day teaching English Literature at the local college to help create young minds, but her own mind she could not get into the groove. Her writing goals diminished, and she sat at her desk frustrated, twirling her long, brown hair, staring at the blank screen. "What's wrong with me?" She said to her Shih-Tzu, Lucy. Lucy jumped on her lap for a stomach rub. Breanna stroked her tiny stomach and Lucy relaxed her paws and closed her big dark eyes. "Oh, Lucy, I wish you could tell me how I can get myself going again. It's difficult, and I've hit a rough patch." Lucy continued enjoying her stomach rub, and it seemed nothing else mattered. "Well, I didn't expect an answer from you, Sweetie." She kissed Lucy's forehead and sighed.

Spooked by a noise, Lucy jumped off Breanna's lap and ran as if she was chasing the neighbor's cat. "Lucy," she called, but Lucy had already left the room.

"Hey, you, Breanna. What's this nonsense? You can't get yourself going? You've had two novels published. What the heck is going on with you, woman? Sit down and get your fingers typing."

Breanna jumped. Her chair fell over and scratched the hardwood floor. "Damn, my nice floor. Who's there? Answer me! I have a mop, and it can be used as a weapon." Breanna held the mop upside-down, so the pole was visible.

"Put that mop down and calm yourself. Don't you recognize me? I'm your favorite red pen. The one you use to make corrections and jotting down new ideas when you're not at your computer or away from home. Well, I must say, I'm disappointed in you. I'm sure the others will feel the same as I do."

"What others?" Picking up the red pen, Breanna studied it. No answer. "I've gone mad! I actually thought my pen spoke to me?" Breanna placed it back into the box and rubbed her eyes. She went to the bathroom and splashed cool water on her face. She looked at her reflection in the mirror: her eyes were puffy; her hair a tangled mess. "I need to get a grip, or I'll completely lose my mind." Then she heard something. She quickly wiped the excess water from her hands and ran to her room.

"How about me, over here? Don't I get a say in this?"

Breanna, wide-eyed, watched as the stapler moved up and down, making its way towards her. It opened its cover and spoke.

"Listen, I agree with the red pen, your writing has been awful lately. Or should I say, lack of writing. You've got to pull yourself together, or you'll never get published again." The stapler shifted its position over to the garbage pail and dropped itself in.

"Hey, I need you!" Breanna took the stapler out of the trashcan and wiped it clean. "Don't do that again! What's happening? Have I completely lost my mind, am I in a dream or do I need more sleep? Maybe all three!"

What happened next, Breanna could not comprehend. The paperclips began unwinding and dancing on top of the desk, each one bouncing up and down, tap dancing. They performed as if they were professional dancers on Broadway. Then the computer began typing: "You should be ashamed of yourself. Why can't you type a sentence? Come on, don't be a wimp." And she could have sworn her desk lamp flickered and laughed. She had enough.

Breanna took her chair and flung it at the door, scratching some of the white paint off the trim. *The noise must have scared poor Lucy out of her wits*, she thought. "Okay, that's enough! Who are you to tell me I'm a disappointment? You don't know anything about writing!"

The paperclips dropped, clanking until each one became still. The pen bounced its way into its box, the chair lay still where Breanna threw it. The lamp stopped flickering. The stapler went back into its place on the desk. The computer stopped typing, and the screen went blank.

The stapler began speaking again. "May I just say we wouldn't have to do this if you just took the time to concentrate as you did on your other novels and not wing it. How do you think we feel? Each day you use us for something, we're considered failures if you fail. Not a good thing to be, in my opinion, and I'm sure the other supplies will concur."

Breanna was done with the nonsense. It was her turn to speak. "Okay, all gather around. I have something to say, and you need to hear it. You're not the only ones who can give a speech, and I'll add that it was rather nasty and uncalled for. Anyway, listen up."

"It's true my writing hasn't been its best lately, but that doesn't mean I'm a failure. I'm only human. Sometimes we humans hit a rough patch, and that's what happened to me. But I have no intention of giving up. If you give up on me, then you're failing us as a team. I have a story idea, protagonist and surrounding characters, but I just need to get it right in my head before I type it down. The problem is, I became ostentatious after the second novel was published. When my novels received rave reviews, I thought I could write anything at the spur of the moment without consequences. But that's not what writing is about. Writing is a sense of purpose and enjoyment. I want my readers to feel the impact of my stories. I want the readers to put themselves in my characters' place; feel their happiness and their pain. It's all for the readers, and the writer must make the readers interested. I must say, that after hearing all of you speak of your disappointment in my lack of writing, I realized I needed that push. Although you were all a bit harsh, it opened my eyes. I'm ready to start fresh, and I hope you are too? And remember, since you're all a part of my team, we need to work together. I want you with me. If you help me, I know I will succeed. I just need a little guidance from my handy office supplies."

The room was quiet. Breanna wondered if she had gotten through to her office supplies and then one of them spoke.

"That was a great speech, Breanna, but don't you think you can pick me up now?" Breanna's chair asked still on its side up against the door. "You need me, too, unless you intend on standing when you type. Boy, you have some arm. I think it'll be weeks before I recover."

Breanna chortled. "Of course, I need you, too. "Here we go." She put the chair back in its place at her desk. It bounced a bit, then settled down.

"Boy, I feel better back in my spot. Next time throw something lighter, like a paperclip."

That did not make the paperclips very happy. "I think I speak for all paperclips when I say that's not a good idea. How about throwing your red pen instead, Breanna?"

The pen jumped out of its box and bounced over to the paperclip. "Hey, watch it clippie, I have your number." They stood facing each other, ready for a fight. It reminded Breanna of a boxing match.

"Relax, I'm not going to throw any of you. At least not at this moment." Breanna grinned. "Okay, let us get to work." Breanna sat and had her fingers ready to type until the laptop started typing on its own again. This time it had some sound advice.

"Breanna, I listened to your speech, and it makes me happy to know that you consider me part of your team. I'll do my best at correcting any spelling or grammar errors that arise. After all, you did say you're only human and humans make mistakes, so it's up to me to help you along. I'll not interfere unless it's to help you. You needn't worry about negativity from me. I'm ready when you are." The laptop ended its speech with a smiley face, and when Breanna finished reading its message, it deleted from the screen.

"Thank you, laptop. You're an inspiration to my writing, and your speech was wonderfully written."

"Before you start, Breanna, I'd like to give a speech." The paperclips stood in a straight line and the one that spoke earlier, which Breanna assumed was the head of the group, stepped forward and began his speech. "It wasn't polite to dance around and say the things we did. We should've taken into consideration the strains a writer goes through. Not every book may be a best seller or even your best work, but the main thing to remember is not to give up. We'll be here for you when you are ready to clip your chapters together. You'll have nothing but positive attitudes from us going forward. Also remember, if this book doesn't get published, there's always another one to write." The paperclip bowed, crept back into the crowd and each one plopped itself back into the box, silent once more.

Breanna had an instinct that if the laptop and paperclip gave a speech, the other supplies would not want to miss out. She waited, and next, the red pen spoke.

"Breanna, I was wrong. Do you know why you use me? It's because I help you put writing down on paper and create a story. Sure, I'm used for mistakes, but once you make your revisions, it's time to get it down in print. Without me, you wouldn't be able to do that, and I should've showed you respect rather than taunting you. It wasn't fair at all. I humbly apologize, and I'm ready to get back to work. Don't forget to replace my cartridge when I run out of ink, and keep jotting down ideas."

"Thank you, pen, and I won't forget to change the ink." The pen slipped back into its holder.

The desk lamp began to flicker, and for the first-time other than the earlier laugh, it spoke to Breanna.

"Breanna, you made one hell of a speech. If I wouldn't have laughed and instead gave you encouragement, none of this would've happened. You'd be on your way to another great novel instead of listening to your lamp apologize. I know you've been tired and that has a lot to do with your lack of writing, but it doesn't mean you're a bad writer. It just means you need more rest and when you're refreshed you'll be ready to give it your all. I'll be ready to give you light when you're up late typing in the wee hours of the night. Remember, if my bulb goes out, I haven't lost faith in you. I just need a new bulb."

Breanna giggled a little, but touched the top of the desk lamp as a thank you. She waited for the chair or stapler to speak next.

Breanna's chair shifted a little, and she knew it was its turn.

"Breanna, I wasn't too thrilled when you threw me across the room. In fact, it hurt a little. Okay, it hurt a lot. I know you didn't mean it. If it wasn't for the negativity in this room, you wouldn't have done it, so I'm willing to forgive and forget. As for your writing, I was the only one who didn't say anything about it, but I'll say something now. Your butt has been sitting on my face for years. That gives me ample reason to believe you're a dedicated writer. My seat is always available to you." The chair repositioned itself.

Breanna stood. "I want you to know I never hold grudges and all is forgotten from earlier. I thank you for your kind, positive words, and I'm ready to start." Breanna cracked her knuckles, and placed her fingers on the keyboard.

"Hey, wait a minute! I didn't get my turn!" the stapler yelled.

"I'm so sorry, stapler. I got ahead of myself. Please give your speech." Breanna waved her hand for it to begin.

"Although you just forgot me, I don't hold grudges either. I can't hold a grudge on a great writer such as yourself. If it wasn't for your writing career, I wouldn't have a place on this desk. I need you just as much as you need me. You'll get no more trouble from me. By the way, your speech really hit home. If I must be so bold, it was the most influential speech I ever heard."

"Well, since I'm probably the only speech you've heard, I don't think you would know if it's the most influential, but I'll accept that compliment. Thank you very much, stapler. Without you, I would have nothing to protect my papers from separating."

The stapler sniffled a little and then silenced itself.

"Okay, now that all of you have given me your reactions and speeches, I'm ready to begin." No cracking of the knuckles this time. Breanna went straight for the keyboard. Once she had her fingers typing, she could not stop. She spent hours each day typing away at her novel. A year passed, and then it was time to hand it in to her agent.

Breanna walked five blocks to her agent Robert Mill's office. The manuscript, heavy in her bag, made the walk slower than usual. She did not care. If good results came out of it, she would deal with the discomfort. When she approached his office, she took a deep breath. She opened the door slowly, and there was Robert, sitting at his desk with his ear pressed to the phone. Breanna took a seat and waited patiently. His two-minute phone call seemed like hours.

"Hello, Breanna, do you have your manuscript?" Breanna pulled it out of her bag.

"Of course, Robert, why else would I be here?" Breanna chortled.

"It took you quite some time to write this, so I hope it's good. Give me a few weeks to read it and pass it along to the publisher. I'll let you know then if the publisher is interested. He liked your other two books, so I'm sure he'll be interested in this one." Robert took the manuscript and shook Breanna's hand. "We'll speak in a few weeks."

****

A few weeks felt like months to Breanna. She tried to occupy her time by reading, writing short flash stories, and cleaning her apartment over and over, but she could not get her novel out of her head. She wanted to succeed. She took a jog to clear her head and that morning when she returned, the phone rang. She let it ring three times, picked up the receiver and took a deep slow breath. "Hello."

"Hi, Breanna, it's Robert. I have good news and bad news. The publisher of your first two novels didn't care for this one. He said it was predictable. The good news is, I sent it to another publisher and he thought your writing was refreshing. He wants to publish your novel. You just have to come down so we can go over the contract together. Breanna, are you there?"

"Yes, I'm here, Robert. When do you want me to come to your office?"

"Tomorrow afternoon at one o'clock will be fine. See you then."

"See you then." Breanna hung up the receiver and patted Lucy on the back. "Hey, Lucy, my third novel is going to be published. Not by the same publisher, but who cares. Not everyone has the same opinion." Breanna gave Lucy some water and dog food. Then she took a long, hot shower. She let the water run down her back, and it relaxed her body.

In the other room, the supplies were acting up, sending Lucy under the table. They were so proud of Breanna.

"See, all she needed was a little push." The stapler bounced.

"Yeah, and we all gave her that push. We should get a medal for our act of valor." The red pen hopped on the desk.

"Oh, stop being an idiot. We're office supplies. We don't get medals." The stapler slid across the desk to the pen.

"Shut up. She's coming." The pen backed away, and it and the other supplies went back into place.

"Lucy, that shower felt so good." Breanna tied a towel around her wet hair and made breakfast. She cooked scrambled eggs, bacon, and wheat toast, and had a pot of coffee brewing on the stove. Most people went for the modern coffee makers, but Breanna preferred the traditional stove top percolator. Her mother always said it made the best coffee and she was right. After she ate breakfast, she spent the day shopping, treating herself to new clothes. She deserved it after all her hard work. She not only bought new suits, but she also bought new shoes, an expensive gold necklace, and a new purse. She spent over eight-hundred-dollars that day and did not care. She never treated herself to anything.

The next afternoon, Breanna and Robert went over the contract thoroughly as usual. Once everything was in order, she signed it. Her book would be published and in all major books stores and online.

"With this new book, you're bound to get even more sales on your previous two novels." Robert seemed confident.

"I hope you're right. You were so sure the original publisher would like my novel, and he said it was, what was it, predictable." Breanna tapped her chin with her finger.

"Okay, so I had one miss. But that was the only time." Robert smiled.

"Very true, Robert."

Robert shook Breanna's hand and laughed. "See you soon."

"See you soon."

Breanna, with a little help and guidance, pulled it off again.

After her success with the third novel, she wrote many more, and some of her books were made into movies. She became wealthy, married, and had two children. Her life was complete, and it was all thanks to her office supplies.

****

Breanna's eldest daughter, Bree, took after her mother and became a writer. She struggled at first, but with the help of Breanna and long hours of writing, she became an author and had her first novel published at the young age of twenty-eight. Breanna could not have been more proud of her. A daughter to follow in her footsteps and continue the legacy. Bree wasn't the only writer in the family. Her younger brother, Brian, became a journalist for a well-known newspaper. His career was thriving as well. The only one who was not a writer was Breanna's husband. He worked in the stock market. They had a happy home and Breanna through the years of moving, took those same office supplies with her. Although they never spoke to her again, she knew they did not need to. Everything was said that one day, long ago.

The Mysterious Call
Cynthia Joyner

As I look around my bedroom, it's difficult to see. I sit up on the edge of the bed, slowly peering around at the shadows on the walls cast by the light of the full moon. As I stand and walk to the window facing the front street, still groggy, I notice an older car's engine just barely humming as it creeps down the street. Slowly leaving the cul de sac. Again, at this point, being half asleep, I'm not sure if I'm dreaming or awake. In fact, I'm confused about the last few minutes.

I decide to start the day a few hours early and brew a fresh pot of coffee. I walk downstairs, almost silently to not wake my husband. Trying not to stir the dog, my feet barely touch the floor as I approach the kitchen. Funny thing is the French doors in the kitchen are wide open, with the sheers blowing in the brisk breeze. As I approach the doors puzzled, Brownie, my one-hundred-pound chocolate lab, runs in from the yard and almost knocks me down. At this point, my husband is coming down the stairs, turning every light on till he reaches me. As we lock eyes, the kitchen doors slam shut!

The darkness was now turning to daylight. Since a thorough search of the house and yard turned up nothing, I decide to start breakfast. But my husband, Dan, just grabs his coffee and heads off to the office. I'm going through the motions of a normal day but just can't shake the feeling of the strange night before. The day went by quickly and not feeling rested, I decide to turn in early. So exhausted, I fell asleep immediately. But soon awakened by what I thought was the phone ringing. As I look down on the floor, the phone is laying there. I then hear that strange sound of an old car drifting down the street. As I get up out of bed, I notice that I'm wearing my slippers. Confused and startled, I jump back into bed, grab my husband and while holding him tightly, drift off to sleep.

The next day, I can't shake the feeling of confusion. Deciding to de-stress, I decide to spring clean and tackle the attic. I start with the old cedar chest my mom left me. Not realizing this will be the beginning of solving this mysterious puzzle. After hours of dusting and sorting through stacks of old photos and clothing, the sun was starting to set. Dan had come home and was coming up the attic steps. This was a welcome break. As I start to close the lid of the chest, I notice a faded, folded picture. Upon pulling it out of the hinge of the lid, I realize it's a picture of my baby brother, Bernie. He looks about seventeen. This just took my breath away, having lost him tragically in a car accident ten years prior.

As my eyes swell with tears, I look at Dan and with lips trembling, whisper, "This is my baby brother, Bernie. My only brother."

Dan lovingly wraps his strong arms around me as we head downstairs. Not very hungry, we both nibble at some Chinese takeout and decide to turn in early. Knowing that I want the perfect frame for my brother's picture, I decide to leave it on my bedside table.

Falling asleep wasn't difficult after the previous restless night and a hard day's work. I drift off to sleep staring at the faded photo of Bernie smiling warmly, pointing off in the distance.

What seemed like just minutes later, I was awakened by the phone ringing. As I tried to get my eyes to focus and my thoughts to come together. I pick up the phone.

"Hello." There's silence.

Just as I am about to hang up, thinking okay, wrong number or some idiots playing games, I hear a male voice!

"Adele, it's me, Bernie!"

I was stunned! Bernie, my brother, my only brother, who had since passed, was on the other end of the phone. I was unable to speak through my quivering lips.

He spoke again, "There is a car waiting for you outside. Get in it, you don't want to miss this."

I jumped out of bed! By this time, Dan had woken up. He was trying to grab hold of me, as I was running down the stairs and out the front door. Stopped at the edge of the yard, waiting for me, was an older model red sedan. As I approached the car, the windows that appeared fogged, seemed to slowly clear. I am frozen with excitement, confusion, and fear. I hear the driver side door opening. As I stood there, unable to move, I was contemplating running to my husband and the safety of our home, or waiting for, well, the unknown.

I closed my eyes, took a deep breath and, looking straight ahead, walked to the car. As I stepped off of the curb, I looked up, and to my astonishment, I was looking at my brother! I felt my legs turn to Jello. My heart was pounding! I couldn't breathe, let alone speak.

He looked at me, smiled, and put his finger in front of his lips as if saying, "don't speak". I am now in complete shock! He walks me to the passenger side of the car, and I get in. Still shaking and crying, I look back at my husband standing in our yard as we drive off. Unable to speak, I sit completely still.

We drive on through the night. I don't know at what point I was actually coherent enough to comprehend what was happening, but as we drove, I realized that with each bit of pavement under the tires was a place, a part, of my life. First, our humble red brick childhood home, our elementary and high school, our grandmas' and our old friends' houses. All leading up to the quaint country chapel where we were baptized, went to Sunday service, the place where I was married and sadly where my brother's funeral service had taken place.

At this point, Bernie stopped his car, stepped out, and walked to my side and opened the door. Again, I am in shock! Almost pinching myself to see if I'm awake or dreaming. He helps me out of the car. We walk through the mist, down the cobblestone walkway that runs along the side of the church. No words or even gestures are exchanged as we walk.

We come to the end of the walkway. I look up and realize that we are standing in the small church cemetery. But that's not all! We are standing at my brother's headstone! Yes, he and I holding hands, side-by-side, looking at his gravesite.

Just as I thought that I may be able to muster up the strength to finally speak to my brother, Bernie let go of my hand. He steps back into the mist. As I try to approach him, thinking there's no way that I will let him go, he puts his right hand up as if he's motioning me to stop.

He smiles so incredibly warmly and almost whispering, yet with a strong tone to his voice, says, "Adele, you are going to get the greatest gift of all!"

At that exact moment, I opened my eyes to realize that I was at home in my bed, next to my husband! I jumped up to look outside for Bernie, his car, something! Just then my husband turns over in bed, hugs me and hits the button on the alarm to turn it off.

Was it all a dream? Was it real? I sat on the edge of the bed, confused, sad, melancholy and missing Bernie. I didn't bring it up to my husband, because of the emotionally overwhelming, heavy-hearted feeling that I was experiencing. I chose to keep the experience locked in my heart, hoping that at some point, I would be able to make sense of it.

Several months pass without incident. No strange nightly calls, no odd dreams. Even the melancholy feeling that I was carrying around had faded. I still missed my brother every day. But, I decided to keep my experience to myself. To consider the visit, or whatever it actually was, as the "Gift". I have to admit I went to bed every night wondering if that phone would ring, that car would be waiting out front, would I again travel down memory lane and, most of all, wondered if I would have that chance to see my brother again. I kept holding on to the fact that, even if it was a dream, it truly was a gift!

****

Dan and I had been through a lot of ups and downs in our marriage. We both desperately wanted children. We didn't lack anything in our relationship. In fact, things were so good, and we were so in tune with each other, that it just seemed natural and right to share the Blessing of a child. We discussed, planned and dreamed of the day that we would bring a child into the world and to complete our family. We even bought our home because it just seemed perfect to raise a family in. It being an adorable two-story cottage that has white siding, yellow shutters, a white picket fence, a huge fenced-in yard and pretty flower boxes under every window. Not to mention the tree-lined, cobblestone street with a park across the street. But not for lack of dreaming and trying, it just never seemed to happen.

Time kept passing by, and Dan and I focused on building our business and even talked about turning our spare bedroom into a home office. We were enjoying our life together. We loved each other and seemed to have everything. But, just like the empty place in my heart for my brother, I longed to have a baby with Dan. The man I loved. It just didn't seem possible.

We finally just put that dream on the back burner. We just accepted the defeat of the dream. We worked, traveled and lived our life.

That is, until the moment that the phone rang and I answered, "hello". This time, it was in the light of day, and I was wide awake.

The dream-come-true was my doctor calling to give me the news that I was pregnant. With this news, I felt my eyes fill with tears, and I trembled with heart-filled exhilaration.

I dropped the phone, grabbed onto my husband, looked him in his eyes while also looking at my brother's picture, and softly whispered to my husband, "We are going to get the greatest gift of all."

Nine months later, on December fourteenth, my brother's birthday, our son was born! Truly, our greatest gift of all.

The Mysterious Call
Serah Demmer

The phone is ringing. Why on earth is the phone ringing? I groan and fumble around the headboard, my hand colliding with the phone cradle.

"Ow." I hold the phone to my ear and groggily mutter, "'Ello?"

An indiscernible voice says, "There is a car waiting for you outside your house. Get inside. You don't want to ignore this."

Mac rolls over and clicks on the lamp. Eyes squinting, he asks, "Everything okay?"

I roll my eyes. "Seriously?" I grunt to the caller, sitting up. "You need to go home and sleep it off." Mac chuckles and runs a hand through his wild hair.

"This is not a joke," the voice continues. "You have been warned." *Click*, the line goes dead. Come to think of it, whoever that was didn't sound real drunk.

I hold the phone for a moment and look over at Mac. He scratches his chest and yawns. "Anyone we know, dear?

"Nah, just some creep wants me to get in the car outside."

"Honestly?" Mac snorts. "What car outside?

I rub my eyes. "I dunno. I haven't looked." My alarm clocks reads 3:00 am. "Honestly, people," I close my eyes, "if you can't hold your liquor, don't drink."

Mac gets on his knees and opens the window shades above our bed a crack. "Babe, there's a car across the street."

"Wha—?" I twist to look up at him. "Oh, no." I cross my arms. "No, no, no, no, no! If you are some super-secret CIA operative on some super-secret mission, and now I'm being dragged into it become some not-so-secretive bad guys are trying to kill us—let's just skip to the part where you shoot everybody so I can go back to sleep."

"What are you talking about?" Mac still has his eyes glued on the car. "You think we should call the cops?" He plops down beside me. "Look, what exactly did this guy say? Maybe it's nothing. Maybe it's one of those reality TV shows—you know, like the taxi one where you enter that taxi and win money?"

"At three in the morning?"

"Kay, good point. Well…" he checks the car again. "It looks like a super secretive bad guy car. You know, the creepy-scary-creepy SUV type?"

"Correct," a human dressed completely in black and a ski mask says from our bedroom door.

"AAAAAAAH!" I shriek and grab for Mac, who loses his balance and topples off the side of the bed to the ground under me.

Mac recovers more quickly than I and tries to sit up. "Hey! Hey! Hey!" He protests to me. "Wait a second, babe! Babe! Chill!" He tries to reason to release my death grip on his neck. I swallow the rest of my screams and look back at the ninja-assassin type creature with some kind of freaky looking machine gun is standing at the foot of our bed.

After a moment of silence, Mac observes, "Well, you look like a super secretive bad guy."

"You were warned," Ninja growls.

"You mean the phone call?" I exhale and rub my smarting elbow. "That was, like, two minutes ago! You can't expect to wake someone out of sound sleep, feed them a lousy James Bond line, and then expect an answer in two minutes! Come on, man!" I smack the side of our bed with my hand and lunge to my feet.

"Alright! Alright! Now, everybody calm down," Mac says grabbing my shoulder. "What do you want with us?"

The ninja jerks his head back towards our door. "That way."

Mac and I look at each other, deliberating. The ninja raises his gun to my chest. *I should probably stall for time,* I think. *We should call the cops, too. And we should disarm this guy. So, much to do, so little time—and skill to do it with.* I groan, "Oh, honestly."

Ninja loses his cool and takes a step towards us. "Oh, okay!" I put my hands up like I've seen in the movies. "We're coming."

Mac whispers in my ear, "So, he must not want to shoot us, or make any loud noise otherwise he would've used his gun just now."

"Or maybe, he's—you know—got something against guns," I shrug.

"Be serious!"

"Okay, I'll be serious," I turn to him and jab my finger in his chest. "Who are you and who are you working for? Let's not even wait 'til the 'big reveal' moment in the movies. Who are these guys? Why would you not tell me you are a secret agent? I'd have been cool with that!"

"Lexie, I am not a secret agent," Mac rubs a hand over his five o'clock shadow. "If I was, do you think I'd be standing in my bedroom, in the middle of the night, at gunpoint, in my Fruit of the Looms?! I'd at least have, I dunno, grabbed a pen at this point and would be locked in mortal combat with Ninja over there!" He glares at me. "Maybe you're the secret agent."

"Me?" My jaw drops open. "No, thank you!"

"Shut up!" Ninja man hisses. "Both of you!" He gestures for us to proceed him out the door.

I look at Mac and he nods to me, so I head into the hall. It is pitch black, and I am blind for a moment. Hearing a scuffle behind me, I whirl around to see Ninja and Mac both toppling onto the floor in a heap!

"Quick, Lexie!" Mac slides the machine gun thingy to me. But, he's overthrown, and it passes me down the dark hall, so I scurry after it. Unfortunately, my eyes haven't adjusted, so I still can't see a thing.

Something cracks against my shin in the dark and I cry out. "Honestly, we have got to find a better place for that desk," I mutter, as I hobble down. "Okay, gun. Where's the gun? Find the gun!"

I switch on the hallway light and see two more ninja people. "Oops," I say and switch the lights back off. I would've yelled for Mac, except that he's already preoccupied. *Serves him right*, I think, satisfied. *Maybe now he'll quit the CIA or whatever occupation he's in, now that my life is in mortal danger.*

One of the Ninja finds me and grabs my arm! I twist and hit at his fingers, but my hand connects with his gun instead. *Perfect! I'll just take his!* Grabbing the barrel with my free hand, I jerk it back towards the general direction where I assume his face is and hear a satisfying crack! Ninja #2 grunts but doesn't release his grip on my arm. Ninja #3 grabs my other arm, and I'm stuck.

Well, I still got my legs. If these are males, so help them... I twist back to Ninja #2 and knee up into what I hope is his (I hope it's a "his") sensitive area and connect. *Yes!* Ninja #2 groans and doubles up, letting go of my arm. Since I am still hanging on to his gun with my one hand, I jerk it backward into what I pray is Ninja #3's face and success! I hit something hard that cracks under the metal and Ninja #3 cries out. I knee him too, just for good measure, and he goes down beside his compadre, who is struggling to rise.

I race back to my bedroom, blinking at the sudden light. "Nooo!" I shriek, as the empty room blankly stares at me. The window has been opened, and the light blue curtains flutter in the hot, humid breeze. *No, not Mac! Not my Mac!*

Suddenly, I am furious! I hear footsteps behind me, so I turn, swinging my gun like a bat. "You took Mac!" I hit Ninja #2 full on in the chest. "I want him back!" I turn the gun on Ninja #3 who skids to a stop. "I don't know the first thing about guns except that to work them you pull the trigger and aim! And right now, I don't think I could miss a blue whale soaking in my bathtub, so you just better park it right there, sonny!" He blinks in confusion at my metaphor, but I don't care.

I grab my cell from the bed while trying to keep the gun pointed at them. "Siri, call 911, please."

"Lady, you're going to call 911?" Ninja #2 drops his hands. "What is up with you?"

"Get your hands back up!" I aim the heavy gun back at him. *Woo-wee, this is a really great work out.*

"911, what's your emergency?"

"Hi, yes, ma'am, uh, my home has just been invaded by these ninja-type guys, and they've taken my husband, who may or may not be a secret agent, so I've taken two of them hostage.

Please, please, please tell me you got a squad car and S.W.A.T team that are just randomly out tonight and are, like, thirty seconds away from my place!"

"Whoa! Whoa! Whoa, okay, chill." Ninja #2 starts rising from the floor. "I would have expected you to use your training, but you're acting like a civilian."

"He's getting up! Can I shoot him?" I demand of the operator.

"Ma'am, please don't shoot anyone just yet. What is your address?"

There is scratching at the window. I don't wheel around because then my back would be to the other ninjas. (See, I watch all the cop shows!) Instead, I back towards my bed so that I can see the window from the corner of my eye.

It's Mac! Crawling through the window. Safe and sound, without a scratch.

"Mac!" I scream, throwing my arms around him. "You're safe!" Then I frown. "Maaaac!" I punch his shoulder. "I cannot believe you wouldn't tell me about all this!" I gesture with the gun thingy towards the other Ninjas.

"Oh, babe, this was all a mistake!" He tries to hug me.

"You bet it was a mistake!" I shrug him off. "It is going to take you some serious chocolate, flowers, and maybe even a vacation to the Bahamas to make up for this."

"No, no, not my mistake—their mistake!" he tries to correct himself.

"Your super-secret bad guy friends!"

"They're not my friends!" he protests. "I'm not a secret agent!"

"Yes, you are! How else did you get away from that one guy?"

"Well," he tries to look modest, "there was a little skill from my wrestling days involved, but I'm not an operative. These guys are trainees for CIA program, and they were supposed to simulate an attack on fellow trainees, but they got their directions mixed up and invaded our place."

"WHAT?!" I swing my gun back at the two in my bedroom. They both jump back.

"I just got done talking to their supervisor outside. That's why they were so easy to get the best of."

"Hey!" both Ninjas protest, as the cops come and handcuff them.

"So, you're not a spy?" I turn back to Mac, hands on hips.

"Not even close," he promises.

"Then why are they arresting them?"

"Because, babe, we're all having to go down to the station to sort this all out." He wraps his arm around my waist and pulls me close. "I'm just glad you're okay."

I'm still not convinced. "This whole thing wouldn't be some massive cover up for a hit gone wrong? I watch all the spy movies, you know."

Mac laughs. "No, babe, this is not a cover up." He kisses the bridge of my nose and smiles innocently. "Honest."

The Scarf
Debansree Banerjee

It was a bleak day; the winds howled through the house, entering and leaving through small nooks. The holes in the attic had to be boarded up because it had been that way since Bob left three years ago. Ours had been a dream wedding, but a nuptial disaster. Now, with the power lines down due to the storm, I ambled through the dimly lit wooden space, narrowly missing more disasters. The old tub of clothes lay in front of the single window that attempted at casting a feeble light on the remains of my earlier days; clothes that would never fit me again. Weary and uninterested, I tugged at the tub, intending to slide it a few inches, so that I could edge towards the window that I found wasn't exactly bolted.

My eyes caught Bob's dress shirts, just staring back at me, as if mocking about how happy he was with his life, while I ruined myself day-by-day, immersing in alcohol and misery. What had gone so wrong between us, I wondered. It was a dream come true, he was a successful architect; me, a promising Doctoral candidate. At first, our decision to respect the other's professional life seemed like a perfect arrangement, but with Bob getting more involved with his wealthy clients and their dream homes, and me taking on the strain of teaching and a doctorate simultaneously; we somehow rifted. It wasn't like we fought, we simply stopped talking, until one day we were like aliens living under one roof.

My eyes stopped on the green polka dotted scarf, that was a tad-bit discoloured with all the years. How I had pleaded with Grandma to give it to me. My hand shot out to touch the silk, and a shiver ran down my spine. It has been twenty years since Grandma went away to join Grandpa across the rainbow bridge; had she been able to tell him about the handsome young man who had gifted her the scarf? It was even possible that Grandpa had taken the information with a good sense of humour, and might even be sitting with Tomas Goetz right then. I remembered how I had listened to Grandma's story, mesmerized with each word, because she didn't want to part with her legacy without passing on the story that went with it.

****

It was 1944, and Hitler's designs towards annexation of Czechoslovakia into Nazi Germany had begun with a march of a thousand young German soldiers into Bohemia in 1939. Grandma, along with her ailing father, mother and three younger brothers, had earlier fled from Lidice, a village that would later during the year gain notoriety for the complete annihilation of all its occupants by the Nazi forces. They arrived at Banská Bystrica earlier, which was the seat of the Slovak uprising that was ultimately crushed with the disarming of the Eastern Slovak Army.

Amid such turmoil, the family subsisted on whatever little they could forage among the burnt ruins of places that used to be somebody's home. The local granary had been destroyed after most of the grains had been shifted. Grandma told me that they lived on raw, stale wheat for a week, amid the ruins of the granary, until one day a young German soldier stumbled upon them. Grandma was sixteen, and he didn't look like more than twenty-one. She couldn't decipher the precise reason why the young man chose to keep their existence a secret, but occasional visits from him would become a routine for the next eight months, until the liberation of Czechoslovakia in May the next year. The scarf had been the most extravagant gift Grandma had ever received.

When I asked her if she felt ashamed that she was in a romantic alliance with someone from the opposite side, she replied in negative. Though neither understood the other's language, their love flourished amid all odds. The feeling of challenging the establishment of hatred that was the war, gave both young people an unprecedented thrill because discovery of their affair by anyone would mean death for them. However, Grandma insisted that she just knew this wasn't a bad person, but before long, she was pregnant. This made her family very worried because, either way, she was on her path to destruction.

As she was to learn on the day when there was an uprising that resulted in the execution of seventy German soldiers by Slovak rebels, Goetz was from Munich and hailed from a well-to-do family. His father's lamp manufacturing business had suffered a severe blow with the war, but they were still well-off until a decree was issued that each family having more than one son had to compulsorily draft one into the Army, or be prepared to pay a hefty fine. This was near impossible for them. So, Goetz had ended up serving in the Army, so that his family could be safe. These words made little impact on the Slovaks, for Goetz was among the seventy killed that day. He had insisted that he wasn't a Nazi, and was just as much a soldier trying to fend for his family as anyone on the opposite side, but his fate had been sealed. Grandma was forced to surreptitiously abort her child by her parents because her brothers would be killed if others knew that their sister had been harbouring a romantic liaison with a German soldier. Grandma had asked a goggling ten-year-old me, to value love every day, whatever the differences be.

****

Bob's shirt beckoned to me; it was my first call to him after our annulment. I was happy to know that I'd been imagining his happily-ever-after life, just the same way he was thinking about me. The faded silk scarf had reminded us that life and love were all about differences, and no dearth of words could rob off our love; after all, Grandma had never spoken a word to Goetz. I ended up mending a lot that day.

The Tag on The Dress
Tiffany Buck

"This is yours."

My sister-in-law, Jaclyn, handed me a large brown box all taped up with no writing on the outside to tell me what I may find. I sat down on my parent's living room floor and opened it. I felt my eyes water as I touched what was inside.

"Thank you," I said to Jaclyn.

"You're welcome."

The box contained clothes that my mother made for me. All of them were beautiful and brought back special memories, but there was one in there that was my favorite. It was a burgundy dress with lace on the collar and wrists; best of all, it had a tag on the back that read Made by Patricia.

I was about to turn ten and thought that I, unlike my fellow students, was sophisticated. I knew things that the other kids just didn't. Things like: Ralph Lauren used to work at Brooks Brothers; the best ballerinas are in Russia; Bergdorf Goodman is the best department store in New York; sophisticated people bought their clothes in a store.

Now that you can see the extent of my knowledge and sophistication, you know that a handmade dress sewn by my (mommy) was just unacceptable. Didn't my mother know I wanted that dress I saw in the Laura Ashley catalog? The mulberry dress with the four buttons down the front. The dress that looks like it belongs to a tween who will be spending Christmas in a castle in

Scotland. Granted, this dress was over one hundred dollars, but surely my parents could afford it. On some level, I believed that if I had that dress, I could mentally transport myself to the Scottish castle and escape the dull suburban holiday traditions of Mass and usually bad food.

For two solid weeks, I begged my mother, three times a day for this beautiful dress, complete with a tag on the back. When my mother had had enough of my constant persistence, she said, "maybe." Of course, if I asked her about it again, I would not be getting it at all. So, the maybe was good. It wasn't a yes, but it wasn't a no either.

November came and went, and I knew any day now I would be getting that dress. I had been good. I didn't ask about it at all, but I did gaze at this dress in the catalog every chance I got. I was a little obsessive back in the day. Two weeks before Christmas, I patiently waited, and nothing came.

One week before Christmas, and the day before my photo shoot with Santa for the grandparents, (my mother promised me this would be my last year of that dreaded tradition) I was given a box to open. I don't rip paper; I wanted to savor the moment. Once the ribbon and paper were off, I oh-so-carefully opened the box and peeked inside. It was not the mulberry dress I begged for with the four pearl buttons down the front. This dress was more beautiful. Instead of being mulberry it was burgundy, it had the four pearl buttons down the front and added lace to the collar and wrists. In my eyes, it was fit for a princess. I took the dress out of the box and hugged it. It was soft velour, and best of all it had a tag on the back that read Made by Patricia.

The whole time I begged my mother for a store-bought dress, I never once heard her sewing machine. She must have made the dress while I was at school and tried to copy the Laura Ashley dress I so desperately wanted and, for a little something extra, she added the lace. Growing up, that was my favorite dress, and I am so thankful I got it back, and hopefully, my daughter will love it as much as I did.

The Wish's Labyrinth
Izabela Jeremus

The shiver running through me wakes me up. I come to slowly, as if I had been drugged. I'm lying on a patch of grass, still wet with dew.

How did I get here?

The last thing I remember is collapsing in bed, still wearing my outfit from the previous night, jacket and all. I had had a few drinks, but I'm sure I had gone home. I had gone to the gay club with some friends and spent the night dancing with a particularly beautiful woman. I still remember her eyes, blue one minute, green the next, then grey. I had declined her invitation to go to her place, though.

"I'd like you to be my companion. I'll show you things you've never seen before," she'd promised.

"I wish more than anything I could," I'd told her, "but I can't."

I had to work in the morning. The office needed me and I had no time for fun. I never had any time for fun. I hated my job, but it made me the money I needed to survive. Both of my parents had died within months of each other, and I had gone into deep debt paying for their funerals. Neither had life insurance. Not to mention the expensive bills that kept coming from my ivy league college. I had lost my scholarships when my parents died, and I went into a deep depression; I had barely graduated. But an ivy league degree is impressive no matter what your grades were, so I got the job straight out of college.

My friends had dragged me out kicking and screaming that night. But it was my birthday, they had argued. So I acquiesced.

Getting up slowly, my joints crack, muscles straining. I must have been out for a long time. All around me are beautiful bushes, covered with creeping ivy. The bushes obscure my view of anything around me; they're a good four feet taller than I am. They're neon green, a color not seen in nature. The huge flowers growing all over them are buttercup yellow. They're shaped with long petals and spiral around, as if a rose and a lily had a child. The scent is sweet and smoky, lavender with a hint of sage.

Rubbing my eyes, I spin around to see a sign hanging from one of the walls. It reads: "You have one hour. Don't touch the walls."

Fear and confusion filling me, I look at my watch. It reads eight o'clock. It must be morning. I take a few steps toward the only opening. Moving through it, my eyes scan the walls. There doesn't seem to be anything particularly sinister about them, but I don't want to take any chances. I keep walking, careful to avoid the walls.

When I come to a four-way intersection, I stop to think. I can't touch the walls, but no one said I can't touch the ground. I stoop down and grab a handful of grass, yanking it out. I dig a small hole in the ground in front of the entrance from where I just came. Then I look around. Each of the other three walkways looks the same. I decide to go to the left. Before proceeding, I dig a hole in front of the entrance.

The sun above paints the ground in gold. I walk for a while before the path begins to wind. I follow the turns, left, then right, then left again. It winds over and over again until I come to another intersection. Annoyed, I recognize the holes I had dug earlier. I have come out one of the other paths. I drop down and dig another hole. Then I dig the fourth hole and walk through that way.

This path also winds, but only toward the right. When I come out, there are only two choices this time, left or right. I dig my holes and go right. The air around me begins to cool as rolling clouds cover the sun. Thankful for my jacket, I pick up my pace. I seem to be going in the right direction, as I have not come upon any of my previous holes.

This path is uneven and covered with sticks. They snap loudly when I step on them, starling me each time. I look around and find the longest one. Picking it up, I move toward the wall of bushes. Shaking, I jab it into the wall. Immediately, the strange flowers closest to it begin to move, their petals unwinding. They grip the stick with the strength of ten men and rip it from my grip. Snapping fills the air as the petals break the stick into tiny pieces before spitting them back out onto the ground. When they're finished, the flowers go back to looking innocuous.

No wonder I'm not supposed to touch the walls.

Turning away from the stick, I continue on my way. I'm once again faced with another four-way. After my holes have been dug, I decide to continue going straight. Some of the paths are covered in sticks, others in small stones. I don't dare to pick up any more.

More choices, more holes. A glance at my watch tells me that I've already used up thirty minutes.

I walk and walk, when, to my horror, I come out into the first four-way where I began. Using my memory and holes, I retrace my steps. When I finally get to my last decision, I make a new one. I'm jogging now to make up for the lost time.

The beating of my heart in my ears nearly deafens me to it, but I hear a melody floating in the air. It's soft and sad, wrenching my heart. I stop for a moment to listen to it. It seems to be coming from one of the paths. I slow down my pace and begin to follow it. I'm so focused on the music that I jump and scream when a roll of thunder blasts nearby. It's followed closely by blinding lightening. A sprinkle of rain hits my face, mixing with my frustrated tears. I only have fifteen minutes left.

I break into a run, the music getting louder the farther in I go. Without warning, I stumble into a clearing. There is a pond in the middle, blue as the ocean in the Florida Keys. Around the pond are grey stones in the shape of chairs, framed by lovely green willows. Upon the largest stone sits a woman with her back to me. I can see the end of some sort of flute, longer than any I've ever seen.

I approach this woman slowly, cautiously. Her long black hair shines, despite the lack of sunshine. Her pale skin glows from the inside out, lithe fingers playing the instrument. She only stops when I'm close enough to see her face. Straight nose, high cheek bones, and full lips are set in an aristocratic face. Her eyes change from blue to green to grey.

"It's you!" I gasp.

She puts the flute down with a smile. "Welcome to my Labyrinth, Hannah."

"Who are you?" I ask. "*What* are you?"

She tilts her head, considering the question. "I'm Mab, queen of the Faeries."

"Why did you bring me here?" I ask, too startled by her revelation to question it.

She flows off of the rock, moving toward me like liquid. "You wished for it."

"So you kidnapped me?"

"I saved you," she corrects.

"From what?"

"From your mundane life."

I stare at her for a moment. "I didn't know Faeries granted wishes."

Her laugh tinkles like bells. "Don't judge by your preconceived notions. You wished for it; I granted your wish."

"And the labyrinth?"

"A test. You passed."

"So now what?" I ask, my heart speeding up.

Mab reaches out and touches my face, sparks flying from her fingers. I gasp, electricity filling every molecule of my body. Her hand finds the back of my neck and she presses her soft body to mine. Our lips meet in a flood of warmth where galaxies collide.

"I told you I'd like you to be my companion," she whispers after she pulls away. "Stay with me and I'll grant you any wish you desire."

I only think about it for half a second. "Yes. I'll stay."

The clouds part and the sun illuminates the landscape. Mab takes my hand and with a wave, parts the labyrinth bushes. A straight cobblestone road appears, leading to a castle that had previously been obscured by ivy. It rises up into the sky, shimmering white quartz in the sun. Mab leads the way, humming softly, to show me things I've never seen before.

We Can Do It!
Patricia Holland

In the troubled summer of 1943, World War II, and a murderer changed everything in our town. The Middleton Community Cannery opened that July, and in August, a good man was found murdered there. A bad man was murdered too, but that will require an explanation.

With most of the men off fighting, Middleton women ran the cannery. One morning, a nasty rumor spread from lady to lady as we worked. Many of the hundreds of cases of canned goods we made for the soldiers overseas had been stolen. We had a thief among us.

My mother said, "We all have good reasons to support the war effort. Even with rationing, here in farm country, we all have enough to eat. There is no good reason someone would steal the food we wanted to send to our soldiers. Another big load of canned goods for the soldiers is on that truck parked out front. We need to make sure all the soldiers' food gets aboard the next train leaving Lexington."

So all of us chipped in our egg money to hire young Peter Gray to guard the loaded truck that night and travel to Lexington with it the next day. Poor Peter was one of the few young men left in town. He was 4F, kept out of the army because he had flat feet.

At fourteen, I was the youngest cannery worker. My two jobs were preparing food for canning and watching my granny. In the morning she might seem as bright as a new penny, but she couldn't remember a thing by afternoon. She was a sun-downer. When her memories hid, she couldn't even remember my name.

My family was almost ready to leave the cannery when Peter arrived to take up his guard post. He said he planned to lie low, watching the truck all night, hoping the thief would come back. "Even though I can't fight the Nazis, this is a way for me to protect our home front."

He was such a good man. As we left, he called out, "Ladies watch out for that oil slick out front. The cannery truck must leak oil like a sieve."

The next morning, as my family trudged toward the cannery, we saw Bull Jones, a truck driver for the County Roads Department, out extra early spreading gravel on Prescott Road. I held on to Granny for she found it difficult to walk on the uneven piles of rocks.

"How many years have we asked for some gravel on this road during the winter time?" Granny grumbled. "Why in the world would he take it in his head to lay down so much rock in the summertime? Why, I've never known Bull to get to work so early, load up a truck full of rock, and get all the way out here to drop it on our road."

Bull finished off his work by piling an extra thin layer of rocks out in front of the cannery. He shut down his truck and swaggered over to talk to us. Bull's gut-bucket hung out over his belt. Even though his wife, Opal, was there, he looked me over as if I had no clothes on.

Granny whispered to me as she pushed me to the back of the pack of women, "Emily, you stay away from Bull. There's a bit of the devil beast in him; he's a rough man." Then she did an odd thing. She walked up to Bull and demanded, "What do you know about those soldiers' cans gone missing?" He mumbled something—nothing we could understand—and went away.

I was the first to go inside the cannery that morning. I found Peter, face down on the floor, lying in a river of blackened blood. When I screamed, the older ladies rushed in.

"After losing so much blood, is he still alive?" I asked.

When they turned him over, I saw a jack knife buried in his throat. His killer must own that knife, I thought. *Find the owner, find the killer.*

Mother hustled me and my equally upset Granny out to the front porch, then sent one of the women for the town constable.

When Constable Able McFarland arrived, he acted like a mystery detective in a pulp novel, talking out of the side of his mouth all the while keeping a cigarette dangling from his lips. He carefully used a towel to pick up the knife. "I'll check it for the killer's fingerprints," he said, sounding very official.

At noon, Constable McFarland sat down on the porch and talked to us. For all of those what, when and how questions, the constable hadn't noticed something important.

My Granny clambered into her cradle and asked the constable, "Where's the cannery truck and all of the cans for the soldiers?"

"Didn't you notice that they're gone?" Everyone gasped. Only Granny had noticed.

"Well, now we know the murderer we're looking for is also the thief," the constable blustered. "In a way, it should be easier to find out who took those cans than to learn who killed Peter."

After Peter was murdered, it seemed as if Granny was comforted by a new friend at the cannery. Every morning Granny followed Opal Jones around and chatted with her as they washed and chopped tomatoes. Nobody else seemed to think it was odd that a very old lady who hardly talked anymore would suddenly befriend a much younger woman. It was a mornings-only friendship as Granny's memories slipped away every afternoon.

The day she met Opal, Granny quoted a bible passage to her, "*Thus said the Lord, Consider ye, and call for the mourning women, that they may come; and send for cunning women, that they may come.*" I was not the only one mourning Peter, so that part of the verse made sense. But why would Granny think Opal was a cunning woman?

By Friday of that busy week, we had canned most of the tomato crop. By then, the ladies felt exhausted. So we didn't realize Granny was missing until we went out on the front porch for our lunch break. Mother noticed that Granny was not in her cradle, so she sent me inside to find her.

I walked through the building and out on the other porch. There I found Bull Jones and Granny. She knelt on the porch floor, her strong, fisted hands holding a garrote, a knotted length of baling twine, tight around Bull's neck. Granny released the cord slowly and got up as Bull's lifeless body slumped over and toppled off the porch.

"Oh Granny, what have you done?"

"That man didn't think I could understand his brag," Granny said. "Call the other ladies out here. Be gentle with Opal Jones. This is going to shock her. I will only tell my story once. I need to remember all of it. It will be gone by afternoon, you know." She sounded so wise and so like the Granny who helped raise me, but she had just killed a man.

Granny said Bull had bragged to her about killing Peter and stealing the canned food. "He thought I was too deaf or too senile to understand what he was talking about."

She struggled to tell her story to the ladies, "Bull said he began gambling heavily when Count Fleet was entered in the Kentucky Derby horse race in May. That horse was born and bred on the stud farm where Bull worked for a time. Bull thought Count Fleet was probably the fastest horse in the world.

Opal Jones broke into Granny's story. "Bull was obsessed with gambling on Count Fleet. Bull won a lot of money on the Derby," she said. "But over the summer, he gambled away all of his winnings and then some. He owed a lot of money to his bookie."

"This morning, Bull told me he had decided to beg, borrow or steal to get money to pay off that bookie," Granny said. "So in July, Bull stole several cases of food for the soldiers right out of the cannery truck and sold them on the black market. The night before Peter died, Opal told Bull the cannery truck was filled with more cans for the soldiers. Bull told me he slipped out of his house in the middle of the night to steal them."

With my hand fisted and my expression grim, I turned to Opal and asked her, "When you told your husband the truck was loaded with those canned goods, why didn't you tell him we had hired Peter to guard them?"

A guilty look crossed Opal's face. "I was married to a gambler and a thief. I didn't want to *stay* married to him. I hoped Peter would catch him so the truth would come out," she admitted.

"Well, today I tried to turn the other cheek, but that's when Bull went after me," Granny concluded. "Sadly, Bible verses do not always work out. But I thought of the twenty-first verse in Exodus for my salvation, '*An eye for an eye, tooth for tooth, and wound for wound*'. So as Bull tried to strangle me, I strangled him."

Looking around the circle, my mother asked, "Well ladies, what should we do now? I don't want my mother to stand trial. Can you keep silent about what you have seen and heard here today?"

The ladies took a vote. All agreed to clean up the cannery mess and to save Granny.

I always thought that Constable McFarland suspected that one of the cannery ladies might have killed Bull, but McFarland wanted the credit for solving the cannery crimes.

At the inquest, he claimed Bull's death was an accident. Very official and important like, Constable McFarland said, "He fell off the porch and must have broken his neck."

After the judge ruled Bull's death an accident, the cannery crew and I prayed Granny's part in it would remain a secret. Granny had already forgotten it.

Then the constable rounded up a huge posse of Middleton men and had them shovel the rocks and gravel off Prescott Road from the cannery steps right up to the Jones' house. They followed a trail of oil drops from the cannery to a big oil slick where Bull Jones must have parked the cannery truck at his house. Some of the exhausted men argued that might prove who the cannery thief was, but left Peter's murder in doubt. They thought the constable didn't have enough concrete proof.

Constable McFarland pulled out the jack knife that killed Peter. When he showed it to Opal Jones, she identified it as her husband's favorite. She said, "Bull lost it about a week before he died."

Using a big preacher's voice, McFarland told his posse, "I matched fingerprints from the knife with Bull's fingerprints." The constable thought he had solved both of the cannery crimes, the theft, and the murder.

Over the years, since that turbulent time in 1943, the Middleton men and Constable McFarland have repeated the story many times. They still believe they were excellent crime solvers. The sworn secret of the cannery ladies has remained just that, a secret to this day.

Which Love?
Sue Ann Whitston

Reflecting the commissary and the four beige vending machines, two gray racks holding paper cups, forks, spoons and knives, and two microwaves placed on a flat shelf, the mirror hung above the pine wainscoting. Though four tables and chairs were pushed against the wall with eight others scattered in the center, only one wall table was occupied by two men and a woman.

The woman wore her auburn hair short. Seated on the blue plastic chair with chrome legs, wearing a yellow short-sleeved cotton shirt, brown pants, and brown oxfords under the table. There was a mischievous gleam in her brown eyes behind the eyeglasses. While her left hand fluffed the pages of a notebook, the right hand toyed with a tassel attached to the zipper pull on her purse as she gazed at the young man across the table.

The young man across the table wore his burnt umber hair shoulder length. His mustache and beard concealed the round face. Bushy eyebrows were obscured by the large, dark eyeglasses perched on a Roman nose. Wearing a green plaid shirt tucked into paint-spattered jeans, he sat in the matching blue chair with feet under the table, near the woman's feet. Both fingers drummed on the table, a short distance from the hand toying with the tassel.

The other young man with black curly hair straddled the blue plastic chair, pushed from the table and right foot planted on the floor. His left foot in a polished oxford shoe propped on his right knee. His white dress shirt spotless as was his black dress pants. A pick protruded from the shirt pocket which he pulled out every five minutes to fluff his hair. He withdrew a handkerchief to polish an infinitesimal spot from his shoe and brush a speck from his pants.

"Are you a couple or not? I see the way you look at each other. You might take easels on the opposite ends of the classroom, but you peek at each other. I've seen you. At first, I thought you were studying the model. Then you sit next to each other. What gives?"

"Is there something wrong with that, Leonard? Can't people stand at opposite ends or sit next to each other?"

"There is if you are not a couple, Keith."

"Why are you asking if we are a couple, Leonard?"

"I want to know, Sarah."

"You aren't the first person to pair me up with someone. The first time was in elementary school when my teacher paired me with Steven for the presentation of the Tom Thumb Wedding at the School Fair. Our mothers got together to coordinate our attire. He wore a red jacket which matched the sash on my dress."

"That doesn't sound too bad. He was a lucky fellow."

"You are right, Keith. Steven had no complaints. The second time Steven chose Gloria for his square dance partner. Fred chose me which set Janet in a tizzy as she had her sights on him asking her to be his partner."

"Lucky Fred. I assume there is a third incident."

"You mean when the church secretary married me to my brother when we would greet incoming parishioners at the sanctuary door on Youth Sunday."

"Wow! That must have been embarrassing, Sarah! I'm glad I have a brother."

"Well, Keith, the secretary did apologize for the error. Of course, everyone in attendance that day saw our names on the bulletin. She vowed she would not do it again."

"Did she?"

"Unfortunately, she did."

"I guess some people never learn to double check their facts. What a history professor urged my class to do."

"All this talk has not answered my question."

"What question?"

"Got ya both! Since you spoke together, you can't talk until I give you permission. But, first, you have to rap fists across the table. That's the way. Now I want you to tap your toes together under the table. My family does that when two of us speak at the same time. Now with that done, I can proceed. What I wanted to know if you two are a couple. First you, Sarah."

"Why do you want to know if Keith and I are a couple?"

"Because if you aren't, I will stake a claim for your affections."

"My affections? I'm not sure about my relationship with Keith. I consider him a *good* friend, not just a friend. You say we set up at different ends of the room and sit next to each other. Is that a crime? Keith is one person I know. We share ideas without worrying that he would take my ideas and not give me credit. I have met people who do that. We laugh and have fun during breaks. I value his friendship and hope it grows. What I don't want is to force it. If we do become a couple, I want it to be natural. As for you, Leonard, you are a friend. You may watch us, but I saw you polish your impeccably shined shoes twice since we sat down. You've looked in the mirror three times to check your hair and straightened a wrinkle on both shirt and pants, a wrinkle that is only in your imagination, as you've done during class."

"What about you, Keith?"

"Here's my two cents, Leonard. Sarah's right. I consider her a *good* friend, too, someone I am glad to know. Whether we become anything more is 'to be determined.' She's right, I don't know whether we become what you call a couple or not. And I don't want to rush. Sarah listens to me and doesn't press me for answers. I like that from her. You, Leonard, want to muscle into the situation and I don't want to be forced making a decision."

"You're a couple," Leonard answered, and the conversation ended.

Wizards and Warriors
Sylvia Matthews

I sat at my desk playing a new video game that I recently found called *Wizards and Warriors*.

Rain was pouring down in buckets outside, leaving crystal-like droplets on the window next to me.

"Wow, it's coming down really hard out there." I murmured as I leaned closer to the window and gazed out at the cloudy sky.

Suddenly, there was a loud boom of thunder and a blindingly bright flash of light.

Warmth flooded my body as I let out a screech.

I felt a searing pain in the back of my head and darkness consumed my vision.

After a while, I opened my heavy eyelids and blinked a few times to clear my vision.

I gasped at what I saw.

I was on a dirt trail in a dense forest with a small village in the distance, the same place my avatar was when I was back at home playing *Wizards and Warriors*.

I struggled to my feet and looked around. On the ground, there was a sword and brown backpack with a note attached to it.

The note read *"Beat me, and I'll send you home."*

A shiver ran up my spine, "Th-this is not good, not at all."

What am I going to do now?

Fear gripped my heart, but I took a deep breath and tried to stay positive. "I-I can do this."

I grabbed the worn backpack and pulled it over my shoulders, pocketed the note, and snatched the sword from the ground.

"Okay, I should head to the town first."

As I made my way down the dirt path, I thought about how I'm going to get out of here.

They said I have to 'beat' them to leave, but I don't know how I'd even do that. Sure, I'm pretty good at video games, but I don't know the first thing about actually fighting, with a *real* sword.

I held the sword close to my face to examine it. "This is *really* sharp."

"Well, I'd hope so," said a voice near me.

"Eek!" I jumped up and turned to face the voice, pointing the sword at them.

"Woah, calm down!" A brown-haired guy stood in front of me, holding up his hands defensively.

"Oh, sorry." I pulled the sword away from him.

"I haven't seen you around here before. Are you new to Tynat?"

Tynat? That must be the name of this village.

"Yeah." I nodded.

"Well, the name's Ajax." We shook hands.

"My name's Salem."

"Since you have a sword, I assume you're a Warrior?" Ajax tilted his head.

I guess this really is the game. Every person has to choose whether they are going to be a Warrior or a Wizard. Wizards fight using magic and spells, while Warriors use non-magical weapons and hand to hand combat.

"Yep!" I chirped.

"Do you have a party? You know, like a group you can travel and fight bosses with?" Ajax asked.

I hadn't even thought about forming a party yet. "Nope."

"We should form one together!" Ajax sounded excited, "We can also look for other people who'll want to join. We should at least get one Wizard, that is, if you want to join…"

"I'd love to form a party with you," I assured him, "In fact, I already have a quest…"

I reached into my pocket and fished out the paper "We need to defeat someone."

"Oh, really? No kidding."

I rolled my eyes. "That's all it says!"

"That's a really unhelpful piece of paper," Ajax said.

Suddenly, a blue, square shaped object popped up in front of me. It said *Ajax the Warrior wants to form a party with you. ACCEPT or DECLINE?*

I slowly reached out and tapped ACCEPT.

"Great! Now we're in a party together." Ajax smiled.

Everything is so similar to the game I was playing... this is strange. I hate to say it, but this is actually quite cool. If I were here under almost any other circumstances, I'm sure I would be enjoying myself. Just not now.

"How about this: we go look for one more person to join us, and *then* we can try to figure out who this is." I proposed.

"Sounds like a plan!" Ajax exclaimed.

Okay, so this note, what's special about it? It's on paper! Yeah, that's not helpful. It's written in red ink, I wonder if that means anything.

"Hmmm." I brought the piece of paper up to my nose and sniffed it. "Ah!"

"What is it?" Axaj whirled around to fix me with a concerned look.

"This is written in blood!" I exclaimed, "It reeks of blood!"

"Did someone say 'blood'?" A girl with short red hair and a black cloak bolted up right next to the two of us with a deranged look in her eyes.

"Uhh. Y-yes." I stuttered.

"Awesome! I want in!" she chirped.

"Okay..." I said warily. *Well someone's full of bloodlust.*

"D-do you want to join our party?" Ajax asked.

"Yeah! My name's Ruby," the girl said.

The same weird blue square that we had seen earlier popped up in front of Ajax, and he tentatively tapped ACCEPT.

I shook Ruby's hand. "I'm Salem, and this is Ajax. We're both Warriors."

"Ooooh, how cool. I'm a Wizard." Ruby smiled, "Now, about the thing that reeked of blood...?"

I handed her the note, which she took and deeply inhaled the scent.

"Well, she's crazy," I muttered to Ajax, who laughed quietly.

"So what were you two trying to figure out?" Ruby asked.

"Who we have to battle," I explained.

"That makes sense." Ruby nodded, "What does it mean by 'home'?"

"Oh, uh... My village, Ryut."

"Did someone use a spell on you to keep you out of your village?" Ajax asked.

I paused for a moment, "Yes."

It'll be hard to explain that I'm actually stuck in this video game. I'll just pretend this is all part of the game.

"So, Ruby, do you know who sent this?" I asked.

"Oh, well I'm assuming it's The Blood Mage."

"Who?" Ajax asked.

"He's a mage who gets his power from spilling blood," Ruby explained.

"How lovely," I said sarcastically, "How difficult do you think he would be to defeat?"

"Fairly hard, but not impossible." Ruby smiled. "Since there are three of us, we have better odds of winning though."

"So, where do we go now?" Ajax asked.

I thought for a moment, "Does this 'Blood Mage', have a lair?"

"Yes," Ruby confirmed. "I can show you the way."

Ajax and I nodded.

Our trio party wandered down a path in the middle of a forest. *I'll be honest, this is the shadiest path I have ever been down. If I wasn't accompanied by another Warrior and a Wizard, I wouldn't want to be here.*

"How much farther is it?" Asked Ajax, "We've been walking for half an hour, and it's only getting darker."

"Ajax has a point. Isn't it strange that we're not finding anything?" I asked.

"Maybe it's a glitch?" Ajax guessed.

"Or it could be an undeveloped area of the game," Ruby suggested.

I was about to agree, but then, I heard a rustling in some bushes to the side of us.

We all looked over at it, Ajax and I pulling out our swords, and Ruby summoned what looked like fireballs around her.

The silence was almost earsplitting, and the anticipation was unbearable.

A small raven hopped out from behind the bush.

"Seriously?" Ajax started, "We were just freaking out over a bir—"

Suddenly, there was a loud sound of cracking bones, and the three of us all stared in utter horror as the raven slowly transformed into what looked like a human. He had silver hair, wore a blood red cloak, and had a warped, blood-stained scepter clutched in his right hand.

"The Blood Mage," Ruby growled with hatred.

"Ah, visitors, what a pleasure," he smirked.

I readied my weapon.

"Oh, Salem, you really should have brought together a stronger group. Was this really *all* you could find? These two imbeciles? Really a shame."

Tension crackled through the air

"Say your final words," I hissed.

"You think you can defeat me? Oh well, I'll be ending your pitiful lives soon enough."

With that, the battle began.

The Blood Mage smashed his scepter into the ground, forcing shocks of electricity across the ground and over towards us.

Ruby dodged it, but Ajax and I both were knocked off our feet by the force of his hit.

I crashed against a tree and slid down it, but still managed to keep a hold of my sword. I stumbled to my feet and lunged at The Blood Mage. Before I could slash him in half, he hit me with another lightning bolt, knocking me away once more.

Ruby summoned a golden fireball and flung it at The Blood Mage.

The fire slammed into him and brightly burning flames enveloped The Blood Mage. He staggered around a bit, before collapsing to the ground, the flames still lapping around him.

After a matter of seconds, the golden flames died down and all that was left was The Blood Mage lying on the ground.

I blinked a few times. I thought this was going to be difficult, considering he trapped me here.

Ruby, Ajax, and I glanced at each other in utter silence and confusion.

"Uh... I think we did it—" Ajax was cut off by a loud roar near us.

The three of us whirled around to face where the sound came from and were met with a terrifying sight.

Before us stood a creature, about eight feet tall, that looked somewhat like a large, wolf with a silver pelt. However, if had no front legs, and relied on its back legs. Stranger still, it had wings.

My voice shook slightly, "This will *not* be easy."

Ajax and Ruby looked just as surprised and scared as I felt.

"Do you still think you can defeat me?" the wolf bellowed.

"O-of course we can! This new form changes nothing!" I called, trying to sound intimidating—but failing miserably.

The Blood Mage burst out laughing, before looking over at Ruby. "You were the one who injured my human form, you'll go first." He raced at Ruby, grabbing her cloaks in between his teeth, before roughly shaking her around.

Ruby let out a scream.

Glancing around, I noticed a branch directly behind The Blood Mage. Slowly, an idea came to mind. I looked over to Ajax and then to the branch. He nodded. We took off running.

Ruby let out a strangled gasp and thrashed around more.

Ajax and I took hold of the branch and jerked it up.

The branch collided with The Blood Mage and he stumbled before crashing to the ground.

Ajax, Ruby, and I cautiously surrounded him. Ajax and I held our swords to his throat.

"You seem to have won," The Blood Mage choked out.

"That would be because we have," I said with confidence.

Ruby, Ajax, and I all smiled.

"That you have."

Three weeks later...

I am currently with Ruby and Ajax, battling a horde of blood elves riding pegasi. Don't worry, I'm not still stuck in the world of *Wizards and Warriors.* I'm back on Earth and in my home.

Even though I'm back in my world, I still play *Wizards and Warriors* with Ruby and Ajax. Our party still consists of the three of us, and that's how we all like it.

The Blood Mage is still alive and wreaking havoc, but occasionally assists Ruby, Ajax, and me on our quests.

The four of us have a deal; we won't try to kill him again, and he'll assist us. He, surprise surprise, isn't much of a help and usually speaks in riddles.

I now have two new friends, The Blood Mage on my side, and I'm back home.

All in all, life is good.

Write This Down. I Want You to Remember It When I'm Gone
Camilla Holland

"...so please do not come on Thursday. You will not be welcome."

Julia folds the A4 typed page and slips it back into the official-looking white envelope. Her stomach clenches and her fingers tremble as they push the sheet in. Still seated at the driving wheel of the car, her boiling emotions preclude any further physical movement.

She waits for the thudding in her chest to subside. She must go now, or she will miss the train. Rosemary will be waiting for her in the restaurant. She folds the envelope in half, careful not to glance at the childish handwriting on the front. Handwriting she had failed to recognise.

The keys jingle as she pulls them out of the ignition. She keeps the crushed envelope in her left hand. She doesn't want it in her handbag.

"How would you feel?" she thinks it says in the letter.

Julia knows how she feels. How did *Eleanor* feel, is more to the point? Eleanor expertly described the violence and drama, and she related the little ways she had developed of coping with his total and aggressive control. Of struggling to meet her sister for a coffee in town before scuttling back home within the hour, hoping to avoid the back of his hand as she sneaked through the front door.

Gripping the letter in her left hand, she gets out of the car, locks it, and slings her bag over her right shoulder. She trudges over the rusty footbridge that leads to platform two. At the bottom of the corroded steps stands a tall litter bin, the type with a flat rubber lid and a dangling transparent plastic sack below. Like a massive condom on the platform.

She drops the folded envelope into the bin and gets on the train.

Waiting and ready in the restaurant with two glasses of wine on this hot sunny day, Rosemary hugs her, steps back and says, "What's happened? You look like you've seen a ghost."

With a dry mouth and battered senses, she tells Rosemary about the letter.

"What does it actually say?" she asks.

"I can't remember much except auntie Eleanor has died, and how the family went through her things and found out about my writing... and not to come to the funeral on Thursday."

"And will you go?"

"Heavens, no."

"But she was like a mother to you, Julia. You can go if you want, you know. They can't stop you. You loved her."

It's the good times she wants to remember. Tea and scones at the cafe by the river, shopping with Eleanor to equip the tiny bungalow the council eventually found for her. A bed, a deckchair to sit on, a second-hand fridge, a new kettle and a set of crockery with some cheap cutlery from the charity shop.

"We scattered mum's ashes together, you know, at South Shields beach."

"I remember," says Rosemary. "You used to go and eat lunch in the restaurant's big conservatory. I've been there myself. Great fish and chips."

"We couldn't decide whether to illicitly scatter mum's ashes in the sea at the back of the cafe or on the beach at the side of the cafe. It was probably illegal either way. So we took turns with the urn, shaking it a little bit. And we said nice things to mum as we dispersed her remains gently, with love."

After her mum had died, she had told auntie Eleanor that she would like her to be mum now.

"I'd be honoured," Eleanor had said. She was eighty. 'You and I were very close when you were little, and your mum would be delighted that I'd adopted my only niece so late in life.'

When she had tried to phone Eleanor one night, her husband answered. "She's gone," he said.

"Gone where? When will she be back?"

"She's not coming back," he said and slammed down the phone.

Eleanor had fled in the night. To a women's refuge. Not to her daughter's house, two miles away, but to an impersonal, emergency refuge thirty miles away, where she was met by strangers.

Julia arranged to meet Eleanor the week after her escape from the violence at home and had taken her for a short break to a bed and breakfast by the sea, only a few miles away. They had walked along the beach and sheltered in cafes from the wind and ladled thick cream onto strawberry scones with their tea. And Eleanor had talked and talked and talked.

"Write this down," Eleanor kept saying. "I want you to remember it when I'm gone."

Julia's pen hadn't stopped writing for three days, and the spiral bound notebook was full.

"Tell the world," Eleanor said. "I want people to know what life is like for abused wives and what happens when they seek asylum in a women's refuge. How the women get there, with their broken noses and taped up fingers, and burned forearms, and split lips. And why the kids have black eyes, and wet the bed, and cling to their mother, and throw up half the time."

And then she added, "And what a high percentage of them pack their things and go back to the bastard that did that to them."

It was only later that Eleanor admitted that she herself had escaped once then returned to her abuser. Her husband had, of course, behaved more aggressively to her, so she was humiliated into fleeing a second—and final time.

Visiting Eleanor after she had left the refuge and moved into the small and damp bungalow became a regular treat for Julia. She would drive down from her home in the north of Scotland, and they would sit up half the night nattering, Eleanor remembering her girlhood at the beginning of the war, how her dad carried on working and didn't have to fight overseas because he was a coal miner. How Julia's mum had made winter coats for them all out of ex-army blankets, scratchy and dull, but warm.

And Eleanor always said, 'Write that down.'

She wrote how Eleanor's grandfather, at only thirty-two, had been shot dead poaching rabbits from the big estate in the middle of the night. But the ghillie was allowed by law to do that. Poaching rabbits was a capital offence.

"Write," she said, "how my grandmother was left with five children when she was twenty-nine, and no man to bring in a wage. No benefits or handouts in those days. We are the lucky ones."

When Julia went on holidays, she sent postcards to Eleanor, sought out special birthday and Christmas cards and mailed them to her, and made photocopies of the short stories she wrote and posted them to her. When the story about her poaching great-grandfather won first prize in a writing competition, Julia sent the newspaper cutting showing Julia being presented with her prize.

"I am so proud of you,' Eleanor had written to her in a letter. 'Your mum would be over the moon. She wanted to be a writer herself."

On one visit to the spruced-up and brightly-decorated bungalow that Eleanor had eventually created, she produced from the cupboard a chocolate box with a pink satin ribbon tied in a bow across the corner.

"I keep all your letters, you know, all your cards, look," Eleanor said. She picked up the housewarming card Julia had sent when she moved into the bungalow five years earlier. And Julia saw and re-read the press cutting of her first competition win.

"I've had another win, auntie Eleanor," she said, "a special win. It's the story I wrote about you escaping to the refuge—and how you put your life back together, went out and met people at book groups, and made dozens of new friends. It's won second prize, and it's being published in an anthology of short stories. Of course, all the names and places are different, but you know and I know who it's about."

Eleanor had hugged her.

****

Over lunch, Rosemary and Julia share Julia's memories of Auntie Eleanor. Rosemary has lived through Eleanor's final years with Julia as her friend. Rosemary never met Auntie Eleanor, but she has often said she feels she knew Auntie Eleanor herself. A sufferer herself of domestic abuse, Rosemary now works as a volunteer, helping witnesses and victims in court. She had to ban her own vicious husband from coming anywhere near her. She admired Auntie Eleanor almost as much as Julia did.

They finish their lunch and Julia leaves for her train. Rosemary had talked such sense and given her a long embrace before they parted.

The letter had been sent to Julia because Eleanor's daughter had been going through her mother's effects and found the chocolate box full of her mother's mementoes. She had read Julia's prizewinning story. Despite the name changes and the different setting of the story, she knew who it was about. But only she understood why a seventy-seven year old would seek sanctuary among battered strangers in a refuge instead of with her own daughter.

Julia didn't understand. But somehow it meant she was barred from Auntie Eleanor's funeral.

All of Eleanor's friends would be there, and her family and the neighbours. But not Julia.

They are all welcome on Thursday, she thinks, *anyone but me.*

When she gets off the train, she has a new perspective. Her heartache has eased, and she remembers her lovely times with auntie Eleanor. She walks across the rusty footbridge to Platform two and retrieves the letter from the plastic refuse bag. A tiny, unmanned station doesn't have much litter, and the letter still sits there on top of someone's discarded Daily Mail. She might read the letter when she is calmer and maybe try to understand.

****

She didn't go on Thursday. She went to her local cathedral and selected an angel in the altar murals to sponsor. "For Auntie Eleanor, a brave soul, from your loving niece," she inscribed in the sponsors' register.

She might even write to her cousin next week and offer her condolences and tell her how she loved her mother, Auntie Eleanor.

Yellow Dress Dancer
Alisha Ritchie

Heavy rain patters on the attic roof as I locate one last box stuffed in the dusty corner of the tiny storage space. I'm hot, exhausted, and hungry but I want to get this project of cleaning out the attic finished quickly. Mom and Dad will be moving out of my childhood home to a retirement community within a couple of weeks. Time is of the essence so I muster up my last bit of energy and pull open the folded flaps of the box.

Flannel shirts and old skirts litter my view, but I see a glimpse of yellow floral fabric peeking out from under the pile of clothes. I hurriedly move the other garments out onto the floor and pull out the small golden dress from the box. Holding the dress up for inspection, I am immediately transported back thirty years ago as the sound of the rain becomes muffled, my senses dulled to my current situation in the hot, stuffy attic.

Memories take me back to my pink bedroom with tall windows adorned with fluffy curtains. Sun streams in through the window onto shag carpet as beautiful music, softly crackling at times, is playing from the record player against the wall.

****

My eight-year-old self, with ringlet curls, is dressed in the yellow floral dress. I can see the detail on the bodice with hints of green and yellow embroidery. The full skirt is lined with an edging of lace that reaches just above my knees. As beautiful as the dress is, I feel even more gorgeous as I dance around my bedroom floor, spinning and swaying to the music.

Smelling the fragrance of sweet fruit in the air, my audience of Strawberry Shortcake, Blueberry Muffin, and an impressive assortment of Care Bears watch my performance intently. They are surely mesmerized by my grace and poise.

In the dress, I am no longer Alisha, but Annie! Of course, my dress is not red like hers but my garment is every bit as elegant and beautiful as the one she wore in the movie. I feel like a princess as I swish and sway around my room, recalling her dance moves from the 80's film.

Now, I am confident and self-assured. Memories fade of my self-consciousness when asked to speak in front of people, especially peers at school. My reluctance to reach out to new friends dims in the bright sunlight. Shyness is backed into the corner and forbidden to show itself again.

Here, in this moment, I am free. Free from worries and insecurities that threaten to weigh me down. No, now, I am light as a feather, gliding and twirling from one end of my room to the other. Happy thoughts invade my mind as I think of the possibilities of what my life might behold, just like Annie's.

The sky is the limit for what I can achieve. I can do anything in this dress. I might try out for the soccer team or be the most outgoing girl in school. I might decide to show off my dancing skills in the talent show or volunteer to pray at church. I am free to be and do anything I want in my beautiful dress. Nothing can stop me because I am invincible—the garment provides a layer of courage in which no criticism or hurtful glance can penetrate through.

I dance and spin, listening to the music for what seems like hours. Finally, exhausted, I flop onto my four-poster bed to rest and catch my breath. Snuggling up on the blanket Mom gave me last Christmas, I am perfectly happy and content with myself.

"I will wear this dress forever," I think as my eyes become heavy and I drift off to sleep.

****

A boisterous roll of thunder booms, bringing me back to present day reality. I look at the dress in my hands and smile. If I could fit into this article of clothing, I would surely try it on. I would run downstairs and twirl around my bedroom, just one last time.

Soon, someone else will move into this space and make memories of their own. But I will always have the memories made in the yellow dress. And I will never forget the gift of confidence that it gave me, even to this very day, a very cherished gift indeed.

www.ingramcontent.com/pod-product-compliance
Lightning Source LLC
Chambersburg PA
CBHW070854250626
47159CB00003B/1061